THE HAWTHORN HEDGE

by the same author

novels

Natana
Kintalloch

short stories

Teresa's Decision

translation

Weir de Hermiston i altres relats
(R. L. Stevenson's *Weir of Hermiston* in Catalan)

THE HAWTHORN HEDGE

A Novel

Mercedes Clarasó

BLACK ACE BOOKS

First published in 1995 by
Black Ace Books, Ellemford, Duns
Berwickshire, TD11 3SG, Scotland

Typeset in Scotland by Black Ace Editorial

Printed in Great Britain by Antony Rowe Ltd
Bumper's Farm, Chippenham, SN14 6QA

A CIP catalogue record for this book
is available from the British Library

ISBN   1–872988–41–5

The publishers gratefully acknowledge
subsidy from the Scottish Arts Council
towards the production of this volume

Everything in the universe goes by indirection.
There are no straight lines.
Ralph Waldo Emerson

1

'Seen this?' John Hodges pointed a podgy finger at the new card that had appeared discreetly on the notice board, then stepped back to let his companions have a look.

'The new appointment, you mean? Scratchley, I suppose?' David Dawe's face bore an expression of resignation tempered by disapproval.

'Dr Herbert Scratchley, you mean. You'll have to show a little more respect. He's going to be head of your department, after all.'

'And that'll give us all a good shake-up, won't it, once we've got that whiz-kid at the helm.'

'You bet,' chuckled John. 'Before you know where you are you'll all be into machines and multiple-choice. Some of you might even be galvanized into reading a new book now and then. Or do I exaggerate?'

Mabel Martin, the latest addition to the English Department emerged from the capacious armchair in which she had been hastily re-reading her notes for the next lesson. 'Do I gather that this isn't a universally popular appointment?' she asked with her usual expression of child-like candour.

'How did you guess?' Colin Parrott, the English Department clown, turned to her in mock earnestness. 'If we'd only thought of it we should all have got together and put up a really good candidate. *Me*, for instance.'

There was a roar of laughter which Colin acknowledged with a formal bow.

'Well,' he continued, 'I'd have stood as good a chance of keeping him out . . . '

David, with his eyes on the door, suddenly stood on Colin's foot and interrupted with the words:

'Anybody know what date that inspector is coming?'

Alan Morley had just come in. Seeing the crowd gathered round the board he nodded towards it. 'Scratchley?' he enquired.

'Who else?' said David, evidently trying to make light of the matter. He knew the disappointment his friend must be feeling.

Alan became aware of the fact that the little group gathered round the board had all turned round to look at him. He felt awkward and venomous.

A voice said jocularly:

'Well, now he's joined the ranks of our betters old Scratchley will have to mind his *p*s and *q*s.'

'Don't know about that,' was Alan's comment. 'It's the haitches that are more likely to give him trouble.'

'Oh, come on, Alan. He's not that bad. We weren't all born in Belgravia like you, you know.' If John Hodges was trying to pour oil on troubled waters he hadn't set about it very skilfully.

Alan gave him a withering look. But the worst of his anger was directed against himself. Fool that he was, to show his pique and disappointment in front of them all. And yet disappointment, he reflected, as he made his way along the corridor towards his classroom, wasn't exactly the word. After all, he hadn't had the remotest expectation of getting the post – not since the interview, at any rate. How could he have been so stupid as not to have thought up some impressive new expansion scheme for the department?

It simply hadn't entered his head. And yet he knew he was up against Scratchley, with his high-powered image and his barrage of new ideas. Alan was clearsighted enough to know that never in a million years could he revolutionize the department as Scratchley would. But he could at least have pretended that he meant to. It wouldn't have been all that difficult to work out some sort of a progressive-looking programme, even though he knew he would never put it into practice. Instead of which he had shown his discomfiture when asked what changes he intended to introduce, and then proceeded to make the worst of a bad job by muttering:

'No changes. I expect we'll all just plod on as usual.'

That, he knew, had clinched it.

He was too upset to face his students just yet, so he slipped into the library and pretended he was looking something up while he tried to work out what it was in him that drove him to spoil his chances so consistently. Not just at the interview, but even now. He had known for days that he wouldn't get the job, that he would have to face his colleagues in the knowledge that he had been passed over, in spite of his seniority, for a younger, more dynamic man. And he had rehearsed the moment again and again – feeling sure he would be able to show, if not magnanimity, at least equanimity. And instead? All he had managed was a childish, spiteful taunt about the man's accent, as if that mattered in a polytechnic!

Bloody Lord Jim complex again, he thought. So busy visualizing how well I'm going to do that I can't cope with the real thing. He had imagined himself saying, 'Oh well, I didn't really want the job all that much. I'm not an organizer, you know. I just felt I ought to have a go. And the money would have come in handy, of course.' That would have given the right impression. Besides, it would have been the truth, though not the whole truth.

And the money would indeed have come in handy.

So would the sense of achievement that getting the appointment would have brought. To be considered a success in the eyes of the world would have been sweet, though not so sweet as feeling he was a success in his own eyes. Being given the appointment would have done nothing towards that. His own private, personal failure remained, whatever his position in the academic hierarchy. But still, the consciousness of having succeeded in one thing might have given him the reassurance to spur him on towards making a start on what he considered his own work. Running the department, of course, would have taken up more of his time; but time, he had realized long ago, wasn't really what was lacking.

Alan had never quite worked out what was missing, what it was he needed before he could start writing. But he felt sure that, in spite of the added workload, the satisfaction of getting the appointment would have given him the necessary fillip.

'More work equals less time equals more incentive equals greater output. Paradox, paradox,' he murmured. And with this reflection he picked up his books and set off for the classroom, ready to face the rest of the day, with the comfort of a paradox to fortify him.

2

Herbert Scratchley knew already that he'd got the job. He had no need to come in early and glance anxiously at the notice board. In fact, he decided it would be good form not to go in till the last minute on that particular day. It would never do to look as if he were hanging about hoping for congratulations. He also had an uneasy feeling that these might not be as hearty as he would have liked, especially from his colleagues in the English Department. They were bound to realize what a shake-up they were in for. Out with all that literature and historical nonsense. No room for that in a polytechnic – not a modern, forward-looking one, at any rate. Practical application of the language, that's what they ought to be teaching.

Not that he'd got anything against literature, of course. He prided himself on being a well-read man, and could pepper his discourse with quotations along with the best of them. But there was a time and place for everything, and he wanted to see the college taking its place in the forefront of modern trends. What's more, he was going to see to it that . . .

Here reality caught up with his thoughts. Take it easy, he told himself, you've not been put in charge of the whole college, you know. Not yet, anyway. Just the English Department.

As Herbert entered the staffroom, John Hodges was coming out.

'Hello, Scratchley,' he said, 'I've just seen the notice about your appointment. Congratulations.'

'Thanks.' Herbert felt irritated. Not because of any trace of reluctance in John's manner. It was the fact that he had called him by his surname, as did all the others. And yet they were all on first-name terms among themselves, including the most recent members of staff. Why was he the exception?

What irritated Herbert most was that he knew the answer only too well. For some reason people just didn't take to him – he never quite knew why. Was it simply their consciousness of his superiority?

Well, it didn't matter that much. The higher he got, the more they would have to be nice to him – like it or not. And he was on his way up. No doubt about that. Only twenty-eight years old, and Head of Department already. And there was poor old Alan Morley, still on the bottom rung in his late thirties, and never going to get a step further. Some people are just losers from the start, he thought with some satisfaction, and made a mental note to be nice to this particular loser, who was really going to be in rather a difficult position. Herbert felt he could afford a little magnanimity in his present success.

Alan, all the way home, was dreading the encounter with Sheila. She must know already, since if he'd got the job he would certainly have phoned. But still, the thing would have to be put into words. As soon as he got in, the girls rushed at him, and he would gladly have stayed with them, answering their questions, looking at their books, asking about the day in school. But Sheila appeared at the kitchen door, and he could tell from her tense, anxious expression that she had not quite given up hope. Without waiting for her to formulate her question he shook his head:

'Scratchley,' he said.

'Oh, no. Not *him!*'

The contempt in her voice exasperated him. To be passed over in favour of someone obviously deemed so worthless was a double humiliation. Angrily he rose to his rival's defence:

'Well, he's at least finished his PhD, and he's got lots of publications, and he's full of new ideas. And he came to the college straight from university, not after a stint in a comprehensive.'

He saw the hurt look in Sheila's eyes as she turned to go back to the kitchen, and he cut his way through the children and their demands and shut himself up in his little study. He might have known she would take the PhD reference personally. How else could she, given that it was because of her pregnancy that he had had to give up his research and take the first teaching job available?

So, he thought, I've messed it up once again. She was going to be depressed enough anyway, without any unwelcome reminders from me. Why on earth did I have to come out in Scratchley's defence?

At table Sheila sat tight-lipped and silent. Alan could see the anger in her eyes, but felt too discouraged to try and put matters right. Even the children realized that something was wrong and sat in forlorn silence. For the first time in her life Tessa, the ebullient four-year-old, sat speechless, occasionally gazing at one or other of her parents, as if looking for signs of a thaw. Her lower lip trembled more than once, but she held back her tears, afraid to break the silence with as much as a single sob.

When the meal was over Alan got up. Instead of making for his study as usual, he crossed the hall to the front door.

'Where are you going, Alan?' Sheila's voice had its usual plaintive, almost reproachful tone, with a touch of added sharpness.

Alan was about to say 'Out', but decided on a more sophisticated form of non-communication instead. 'I'm going to join the Carthusians,' he said. Just before closing the door he heard Jane's eager voice saying:

'Mummy, what are the Carthusians?'

He felt a certain satisfaction at the thought that Sheila probably didn't know the answer. He suspected that Jane, the eldest, who was very bright for her ten years, was beginning to realize that her mother's knowledge was not as encyclopedic as could be desired. The suspicion afforded him a certain amount of satisfaction. It occurred to him that perhaps he was beginning to use the children as a weapon against Sheila. Well, I suppose she does the same in her way, he thought. But even that supposition didn't quite dispel his moral discomfort. He felt that, from start to finish, his reactions to the day's events had been unworthy.

He spent a long time wandering about the neighbourhood, bored and dissatisfied with what he saw, yet unwilling to go back home. He longed for green fields and untamed trees instead of tidy lawns, bird tables and herbaceous borders. I suppose suburbia has its own poetry, he told himself. Just wish I could feel it. And all this noise! He shuddered as two rival grass-cutters exploded into action almost simultaneously.

What's happened to the sound of summer? he asked himself. He remembered the measured, soothing whirr of the old-fashioned lawn-mower, and compared it nostalgically with this inhuman cacophony. By the time he got back to the house he had decided that he hated his job, hated his surroundings, and wasn't all that fond of his wife. If it weren't for the children . . .

Jane met him in the hall. 'Oh, you're back,' she remarked. 'Would the Carthusians not have you in their order?'

'Who told you about the Carthusians?'

'Mummy, of course.' And Jane looked at him defiantly. One up for Mummy, he thought, and went up to his study feeling that perhaps he wasn't all that fond of his children either. If they were going to take Sheila's side . . .

After she'd finished clearing up in the kitchen Sheila went into the sitting room, leaving the door open. She felt too discouraged even to switch on the television, and just sat doing nothing till she saw Alan coming up the drive. She overheard the exchange with Jane, and it brought a brief, thin smile to her lips. She had been lucky over the Carthusians, having come across the word in the papers a few days earlier and, true to her self-improvement discipline, had looked it up in the dictionary. So she now felt some satisfaction in knowing that Alan must realize he hadn't succeeded in scoring over her this time in the general-knowledge stakes. And she had no doubt whatever that this had been his intention.

But her satisfaction soon faded as she realized that Alan had gone straight up to his study. The gap between them seemed to be widening. His disappointment over the job might have been an opportunity to draw a little closer again. If only she could think of the right words to comfort him. But for a long time now she had realized that everything she said, even with the best intentions, seemed to act as an irritant. And his going straight to his room was a clear indication that he didn't want her near. She sat gazing gloomily at the lifeless television screen, thinking over the fifteen years of their marriage.

3

It had all looked so promising, except for the cultural gap between them – and Sheila was determined she was going to do something about that. But they had got off to a disastrous start. And it wasn't because of her pregnancy. Alan had accepted that stoically enough.

Sometimes she still wondered why he had agreed so readily that they must marry as soon as possible. He had gone to London to spend Easter with his parents when she began to suspect what had happened. At Christmas he had stayed on in Edinburgh with her, as they had just got engaged. Now he felt he really had to spend some time with his parents.

'I hate leaving you, even for ten days. Especially now, now that you really belong to me. I don't know how I'll get through ten days without you,' he sighed.

'And me? How do you think I'm going to manage with you away?' She looked up at him with a hint of tears in her eyes. 'Especially now?' she added.

When they got engaged they had decided not to marry till Alan had completed his PhD and got a job. But two years was a long time to wait, and for the last few weeks they had been sneaking back to his digs and spending an hour or two in bed together. Sheila was enraptured, amazed, and horrified by turns. What if her parents were to find out? And how could she have brought herself to do anything so immoral? And, above all, enjoy it? She spent the next few weeks in a daze – a love-soaked daze, telling herself that her love for Alan justified her. After all, how else could she prove that she really did love him above all else? Now that she had sacrificed her principles and her virginity to him she knew that they were bound to each other for ever.

In spite of this conviction she was trembling with apprehension, when, at the end of the ten days, Alan came back and she had to tell him her terrible secret. Just before leaving Alan had said he would write to her. 'No, don't write, phone,' she said. Then, seeing his surprise, she added, 'I want to hear your voice.'

'Of course, darling, that will be better. If I can't have you, at least I'll have your voice across all those miles.' He sighed with longing and she sighed with relief. A letter from Alan would mean she had to write to him in return. And ever since the first time she had seen his writing, when he sent her a note at the office, she had realized what the immense difference between their two styles of handwriting meant. His was an irregular scrawl – ugly, none too easy to read, but the writing of someone who writes as naturally as he speaks.

Writing, for Alan, was evidently something he did as spontaneously as breathing, with no concern as to *how* he did it. For Sheila, writing was a laborious process, which she did with great attention, and in which she took some pride. At school she had always been commended for her writing – large, clear, regular. And that was the way it had remained, the product of a special skill, seldom used, never taken for granted, undeveloped. One look at my writing, she thought, and he'll realize at once what an illiterate little goose I am. Sooner or later, of course, he would have to see it.

But she was playing for time. Since they had started going together she had drawn up a self-improvement programme. She was going to make sure that no grammatical mistakes marred her speech, she was going to read – literature, for that meant so much to Alan, and newspapers and books for general information. She would do her best to turn into the sort of woman who wouldn't let him down, not even in front of his awesome-sounding parents. She just hoped for plenty of time before she had to meet them. If she worked hard she might just manage not to shame him at the inevitable encounter. She knew Alan must be aware of the social and cultural difference between them, but he never spoke of this, and she was grateful. In time she hoped to narrow the gap, to rise a little closer to his level.

She hadn't dared mention anything of her terrible suspicions to him on the phone. The days dragged on, and her share of the telephone conversations became increasingly stilted as her gloom deepened. But she dared not tell him the cause of her misery. What if someone else came into the room and overheard her confession? And how did she know that one of his parents wasn't in the room with him?

'But we were so careful!' he exclaimed in outrage when he heard her news.

'I know,' she said, and suddenly she felt as if she'd dropped into a bottomless pit. What if he didn't believe it was his child? Could he possibly think she'd been having sex with someone else? Seeing her pitiful, frightened little face, Alan put his arms round her and began stroking her hair gently.

'Never mind, darling. It just means we'll have to get married much earlier, that's all.'

Gradually Sheila's trembling subsided. The pit wasn't bottomless after all.

'I'll have to find a job,' he continued. 'My grant's not big enough for two to live on.'

'Three,' she whispered.

He gave her a startled look. 'Three, of course. It's amazing, isn't it? In fact, it's really rather exciting, when you come to think of it.'

Sheila looked up at him with the first spontaneous smile she had managed for days.

'I'm so glad you think so too. In spite of everything, it's really very thrilling, isn't it? But what about your research?'

'I'll have to give that up.'

'No PhD?'

'No, 'fraid not.'

'Oh, Alan, it means so much to you. And you won't get such a good job without it, will you? I wish . . . I almost wish we'd waited.'

'Well, it's too late now.' There was almost a note of grimness in Alan's tone. 'We'll just have to make the best of things as they are.'

His reply left Sheila feeling a little flat. She would have liked something more like a passionate refutation of the idea that they should have put off the final act of possession. His words sowed the seed of a conviction that their marriage was to be an act of reparation rather than a joyful, authorized union of two lovers.

The weeks that followed were dominated for Sheila by a combination of anxiety and shame. Her parents did not hesitate to let her know that they were shocked by their daughter's immoral behaviour, it was clear from what Alan said that his parents were equally dismayed, if for different reasons, and they soon discovered that finding a job wasn't as easy as they had expected. Alan had applied for several university posts and, just to be on the safe side, one or two school-teaching jobs. The wedding had been fixed for early June, and by late May there were still no offers coming in.

Then he was called for interview by two comprehensives, one in Liverpool, the other in Leicester. As there was only one day between the two interviews they decided he'd be better to make just the one journey. It meant he would be away for the best part of five days, not getting back till three days before the wedding. It was very inconvenient, but at least it would mean that by then they might know that he had a job to go to.

The morning after Alan had left, Sheila woke up from a troubled night's sleep and discovered she was bleeding. She lay in bed alarmed and undecided for a while. Was this really important? Should she do anything about it? In the end she decided to tell her mother, who insisted on getting the doctor right away. She was rushed to hospital, but it was too late to save the child. As Sheila's pregnancy was not yet an admitted fact outside the family circle it was agreed that nothing should be said about the miscarriage.

Sheila went home feeling shocked and numb. Sorrow over the loss of the child was mixed up with an awareness of the irony of the situation. If this had to happen, could it not have occurred earlier, before all the plans for the wedding were so advanced, before Alan had formally given up his studies? They could have gone back to their original idea of marrying after he had finished his thesis. How much better that would have been! He would have the qualifications for a better job, she would have had more time to bring her education up to his level and, most important of all, they would be marrying without this cloud that was hanging over them, this blend of anxiety, regret and . . .

She couldn't quite find words for the indefinable something that seemed to be separating them. Indifference? Could that possibly be what she had felt in Alan during the past weeks? A terrible fear – that he now loved her less than before – took possession of her. Perhaps he was just marrying her out of a sense of duty. Of course, she thought, they didn't really need to go ahead now. They could call the whole thing off. The need for an immediate wedding had now disappeared. But the thought of giving Alan up was more than she could bear, and she feared that, if they didn't marry now, they never would.

Besides, she felt sure that, once they were married, once all the present muddle and uncertainty was over, his love would recover all its old freshness and fervour. No, she was sure that the thing to do was proceed with the wedding, and wait for better days, which would follow automatically from the mere fact of being married.

But what if Alan didn't see things this way?

What if he himself suggested postponing the wedding, now that the urgency had disappeared?

The more she thought about it, the more she came to dread this possibility.

When Alan stepped off the train he was greeted by a pale and ghost-like Sheila.

'Well, we've a job to go to at least, in Leicester,' he said in greeting. 'But darling, what's the matter? You look terribly pale.'

'Oh, nothing, really. I've not been terribly well. I think I've missed you too much.' She couldn't possibly tell him here, in the station, among all these people. 'Tell me about the job. Does it seem all right?'

'It'll do.' That was all he had to say on the subject, and Sheila suspected he wasn't really very happy about it. 'Melville's coming tomorrow,' he added. 'You'll like him.' His friend from Cambridge days was to be best man.

Sheila sighed. 'Oh Alan, you know how scared I am at the thought of meeting any of your posh friends.'

Alan laughed. 'Melville's not posh. His father's only a country doctor, and they're a very simple, straightforward family. Nothing to fear there.'

Sheila was not reassured. The fact that Alan couldn't see that a doctor, even a country one, was on a much higher rung of the social ladder than her family worried her. How infinitely high up his own people must be for him not to see the distinction. And the knowledge that in a few days she was to meet these elevated beings added to her insecurity and apprehension.

Melville came the following day and proved Alan right. There was nothing fearsome about him. He certainly seemed rather an original character, with some odd ideas, but he was friendly and natural and soon broke down the barrier of mistrust that Sheila had erected. What with Melville's presence, and Sheila's uncertainty about the nature of Alan's feelings for her, the night before the wedding arrived and she still hadn't told him about the miscarriage. She hadn't exactly decided not to tell him; but she had persuaded herself to wait till Alan himself mentioned the child, and tell him then. As it happened, because of Melville's visit and all the wedding arrangements, Alan simply hadn't said a word about the baby.

Late that night Sheila and her mother were having a final cup of tea before going to bed, checking up that all the necessary arrangements had been made for the next day. She felt a mixture of relief at not having had to tell Alan about the miscarriage, and apprehension over the fact that sooner or later he must be told, and would probably reproach her for not having done so before.

Mrs Barton's thoughts must have been on the same subject, for she broke a long silence with the words, 'Well, and what does Alan think about your losing the baby? Was he upset?'

'Nn . . . no, not really.'

'Well, what did he say?'

'Nothing much.' Sheila felt she was on dangerous ground, but so far at least she hadn't uttered a lie.

'Sheila!'

The girl looked up to face her mother's level gaze. 'Have you told him?'

Sheila's eyes dropped in confusion. Then she shook her head. 'Not yet.'

'What do you mean, "Not yet"? You won't be seeing him again till the wedding. Don't you realize that?'

Sheila nodded. Her eyes were fixed on her own tightly clasped hands. After a moment's silence her mother sighed and then said:

'Oh Sheila!'

Nothing else. The silence that followed was too much for the girl's strained nerves. She buried her face in her hands and burst into tears. Everything had become so ugly and twisted and complicated. She couldn't understand what had happened to her beautiful, radiant love. After a while she tried to express this thought to her mother.

'I don't know what's happened,' she sobbed. 'Everything was so good and we were so happy and suddenly it's all . . . all wrong, and miserable and muddled.'

'And you don't know why? Think, Sheila, think. You did wrong, and this is the punishment. It's as simple as that.'

For a moment Sheila was tempted to accept her mother's explanation. All she need do was repent and everything would come all right. But in spite of the appeal of this viewpoint she had a nagging suspicion that perhaps things weren't really that simple. After all, if she hadn't given herself to Alan would he have gone on loving her?

He might have taken her refusal as a proof of her indifference and given her up in despair. In the midst of all her present misery and distress she hung on to the one certainty she had had since meeting Alan – that her only possible happiness in this life would consist in being married to him. No price was too great to pay in order to secure this prize. Her virginity and peace of mind, Alan's future, the trust she and Alan had shared up till now, all these had to be sacrificed. Come what may, she must be Alan's wife.

Nothing else mattered.

4

Alan sat in his room and stared at the pile of essays on his desk. They were to be marked by the next day, so he'd really have to get started on them. His long walk had done nothing but put off the evil hour. He picked up the top essay and started reading, but soon put it down again. Once again he regretted not having got into university teaching. He felt sure that the standard, even in the first year, would be miles higher than this inept rubbish. He forced himself to start reading again but no, it wouldn't do. His mind was too far away from everything except his own troubles to take in any of the simplistic and rather disjointed statements in front of him.

'Wordsworth's obvious sincerity . . . ' he read as he put the paper down. Stupid idiot, he thought. Sincerity is never obvious. Then he turned the sheet of paper sideways and scribbled in red ink on the margin, '*Il faut longtemps pour être sincère.*' He won't recognize the quotation, of course, he thought with some satisfaction. Probably won't even recognize the language. He felt tempted to give each essay a random mark, just to be done with the lot. He could perhaps scribble 'Relevance?' in the margin at intervals, just to give the impression that he had actually read the thing. The chances were it would hit the mark in most cases. If I weren't such a coward, he thought, I could save myself a lot of time. Or was it professional integrity? Gloomily he decided that this was the less likely explanation.

He had been sitting gazing into space for some time when he heard the girls coming upstairs, running as usual. The sound of their feet on the stairs mingled with the giggling and squealing that seemed to accompany them wherever they went. Hastily he seized his pen, and was bending studiously over one of the essays when the girls came in to say good night.

He dismissed them soon, kissing each in turn. 'Got a lot of work to do,' he explained. The girls left in comparative silence, but as soon as they got out of the room the storm of giggles exploded again, and he could hear its muted outbursts coming from their bedroom at the far end of the corridor. He sighed. Well, it was natural, he supposed. They all did it.

Then he found himself wondering whether Sheila and her sister had giggled like this in their turn. He could hardly visualize Sheila behaving like this, even twenty-five years ago. She had always been so quiet and self-effacing in the early days, as if she were trying to melt into the background. She was still quiet now; but the early gentleness had been replaced by a plaintive, sometimes nagging quality in her voice. She never raged, she never shouted, but she knew how to scratch, she knew how to hurt. And marriage seemed to have brought out this quality in her. It's not been a happy marriage, he thought. Not for her and not for me.

What else could you expect, after such a start?

5

The wedding day itself had been quite a strain, but then, he'd expected it would be. The only thing that had made it tolerable was Melville's presence. Melville had a talent for defusing tense situations. He could always see the funny side of things, and if there wasn't one he could create it. He had been the life and soul of the reception, somehow managing to bridge the gulf between the two strained and anxious families. Unfortunately, they could hardly have him with them on the honeymoon. And it was that night, in the hotel, that disaster really struck, when Sheila burst into tears and confessed about the miscarriage. For once Alan felt not the slightest urge to comfort her. He stood and stared at her weeping form, and felt as if the earth had crumbled to dust beneath his feet. After a pause he said:

'I already felt like a character in a Hardy novel. Now I feel like two.'

Sheila stopped sobbing and sat silent, evidently waiting for him to explain. Alan walked over to the window and gazed at the darkening landscape. After a while he heard a combination of speech and sniffs. 'I wish,' sniff, 'I wish you'd sometimes,' sniff, 'just tell me what we're talking about.'

'Right then, I'll tell you. I'm talking about Jude the Obscure and Angel Clare. Does that help?' he asked acidly.

Sheila's reply was another burst of tears. Alan felt a flood of anger rising in him. For a moment he was tempted to take hold of Sheila and shake the life out of her. He controlled himself and walked over to the door. Before opening it he turned and exclaimed:

'You're so bloody supine, that's what it is. *Supine!* Just do nothing, and you'll get your way in the end. Well, you've got it. I hope you're pleased.' And he walked out, closing the door none too gently behind him.

He spent an hour walking about the little town, crossing the centre again and again. Then, tired out, he stopped on the bridge and looked at the dark water below him. That would be one way out. But he told himself he wasn't seriously prepared to consider such an idea. Not just yet, anyway. But if the future turned out to be as black as it promised . . . ?

Meanwhile he had to decide what to do, which of the two actions open to him he should take. Still seeing himself as a Hardy hero, he wondered whether to accept the situation, as Jude had, or to adopt Angel Clare's drastic solution and refuse to consummate his marriage.

Except that this marriage *had* already been consummated. That's where all the trouble had arisen. If it weren't for that he would still be single, working on his thesis, engaged to Sheila, still in love with her, and with nearly another two years in front of them of the sort of happiness they had known to begin with. And if after that time they discovered that they were no longer in love, well, they could have parted without any ill feelings. It would all have been so simple.

And reversible.

No use in day-dreaming over what might have been, he told himself. I've got to decide what I'm going to do. He felt very tempted to adopt Angel Clare's heroic measures. Serve her right, he thought. She'd have a job explaining it all to friends and family, wouldn't she? And serve her bloody well right, too. And then it occurred to him that he too would have rather a job explaining things to his friends and family. That would

27

be distinctly awkward, he had to admit. And awkwardness was a thing he wasn't at all good at coping with. Alan never liked to have to justify himself in any way. Which meant that he was inclined to give in, even if resentfully, whenever a conflict arose. Just then the word 'supine' came into his head again. Could it possibly apply to him too?

That settled it. He certainly wasn't going to accept the situation. He would leave her. In fact, what was the point of going back? There would be more recriminations, nothing would be gained. If he just never went back, Sheila would know very well why. Then he thought of a practical problem. All his things were in the hotel, in the same room as Sheila herself. So immediate flight would mean abandoning most of his personal possessions, including some books he had been looking forward to reading. While he hesitated over this difficulty, another aspect of the situation struck him. How was he to get away?

It was now nearly eleven o'clock and everything in the little town seemed closed for the night, including the station. That was the trouble with these quiet, picturesque little places. Everything closes down in the early evening. So . . . There was really nothing for it but to go back to the hotel.

He could always spend the night in an armchair in the lounge. Then, in the morning . . . well, he'd see what he wanted to do then.

But he certainly wasn't going back to Sheila tonight. Nothing else would show her how bitterly he resented her deception, her trickery. For he saw perfectly well that she had held back the news of the miscarriage just in case he used that as a reason for putting off the wedding. She could hardly have failed to see that, without the need for a hasty wedding, there might be no wedding at all. After all, it was true. Over the past few months the thought of marriage had lost most of its charm for Alan.

So, that was the matter decided – as far as tonight was concerned, at any rate. He would just slip quietly into the hotel and either go off in the morning before Sheila was up (abandoning all his possessions), or else see her in the morning and explain that he could not possibly live with a woman who had so completely failed to live up to the mutual trust on which every marriage had to be founded. Then he would go with dignity – and with his possessions.

As he made his way back to the hotel he felt satisfied that he had made the best possible decision in the circumstances. Just slip quietly in . . . But the hotel, like the rest of the town, was locked up for the night. He tried the door, he walked round to the back and tried the tradesmen's entrance, he tried the french windows. You'd have thought they were expecting a siege. The place was impregnable. He sat on the front steps of the hotel, wondering what to do.

Then it began to rain.

He wandered about for a while, hoping some charitable policeman would lock him up for the night. But the town was evidently too law-abiding to need a policeman on duty at night. And the rain was getting heavier.

It was being blown at him by a rather icy little breeze. Ten minutes sheltering in the doorway of the town hall decided him.

He went back to the hotel. The only hope was that Sheila might still be up. If he could only attract her attention . . . He walked round to the side of the hotel where he thought their room was. He knew it was on the first floor. At first it looked as if all the lights were out. Then he noticed a chink of light at the side of one of the drawn curtains in what seemed a likely room. It's not easy to find a small stone in the dark in the middle of an urban street. He gave up the attempt and decided to use a coin. He took a two-pence piece out of his pocket and threw it at the chosen window. It missed, hit the wall, fell back on the pavement and got lost in the shadows.

Next he decided to try with a ten-pence coin. If the same thing happened he'd at least have a better chance of seeing it. Exactly the same thing did happen. Only this time he saw the coin beautifully as it rolled into the gutter and disappeared down a drain. This is getting a bit expensive, he thought, as he tried again. His third coin hit the window with a sharp tap, rather louder than he had intended. He half expected to see several heads looking out to see what the noise was about, but nothing at all happened at first. Then, to his relief, he saw the curtain being drawn, a form appeared and opened the window, and a fair head – Sheila's, he fervently hoped – was stuck out.

'*Sheila!*' he called in an urgent stage whisper, 'Come *down* and let me *in*.'

The head disappeared, the window was closed and the curtain drawn. Alan made his way to the front of the hotel and waited, not at all sure whether Sheila would come or not. After all, she had said nothing. If it was Sheila, of course. It might have been someone else who was on her way to complain to the manager.

But after a while the door was opened stealthily by Sheila. They both crept up the stairs in silence, and in silence they faced each other in the bedroom.

At last Sheila spoke. 'You're wet,' she said.

'How perceptive of you!'

Ignoring his irony she told him he'd better get himself dried and handed him a towel. When he'd taken off his jacket and dried his hair she said stiffly:

'Perhaps you'll be good enough to explain all those literary references you flung at me before going out. Hardy, you said.'

This is what I'll have to do for the rest of my life, he

thought, at home and at work. Explain to the ignorant things that every normal person knows anyway. 'Right!' he said. 'Jude had to give up his studies in order to marry a girl who was expecting his child – and then it turned out she wasn't pregnant after all, so the whole thing was unnecessary. And Tess of the d'Urbervilles told Angel Clare, on the very day that they were married, that she had had a child by another man.'

'I don't see the connexion. I haven't had a child by another man.'

'She waited till they were married before she told him. And he assumed that she had done this because she knew he wouldn't marry her if he knew. See the connexion now? You held back vital information. Just like Tess. Only, in fairness to Tess, I must say she tried to tell him.'

For the first time ever he saw Sheila's eyes flash with anger. 'And how do you know I didn't try? Why don't I get the benefit of the doubt? "In fairness to Tess," you say. What about fairness to me? But that's you all over. All you really care about is those people in your damn books. They matter more to you than I do. They're more real to you than I am.' Once again she burst into tears and flung herself on the bed, burying her face in the pillow to stifle her sobs.

Alan was completely nonplussed by her outburst. What affected him most was the suspicion that there might be just a grain of truth in Sheila's accusation. He thought of the great pity and tenderness he had always felt for Tess, and was assailed by the suspicion that perhaps he knew Tess better than he knew Sheila. And there was no doubt that, at this particular moment, he certainly liked Tess better. It struck him that perhaps he ought to pay some attention in future to straightening out his priorities. Meanwhile, it was Sheila, not Tess, who lay smothering her sobs in the pillow.

He sat down on the bed beside her and put a hand tentatively on her shoulder. She made no move to repulse him. Slowly he started to stroke her hair, and her sobbing began to subside.

'Look, Sheila,' he said, 'it's been a hell of a day for both of us. Let's try to forget it all – all the past, and all the future. Just think of the present. Here we are together, and that's what we wanted, isn't it?'

A nod into the pillow, and the sobbing ceased completely.

Alan was running his fingers through her long golden hair. 'Right, then,' he said, 'let's kiss and make it up.'

Sheila shook her head. 'No, I can't.'

'Why not? Are you still angry with me?'

'No.'

'Well then, why won't you let me kiss you?'

A muffled reply came from the pillow. 'Not unless you put the light out.'

'What on earth for?'

'Because I've been crying for hours and I must look absolutely terrible.'

When he woke up next morning Sheila was still asleep. He got up and drew the curtains, just to have a good look at this woman beside him who was now his wife. Her face was still swollen from her hours of crying, and the usual delicacy was lacking from her features. Perhaps this is what she'll look like in another ten or fifteen years, he thought – blunted and coarsened. Or perhaps she'll get thin and waspish. While meditating on the Sheila of the future it struck him that he knew very little of the Sheila of the past. After all, less than a year ago they hadn't even met.

6

Alan had been getting on with his research in Edinburgh, looking forward to a good evening's work, when his mother phoned.

If it hadn't been for that phone call he would never have thought of going to that dance. His mother, it appeared, was worried about him: sure he was working too hard (which was possibly true), and sure he would damage his health – which was probably not true. Alan was a fairly temperate type, even in his excesses.

'Yes, mum, I do go out at times . . . No, I don't spend every evening poring over my books. Yes, of course . . . no, not every evening, just sometimes . . . ' He could see he was in for one of her long worry sessions. Then he thought of the dance at the Union that Mary had been trying to get him to go to. 'Yes . . . yes . . . actually, as it happens, I'm going out this evening . . . just a hop at the Union. Some of the other research students are going. Well, you didn't give me a chance to tell you, did you? You were so sure I wasn't going out. Oh, well, I may have given the wrong impression, but yes, I am going out tonight . . . yes, to this dance . . . '

Bit of a white lie there, he thought, but it's in a good cause. It'll keep her happy and get her off the line, and me off the hook.

After his mother had rung off to go and worry about something else, Alan began to wonder whether he really ought

33

to go. He had just got hold of an article he had been chasing for some time and felt in the mood to do a good demolition job on it, as it totally contradicted the main contention of his thesis. It was very tempting just to stay in and get on with it. But he had said he was going to the dance, and he still had enough respect for truth and for his mother's ability to ferret out inconsistencies to feel uncomfortable about telling her an outright lie. Reluctantly he put his papers away and got ready. At least it would get him into Mary's good books. Mary worked in the cubicle next to his, and was useful for such tasks as making coffee and sewing on buttons.

She was standing near one of the doors, watching the dancers with a rather gloomy expression. He went up to her and was gratified to see the gloom suddenly disappear.

'Oh, you've come after all. I'd given up expecting you.'

'I've been working. Some of us take our research seriously, you know.'

'And some of us don't. Some of us prefer to take our pleasures seriously.'

'Come on then, let's do some serious dancing.'

Seriously or not, they danced together for a long time, then decided to go and have a drink. The bar was crowded to bursting. Alan got the drinks and they looked for somewhere to sit. They found a table for four with only one couple at it.

'Mind if we sit here?'

'My pleasure – our pleasure,' beamed the young man, with a lordly gesture of welcome. He seemed to have reached a stage of near euphoria.

'Allow me to perform the introductions, as they say. This is Sheila. And this', he said bowing, 'is Patrick.'

You sound like a Patrick, thought Alan, as he introduced himself and Mary. Patrick, it appeared, was a final-year undergraduate, reading English, and wholly delighted to meet two research students in the same department. When Alan politely asked Sheila what she was reading, Patrick burst in with a guffaw:

'Oh, she's not reading anything. No longer part of our gilded youth, so to speak, Sheila *works* for her living. Typist.'

Alan thought he detected a slight touch of disdain, or at least condescension in the faintly blurred utterance.

'That means you're the only real adult among us,' he said, turning to Sheila.

Patrick roared his approbation:

'The only real adult! That's good, that's rich! And she's the youngest of the four of us. Bound to be – she's only nineteen, and we're all older than that – I mean, you two doing research . . . bound to be older . . . So she's the youngest and yet she's the oldest, ha-ha.'

'That's not what I said,' retorted Alan, annoyed to find that his attempt to champion the girl had misfired. However, Sheila herself steered them out of what, to judge by Patrick's expression, might have developed into an altercation.

'What's the subject of your research?' she asked Mary.

'Chaucer. Rather a bore, really. He's doing Scott,' with a nod in Alan's direction. Sheila looked as if she hadn't much to say on either subject, but Patrick had.

'Scott? Really?' The touch of faint incredulity in his voice was calculated to show that, while aware of the academic hierarchy, he wasn't going to be intimidated by it. 'I'm a Dickens man, myself. Can't beat old Dickens, you know.'

For a while the conversation centred on Dickens. *David Copperfield* and *Bleak House* were discussed, with a view to establishing the absolute supremacy of one or the other.

'What do you think?' asked Alan, turning to Sheila, in an attempt to bring her into the conversation. She was fair and very pretty, with a timid, rather childlike look about her. She blushed, hesitated, and then blurted out:

'I don't really like Dickens.' This was a damaging admission to make in such company. Patrick broke in again, innocent of any intention of covering up her embarrassment.

'Tell you what, old boy,' he said, 'the best of them all would undoubtedly have been *Edwin Drood,* if only he'd managed to get it finished. One of these days,' he declared modestly, 'I'm going to finish it myself. In fact, I don't mind telling you,' he admitted confidentially, 'I've already started. But I haven't really much time at the moment. Once I've got this little matter of Finals off my chest I'll really get down to it. But I've already got it all worked out. I've cracked the mystery, as you might say. It's just a case of finding time for the actual writing. But I've at least made a start. I see the task as a combination of research and creative writing. And once I've got it done you'll all stop arguing about the merits of the other novels. As for Scott . . . ' He made a gesture of unbounded scorn. He had been diligently attending to his wine bottle during the conversation, and it was now clear that anything in the nature of rational converse was hardly to be expected of him.

Alan got up. 'Come on, Mary,' he said, 'Let's dance. That's what we came for, isn't it?' He said goodbye to Sheila. But as he was leaving the table he was unable to resist the temptation of turning back to Patrick and saying very earnestly:

'Let me know when you finish finishing *Edwin Drood.* I might be able to help you find a publisher.'

'Now, that was naughty,' said Mary, with a delighted giggle.

'Well, he'd earned it, the silly sod. I'm sorry for that nice girl he's got with him, though. I think she deserves something better.'

'Yes, she is nice, isn't she?' Mary spoke without enthusiasm. 'Perhaps a bit on the quiet side, don't you think?'

Alan didn't answer.

They danced. Between dances Mary spoke wittily about

their bibulous neighbour and about the callowness of under-graduates in general. At first Alan was amused. But Mary was evidently determined to sparkle, and the humour began to wear a bit thin. Alan wasn't fond of dancing at the best of times, and this, he decided after a few more rounds, wasn't one of them. He felt Mary was becoming possessive, and she obviously expected him to stay with her for the rest of the evening – and then take her home, no doubt.

It was a bleak prospect, not to say an alarming one. Mary wasn't exactly his idea of the perfect woman, and besides, he didn't want to get involved with anyone just yet – not till he'd finished his thesis and got a decent job, preferably lecturing in some university. This was what his parents expected of him, and what he expected of himself – at any rate since getting his unexpected first. He had hardly dared hope for such glory, and he suspected his parents had been just as surprised as he was.

Eventually he saw a friend standing looking on at the dancing. In frantic dumbshow he managed to signal his distress. At the end of the dance Brian duly appeared, joined them and led Mary out to the dance floor.

'See you,' said Alan with relief, and made his way out of the building for a breath of fresh air. He was tempted not to go back in, but just hadn't the courage. Mary would be furious, and would take it out on him next day – and for how many days after that? No, he'd better go back in. But at least he could hang on outside for a little. If one or two other chaps happened to dance with Mary it would no longer be unarguably 'their' evening, and he would feel less tied.

He was standing there, just outside the building, enjoying his respite, when he saw a small figure pushing through the crowd round the door. He recognized Sheila, alone, looking rather upset, and wondered what was the matter.

After the new couple had gone, Sheila and Patrick had

remained sitting out. She knew he was too unsteady to dance; and he was busy drinking, not even bothering to go through the motions of offering any wine to Sheila. She would have refused it anyway, but it was humiliating to be ignored so completely. Patrick was talking all the time, but not to her. Just talking. And Sheila sat silent, thinking of their deteriorating relationship.

Things had gone so well for the first year, before he started this heavy drinking. He was an entertaining companion, and the prestige of having an Honours student as a boyfriend had done a lot for Sheila's rather shaky self-esteem. None of her family had ever gone or would ever go to university, and Patrick was the open sesame to a different, glamorous world. It was perhaps this more than her diminishing feeling for him that had kept them together over the past months. She hated to see him drink, and feared the consequences at home if anyone should report back to her parents that their daughter had been seen with a tipsy companion. They too had felt flattered that their daughter had a boyfriend a few cuts above their own social standing. But no amount of social advantages would make up for the disgrace of tippling.

She spent many miserable hours puzzling over the problem, knowing that the sensible thing would be to break it off. But the thought of the loneliness that would ensue, with no one to go out with, was daunting. No doubt someone else would turn up in the long run . . .

But in the meantime . . .

Louts, she thought, running through a mental list of all the other young men she knew. Louts. Never open a book. Don't believe anything exists unless they've seen it on the telly.

Sheila wasn't exactly a reader herself. Dickens wasn't the only author she had problems with. But perhaps just because of this she felt in awe of anyone clever enough to have acquired some book learning. So she kept putting off telling Patrick she wasn't going out with him again. Besides, he seemed fond of her – when he was sober. But he always behaved truculently to her when he had been drinking, and today things were worse than usual because early in the evening she had begged him earnestly to stop drinking.

Her train of thought was interrupted by a sudden silence on Patrick's part. She saw he was struggling up from his chair.

'Where are you going?' she asked.

'Bottle's empty, isn't it? Bloody bottle's bloody empty.'

'Oh, Patrick, don't. Please don't get another.'

Paying no attention, he stood swaying and rummaging in his pockets.

'Tell you what, darling, lend me a fiver, will you? Jush till tomorrow.'

'No, Patrick. Please, sit down. I'll get you some coffee.'

'Coffee!' he bellowed.

Some people from a neighbouring table turned and stared. Encouraged by this mark of attention Patrick gave free rein to his indignation:

'Coffee, she says. Coffee! What's the use of coffee to a thirsty man?'

A few appreciative cheers encouraged him further.

'Coffee,' he pursued, 'is a venomous drink, a vicious and venomous drink, a poison. And this viper in my bosom, this Borgia, wants to give me coffee to drink. La-ish an' genelmen,' his voice became maudlin, 'I call upon you to witnesh whatsh happening here.' What happened here was a majestic hiccup, which in its turn raised a modest round of applause from the cognoscenti about him. 'It'sh a bitter thing,' he blubbered on, 'inn . . . nordinately bitter, when your own woman takesh to nag, nag, nagging and triesh to poison . . . '

Here he was interrupted by a suddenly fiery Sheila, who stood up so violently that she knocked her chair over. 'I am *not* your woman,' she cried, then turned and made for the door. It was hard work getting through the crowd, all the harder because people were surging forward to see the cause of the commotion. The chair had made a noisy landing on the parquet floor, and Patrick's wails were keening rhythmically above the general uproar.

Nobody wanted to miss the fun. Sheila ran to the cloakroom, struggled into her coat and back along the corridor to the main door. There she saw two hefty chaps making their way to the bar in answer to a signal from one of the bartenders. 'Bouncers!' she thought, and shuddered. For a moment she wondered whether she should go back and intercede for Patrick, but the mere thought of it made her feel faint. Blinking through her tears she made her way through the crowd hanging around the main door. She felt conspicuous and unprotected.

In a few strides Alan had caught up with her.

'I say, er . . . Sheila, where are you off to?'

Without stopping she looked round and recognized him. 'Home,' she said, almost managing to stifle a sob.

'But what about your boyfriend?'

'He's not my boyfriend, not now, not after tonight.' She explained what had happened. 'I think they're about to throw him out,' she added and hesitated, as if about to go back.

'Come on,' said Alan. He seized her arm and walked her rapidly away from the hall. 'It's what he deserves. And you couldn't stop it even if you tried.' Just then they heard a mocking cheer coming from the hall behind them, suggesting that it was now too late even to try.

They walked on in silence for a few minutes, then the girl stopped abruptly. 'But what about your girlfriend?' she asked.

'She's not my girlfriend. Never has been.'

'Well, your partner, then.'

'No, she's not even my partner. We went there indepen-
dently.'

'You mean she won't expect . . . '

'Certinly not. And anyway, I can't let you go home alone
at this time of night.'

This would mean, he reflected, that Mary would have to
go home alone, unless someone else took over, or unless he
himself went back to the dance after escorting Sheila home.
Quite unnecessary, he decided. This poor little thing was alone
and unprotected. Mary was a very different cup of tea. It took
him years to work out the mechanism of this piece of apostasy
on his part. Mary, by her very self-sufficiency, always made
him feel a little ill at ease, almost on the defensive, a feeling
he was only too conscious of being familiar with in most of the
relationships of his life. But with Sheila – this fragile, almost
waif-like little creature – it was quite different. Beside her he
felt strong, serene, competent and decisive.

This new, strong, Mills & Boon type of self-image buoyed
Alan up during the ensuing days, spent unavoidably at times
in the company of a very cold and distant Mary. Normally he
would have apologized, explaining about the predicament of
the nice girl they had met earlier. But in his present elated
mood he felt he had done enough explaining and apologizing
in his life. Besides, his thoughts were too occupied with Sheila
to leave much time for worry over Mary's feelings, which he
assumed, from her tight-lipped, angry expression, were not of
the tenderest. He simply couldn't imagine Sheila with such an
expression, no matter how much cause she might have to feel
offended. She was such a gentle little thing!

7

When Sheila's mother learned that her daughter was no longer
seeing Patrick but was going out with another young man she
showed a certain amount of surprise mingled with a suspicion
of disapproval. Sheila had assumed that all she need do was
tell her mother she had given up Patrick because he was
drinking too much. But her mother did not sound convinced:

'I don't know,' she said, 'it all seems a little too pat.'

'What do you mean, too pat?'

'Well, you were fond of Patrick, weren't you?'

'Yes. But not after he started drinking like that. Are you
saying I should have stuck with him, in spite of the drink?'
she asked incredulously.

'No, you were right to give him up. It's just this other one,
coming so soon.'

Sheila looked at her mother in amazement. To her it seemed
a stroke of the most unbelievable luck that Alan had arrived at
the very moment when she needed someone most.

'I mean,' went on her mother, evidently struggling with
a concept she found it hard to express, 'don't you think
you should perhaps have . . . well, grieved a little? After
all, you were fond of him. Or at least, we all thought
you were.'

Sheila was silent, wrestling with a new idea. Did this mean
she had never really cared for Patrick? After a moment of
self-examination she said tentatively:

'I think I've grieved enough already. The last few months have been terrible. I've done my grieving.'

Looking at her daughter's troubled face Mrs Barton decided that perhaps she'd been a bit hard on the girl. She remembered the misery of her own broken first engagement and the many desolate months that followed. She ought to be glad that Sheila had been spared this ordeal. And, after all, she hadn't even been engaged to Patrick, though they had been going together for at least a year.

'Well,' she said after a pause, 'let's hope it's all for the best. You must bring your new young man round to tea some day. Another student, did you say?'

'A research student. He's already got his degree,' she added, seeing that her mother didn't seem to appreciate the difference.

'Then what's he still studying for?'

'A second degree.'

'What was wrong with the first one? Or is one not good enough for him?'

Sheila sighed. She foresaw difficulties in bringing Alan home to tea.

'His father is a barrister,' she explained. 'They have much higher standards than we have – educationally, I mean,' she added hastily, seeing her mother beginning to bridle. 'If he wants a good job he'll need a PhD.'

Mrs Barton made no further enquiries. She too foresaw difficulties.

8

For the next few months Alan was happier than ever before. Not that he had had an unhappy childhood. As the cherished only child of a late marriage he had been given everything that could make a child happy – affection, attention, intellectual stimulation, and an abundance of material good things. His father Michael Morley, had also been an only child. But there the similarity ended, for his parents had spent their lives propping up the outposts of Empire, and Michael had spent his childhood at boarding school, with so-called holidays spent at the house of an elderly aunt.

Nothing was permanent; nothing was 'home'.

When his parents came home on furlough they stayed with the aunt, quite content not to have a place of their own in England. So young Michael grew up feeling provisional, not much wanted and, above all, not much known. Early in life he had decided that if he ever had a son he should not be sent to boarding school. He would keep him at home and do all he could to provide a stable background to which the child could feel he belonged.

By the time he had left school he had settled on the law as a career and devoted the best of his energies to it, with few other interests to distract him, till he was in his late thirties. Then he met Georgina Maitland, and became suddenly and profoundly distracted by her beauty and sensibility. Georgina had spent the whole of her adult life looking after an ailing widowed mother, and writing poetry as a solace. When she met and fell in love with Michael Morley, and learned of his love for her, she knew she was going to have to make a momentous change in her life.

She could no doubt have tried to combine marriage with her mother-caring and her poetry but she was convinced that she couldn't possibly do all three things well. So she made her decision. She would marry Michael, look after the old lady as usual in the family house, and give up her poetry. 'It is essential to know one's limits and to work within them,' she would say to those who regretted her decision to stop writing. And there were many who did regret it, for she wrote well. But with characteristic determination she put her poetry out of her mind, and concentrated on her home. When, a few years later, her mother died, the gap that might have been filled by a return to poetry had already been filled by Alan.

Both parents, for different reasons, made the boy the centre of their universe; Michael because he saw in him a substitute for the young Michael, and was determined that this time the child should have the love and security that had been missing in the earlier version; Georgina because all the passion and dedication that had formerly gone into her poetry were now focused on her son.

And so Alan had grown up as the centre of his own universe. Not that he had been spoiled. He was by no means what you could call a spoilt child. But he did realize early on his own importance in his parents' scheme of things. Instead of giving him security, this fostered a certain diffidence in him. He was always a little afraid that he wasn't coming up to their expectations, though they were careful not to show disappointment over his performance at school. His marks were always better than average, but never brilliant.

And brilliance, he felt sure, was what was hoped of him.

It was an immense relief when he made it to Cambridge.

The joy of success was slightly marred by his perception that this relief was as fervently felt by his parents as by himself. He couldn't help feeling slightly shaken by the nearness of the thing. It was as if all three of them had been walking along the edge of a precipice, the depth of which he hadn't fully realized at the time. One false step on his part would have plunged them all to perdition, or so it seemed to his uncertain mind.

So now he was, and they were, on safe ground. He was going to read English, always his favourite subject, and he had a vague idea that after that he would *write*. What he would write, and why he would write it, he didn't quite know. Not journalism, anyway. He knew he wasn't competitive enough for that. Besides, what he was really interested in was literature, especially fiction. So he would write novels, no doubt.

He had never quite understood why his mother had given up writing poetry. Simply having a home to look after – even one that included a husband with an exacting career, an invalid mother and, later, a child – seemed to him an insufficient reason. After all, they could afford plenty of help in the house. The complexities of psychological demands eluded him at this stage, even though he himself was caught in the same net of alien hopes, desires and expectations. But at that time he did not know that they were alien. He took it for granted that what his parents hoped for him was what he himself hoped for.

After the initial excitement of his first term at Cambridge had worn off, he began to realize that there were higher hurdles ahead. If he didn't leave with a good degree he knew he would consider himself a failure. And he soon realized that, intellectually, he was outclassed by most of his companions. The only thing for it was to make up for his lack of brilliance by sheer hard work. This was when his mother began to worry about his health, and he took to wandering rapidly about the colleges every evening for twenty minutes, just to be able to assure her that he was getting fresh air and exercise.

Before the sudden, unexpected glory of Alan's flash-in-the-pan First, the highlight of his Cambridge career was his friendship with Melville Wilson.

9

It was on one of Alan's fresh-air gallops that they met. Both were going round the same corner at speed, but in opposite directions. The collision was so violent that they bounced off each other like billiard balls. Alan, with his slight build, got the worst of the encounter. He lost his balance and, before he knew what had happened found himself sitting on the grass with a burly young man bending over him.

'You all right?' The accent was decidedly Scottish.

'Perfectly, thank you.'

'Not concussed, or anything?'

Alan laughed. 'If I am, you should be too.' He scrambled to his feet, ignoring the proffered hand of his companion.

'Doesn't follow. It would depend on the relative hardness of the heads concerned. This one,' and the stranger tapped his own forehead, 'this one is made of sterner stuff than most.'

'A hard-headed Scot, are you?'

The stranger laughed. 'How did you guess?'

They chatted for a while, then decided to go for a drink. More than half an hour later Alan remembered about his twenty minutes. He had been away from his books for more than double the usual time.

'I'll have to get back,' he said, 'I've got work to do.'

'Haven't we all? But you don't have to do it *now*, do you?'

'I'd really . . . better get back.' Alan saw his companion eyeing him quizzically. 'Some work I've to hand in tomorrow,' he lied. As he stood up he added, 'Perhaps we'll bump into each other again some time.' He hoped they would. He had thoroughly enjoyed Melville's zany humour, and reflected that since coming to Cambridge he'd really laughed very little. But he couldn't quite bring himself to suggest another meeting – just as he couldn't accept the other's outstretched hand to help him up after his fall. Again and again he had noticed this trait in himself, this inability to let himself do the very thing he wanted to do. It had cost him many a possible friendship, this reserve of his.

Melville, however, suffered from no such inhibitions. 'Let's do it metaphorically next time,' he suggested. 'See you here at nine tomorrow evening. Okay?'

It wasn't long till they were meeting nearly every day, rather to Alan's surprise. He had always got on well with his companions at school, but had never made any close friends. There was always a point beyond which he retreated into his privacy. The flamboyant Melville seemed to have the trick of overriding Alan's inhibitions. He was certainly very good at combatting his own, assuming he had any. Not the sort of person Alan had imagined as the typical Scot.

Quite early on in their friendship Melville discovered how hard Alan was working, and raised objections. 'That's no way to live,' he said, almost shocked. And Alan found himself explaining how difficult he was finding it to keep up. 'I'm just not as brilliant as most of the other chaps here. My only chance is to work extra hard.'

'Quite right,' said Melville approvingly.

'So, you see, I just have to spend nearly all of my free time working.'

'Quite wrong!' declared Melville.

'Now you're being contradictory. Self-contradictory, I mean.'

'Oh no I'm not. I agree you must work hard, extra hard, if you like; but you certainly shouldn't think of spending all of your free time working.'

'I said, *nearly* all.'

With a lordly gesture Melville dismissed this unworthy quibble.

'Well,' insisted Alan, 'what's wrong with that, if I'm prepared to do it?'

'Simply this: it leaves you no time for living.'

'Living!'

'Yes, living, you revolting little Calvinist. Anyone would think you were the Scot, not me.'

'I must say, you've certainly overcome your Calvinist background all right. Seriously though, it's all right for you. You're one of the brilliant ones. You can do it all without working – or almost without, anyway.'

'All right, so I'm one of the lucky ones. But it's also a question of having a sense of proportion. What are you doing all this work for? Why is it so terribly important to get a good degree?'

'Why? Well . . . I don't know. It just is.'

'To please your distinguished parents?'

'Partly, perhaps. And why not? One doesn't want to let the side down, does one?'

'There again I'm lucky, I suppose,' admitted Melville. 'No side to let down, in my case. My father's just a village doctor with no pretensions. And I'm one of eight children, so the investment in me is correspondingly smaller.'

'Yes, you're lucky.' Alan thought longingly of the wonderful freedom from responsibility of not being an only child. Then, fearing to seem disloyal to his parents, he added, 'It must be fun to have lots of brothers and sisters about.'

'Some of the time. Relative fun, you might say. But, to return to our muttons, I'm not such a frivolous character as you might think. I have a *mission in life*.'

'Which is?'

'To prevent people from working too hard. I spend a lot of time prising people away from their books. It does them a world of good.'

'Shouldn't think it would do their degrees much good.'

'On the contrary, it's an enormous help. I'm seriously thinking of asking the college to take me on as a full-time interruptor. I'm sure the proportion of firsts would go up dramatically.'

Alan laughed. 'All right. I'll let you help me get my first. I'll come to the picnic tomorrow.'

'Good man! Arcadia awaits, with its full complement of shepherdesses, of course.'

The shepherdesses turned out to be highly sophisticated young women, one of whom evinced a desire to explore the country-side in Alan's presence. They found an idyllic spot in a little grove, and sat down on the green grass beside a brook that could only be described as purling. Alan wondered what sort of romantic preliminaries might be required – what sort of, presumably fake, opposition he might have to overcome. He visualized the nymph quoting to him, 'Nay sweet, now nay, now nay, I am not ready.'

Nikki, it appeared, was ready, and no preliminaries were required. She evidently expected her advances to be wel-come, and plunged *in medias res* without delay. When they rejoined the others some time later she seemed as poised and unconcerned as ever. Alan was divided between a feeling of elation and a mild sense of disappointment. Well, he thought, he'd done it at last, proved his manhood, as they say; another hurdle cleared. But mingled with his relief was a suspicion that the experience hadn't been as wonderful as he had been led to expect. Perhaps it was something that improved with practice.

So he practised: diligently, as with all things. By the end of his second year at Cambridge he had acquired something of a reputation as a budding Don Juan. It was his one outstanding success so far, and he regretted that, in the nature of things, he could hardly boast to his parents about this achievement. Still, it gave him a certain amount of superficial assurance. The irony was that it was precisely his insecurity and fear of being committed that contributed to his reputation. He made a point of never going out more than three times with the same girl, for fear of becoming involved.

He was playing it very cool indeed. Paramount on his agenda was the final outcome of his studies. He simply must leave Cambridge with a good degree. And anyway he found not getting involved relatively effortless. None of the girls in question stirred in him anything more than an easily satisfied sexual interest. He really didn't at all mind not seeing them again after they had had their quota of dates. Not one of them could be compared to Lisha. Yes, perhaps it was his admiration of Lisha that made it so easy to love and leave the others.

10

During his first summer vacation at Cambridge Alan had
spent a week at Melville's house in south-west Scotland,
and had completely fallen in love with the place – the house,
the village, the family and the open, noisy, seemingly dis-
organized way of life. Melville's brothers, sisters, and an
unspecified number of boyfriends, girlfriends and just plain
friends, swarmed about the house. Before every meal a scout
had to go through the rambling house and the extensive garden
to count heads. Alan thought of his own mother's worry and
tension if even one guest had to be taken into account, and
wondered at Mrs Wilson's serene acceptance of the risk that
the scout might well have miscounted. After all, as she said,
an extra one or two made no difference.

'My mother would die,' he exclaimed the first time that two
uncounted members of the household turned up for the meal.

'Oh well, with numbers like this it's different. There's
always plenty.'

'And two out of twelve is a much smaller proportion of
excess, as it were, than two out of two or three,' pointed out
the doctor with a jocular nod at the two excess members in
question.

'Yes, I know. But yet . . . No I don't think it's a matter
of proportion, or even of plenty. I think it's that my mother
likes to have everything rigidly planned beforehand. I think if
she was organizing a meal for thirty – which, by the way, is

inconceivable – she would still be terribly upset if one extra turned up.'

'I expect her standards are higher than ours,' remarked Mrs Wilson. 'She would probably find us terribly slapdash and unsatisfactory.'

Alan tried to imagine how his mother would react to the Wilson household. She had met Melville and liked him. But Melville in isolation was not quite so riotous as the whole household in operation. Would she be horrified? Or would some part of her manage to escape and enjoy it all thoroughly, as he did?

'I don't know,' he said, 'I'd like to think she might just enjoy it all immensely.'

Melville's sister Lisha looked at him enquiringly. 'A kind of liberation?' she suggested.

Alan felt something click inside his head. That was it! A kind of liberation. That was just what he himself felt in this household. He looked at Lisha with glowing eyes. 'Yes,' he said, 'that's just it.'

Later on Lisha found him in the garden, sitting on a bench watching some of the others playing tennis. She sat down beside him and reminded him of the conversation over the tea table. 'What is it your mother needs to be liberated from?' she asked. 'Her own self-imposed rules and regulations and high standards?'

Alan thought for a little. Then he said:

'Well, she has to keep up a pretty high standard because of my father's profession. But yes, I think you're right. It would all be self-imposed anyway. She's like that.'

'And you?'

'What about me?'

'Whose high standards do you need to be liberated from?'

'You've been talking to Melville.'

'I often talk to Melville. But not about this.'

'Oh, I thought . . . It's just – that's the sort of thing he says.'

'We're pretty close, Melville and I. It's not surprising if we come to the same conclusions.'

There was a pause, and then Alan resumed the conversation:

'What makes you think I'm in need of liberation?'

'I don't quite know. I just feel, somehow, that you're not as free as we are. And it just occurred to me, when we were talking about your mother's way of life, that perhaps you're a bit too much influenced by her standards. They don't seem to be exactly flexible.'

He laughed. 'You can say that again. But just in case you're ready to put all the blame on her I think I should point out that my father isn't exactly the soul of flexibility either.'

'There you are, you see!' exclaimed Lisha.

Suddenly stricken once again by the feeling of being disloyal to his parents, Alan said:

'I think I seem to be giving the wrong idea of them. They're really splendid people.'

'Of course they are,' she agreed. 'That's just it.'

Alan nodded. That, he felt, was indeed the trouble. His parents' virtues, he suspected, had made him incapable of following any course of which they would disapprove. Then he thought of his recent sexual adventures, and rephrased his statement. Because of his parents' virtues he was incapable of following a course of which they would disapprove unless he stood a pretty good chance of not being found out. He had to admit that this was an accurate assessment of the situation, but it certainly didn't show him in a flattering light. Spinelessness tinged with hypocrisy – that seemed to be a realistic description of his character.

For a moment he felt depressed; but it was difficult to indulge in self-pity in this family. There was always too much going on, and he gladly succumbed to the first distraction that was offered, and recovered his good spirits.

During the remainder of his time at Cambridge he spent some part of every vacation in Galloway, staying with the Wilsons at Auchentoull, and their home became the epitome of all that a home should be. Galloway was for him paradise, the promised land. And it was largely because of his love of Scotland and the Wilson family that he chose Scott as the subject of his research. To be based in Edinburgh, with the possibility of frequent visits to Galloway, seemed an ideal arrangement.

But, as luck would have it, just before he was due to start his first term in Edinburgh, Melville got a job with a publishing firm in London, so the visits to Galloway were less frequent than he had hoped. And Lisha had got a job in York, so she wasn't around much either. Gradually, Auchentoull and the Wilson household faded into a sort of golden dream, something as precious and as irrecoverable as youth.

11

Never in his life had Peter Eward seen such a hedge. It was at least twelve feet high, white with hawthorn blossom, like a great, frothy waterfall. In the rays of the evening sun it shone with a soft radiance that seemed to suggest that the light was coming from the blossom instead of being received by it. He thought he would like to come back and see it at night. Even in the dark, he imagined, it must still shine.

He crossed the road to have a closer look at the flowers. It occurred to him that he hadn't looked closely at hawthorn blossom for many years. Perhaps this is what has been missing in my life, he thought. And the words that he had strung together almost frivolously seemed to take on a more serious meaning as he gazed into the heart of the tiny white florets with the little dark marks near the centre. Was it these darker spots, he wondered, that gave the white of the hawthorn its wonderful softness? Or perhaps it was because each minute flower was surrounded by a suspicion of shadow from its neighbours, so that the white of each cluster was never unbroken.

He heard a car approaching on the main road and wondered whether he ought to cross over to the other side of the lane, where there was a wider grass verge. But from the speed of the car he decided it couldn't possibly be about to turn into the side road he was on. He would stay beside the hedge, drinking in its incomparable beauty.

Too late he realized that the car had indeed turned into the side road. It had taken the bend far too fast, and was hurtling towards him, evidently out of control. For a moment it seemed to be heading straight for him as he flattened himself against the hedge. Then, with only feet to spare, it skidded away from him, and the front wheels missed him narrowly. But the car was still out of control; as it passed him the rear swung round, hit him on the side and threw him into the hedge, where he slid down, deep into the soft whiteness.

Half an hour later a passing motorist found him, unconscious, with his face covered in blood.

The next day the following item appeared in the local press:

Yesterday evening Mr Peter Eward, (47), of The Mount, Castery, N. Yorkshire, sustained serious injuries when hit by an unknown car. The injured man, who was on holiday in this area, was found by a passing motorist, who alerted the police. The victim was taken to the local hospital, where his condition is said to be stable.

When Peter recovered consciousness all he was aware of was whiteness and pain. Great waves of pain crashed down on him, blotting out everything else. Then he would become aware of the whiteness again; it was there when he opened his eyes, there still when he closed them in weariness. After a while he began to distinguish between the two whitenesses – the outside glare of the hospital room, and the inner, softer white that surrounded him when he closed his eyes.

Slowly he began to remember the wall of hawthorn blossom and the sensation of being flung into its depths. Later he became able to identify another kind of wall, the bare, aseptic wall of the little room attached to the casualty ward. Then another whiteness moved towards him, with a blur above it that resolved itself into the face of the staff nurse. She said something to him, but he couldn't make any sense of the words. Gradually the face became blurred again, the voice receded, and he sank back into unconsciousness.

A few days later his first visitor came. By this time he had a clear idea of what had happened and of the extent of his injuries – fractures all down the left side, from upper arm to thigh, and several deep scratches on the face inflicted by the thorns of the white wall as he sank into it. They told him he was lucky, there had been no internal injuries.

His visitor was Mrs Barnes, his landlady. At first he wondered whether he was up to carrying on a conversation, but soon discovered that little participation on his part was called for.

'Oh dear, Mr Eward, this is terrible, terrible. And you on holiday, too. You've no idea how upset I was when I heard. But that was nothing, of course, to what I'd gone through with you not coming back that night. I simply didn't know what to do. Nothing like it ever happened to me before, and I've been taking in summer visitors for years and years. So I waited till the next day and then I phoned the police – I hope you don't consider that was taking a liberty, I mean . . . '

'No, not at all,' he managed to murmur, 'quite right.'

'And I've brought you some grapes – and nobody seems to know who did it, which is terrible, quite terrible. We all thought it might be the young farmer at the crossroads, he's a wild young man. But it seems it wasn't him – he had an alibi, anyway. You didn't happen to see the driver, did you?'

Peter shook his head.

'Or take his number?'

Another headshake.

'I thought as much. I mean, you'd have said, wouldn't you? So you'll just have to stay here till you're better, and perhaps we'll never know, will we? And by the way, about your room, I might as well let it while you're away, don't you think? I mean, it's the busy season, and I hate turning people away, and I've had so many asking.'

'Yes, of course,' put in Peter, wondering how many of them she proposed putting into that one small room.

'So I can just pack your stuff and put it away somewhere, to use the room, I mean? If it's not taking too much of a liberty, that is.'

Peter was relieved when she left. Even his few brief interventions in the conversation had left him exhausted. But he was glad she had come. It seemed to suggest he had made some progress in his efforts at getting in touch once again with his fellow men. Then he remembered what she had said about needing the room, and wondered whether perhaps he was being over-optimistic. Her visit might have been prompted purely by self-interest. He looked at the grapes and wondered how much significance to attach to the offering. He suspected that no self-respecting member of her class could possibly think of making a hospital visit without bearing grapes. Still, you never know, he told himself. She said she would come back, so perhaps . . .

Mrs Barnes did come back the following week, with more grapes and no requests to make, so he took it that they had established some sort of contact. That, he told himself, was satisfactory as far as it went. As for the hospital staff, he felt he was acquitting himself reasonably well with them. He hoped they didn't find him too distant. They were all obviously trying to be nice to this poor, solitary man, who had no visitors except for a once-a-week landlady, and who received no post from anyone. Not a single get-well card, poor thing! Yet, in spite of the realization that they must think him very odd, Peter felt he was getting on quite well with them.

Things became more difficult when he was considered well

enough to be transferred to the main ward. He found the continuous noise tiring, and attempts at conversation with his neighbours frustrating. On one side he had a retired Nottinghamshire miner, whose language was a closed book to him; on the other a chirpy little Cockney, whose accounts of himself were as profuse as they were bewildering.

This Protean character seemed to have been chimney-sweep, rag-and-bone man, post office clerk, plumber, bookie and barman, to say nothing of certain other occupations, hinted at with a broad wink rather than actually defined. Despite the wide range of his neighbour's experience, Peter found that they had little in common, no doubt due to the narrowness of his. He had trained and practised as a civil engineer, that was all. None of the little Cockney's avocations seemed to have covered any of the ground with which Peter was familiar. Even that national mainstay of indifferent conversation, the weather, failed them. In hospital there is no weather. It forms part of the outside world, from which the patient is temporarily exiled. To talk about the weather outside, even though it was only a few yards away, on the other side of the wall, seemed as irrelevant as to make a comment on the current monsoon in Bangkok.

After the first day or two in the big ward Peter found himself retreating into his shell again. Even the nurses seemed more remote. With all the other men vying for their attention, they had less time to spend on Peter. Besides, not only was his condition improving, but he had been relieved of what, to them, seemed the most painful part of his ordeal, solitary confinement. He now had plenty of company, so he couldn't possibly be lonely. It didn't occur to them that he could just about manage a one-to-one relationship, but not much else. He found that the only way he could cope with life in the ward was by shutting it out of his consciousness as much as possible.

So, instead of continuing his efforts at establishing some sort of human contact, he found himself going over and over again in his mind the events that had led to his gradual withdrawal from society. And then, of course, there was Andrew to think about. But the problems raised by his connexion with Andrew were too bewildering and, above all, too new, for him to cope with at the moment. Instead he preferred to concentrate on the origins of his predicament.

12

Peter had never set out to be a hermit. It had happened by degrees, and without his even noticing. First of all his wife had left him – no quarrel, nothing like that. She had just gone off with another man one day. It had not been a particularly happy marriage, but it hadn't struck him as worse than most. Almost at once Alicia had come into his life, and all had been well for some time. Then they had begun to drift apart, and at the same time he and his business partner had started to get on each other's nerves. It was then that his father had died suddenly, leaving him the large, threadbare house in the country.

Peter realized that this was an opportunity for a complete change of lifestyle, and sold his share of the business. He would live in the country, in the family house. Even then, total isolation had not been his intention. Friends were to come and stay with him, and some did, at first. But he found their presence, on the whole, rather irritating. He was amazed at the difference between seeing these people in town, for the odd evening's entertainment, and having them staying in the same house.

It altered the whole relationship.

And it also upset what had now come to be his normal way of life. Having to take someone else into account was really rather a strain. Worse than marriage in a way, because of the spasmodic nature of the tie. You had no sooner worked out a *modus vivendi* than that guest left and you had to start all over again with the next one. Life was pleasanter wandering about on your own, and reading quietly by yourself in the evenings.

It was some time after he had settled down into this routine that his car packed in, and he decided it wasn't worth getting another one. For the past year he had only used it to get provisions from the village. So he made an arrangement with one of the local grocery vans to bring him an order once a week and to pick up anything else he needed from the shops in the village. That saved him the bother of his weekly trip for supplies. In the course of the average week he had a few minutes' conversation with the van driver, made one or two telephone calls to other tradesmen, and that constituted the sum total of his dealings with his fellow men.

One day he thought: they must think I'm quite a misanthrope. It seemed a funny idea. He had never set out to avoid people in general. That was just the way it had happened. Although he had considerable respect for the solitaries of this world he had never thought of himself as belonging to that élite. They had chosen solitude in order to be able to fulfil their destiny – to meditate, to pray, to create some work of art or new theory. With him it was different. He had become a solitary more or less by accident.

Not that this worried him. He enjoyed his leisure and his solitude, the endless ability to choose what and where, and when and for how long, without having to take anyone else's needs or desires or expectations into account.

As his solitude deepened and his few last friends stopped coming to see him he had experienced no sense of loss. Alicia was perhaps the one exception. He did miss her after she stopped coming. And her last visit, the one that the mirror over the mantelpiece had announced, often came back to him with a tinge of nostalgia. And the day he left home, the day he made his revolutionary decision, he had relived that last meeting with Alicia in its every detail.

It was a cold day, and he was advancing towards the fire to put more coal on, when the mirror above the mantelpiece showed him the figure of Alicia coming through the doorway.

He met her halfway across the room and took her hands in his. 'Come and sit by the fire.'

'I rang,' she said. 'I rang but nobody came, so I just walked in. I thought I'd find you in this room.'

'I must be getting deaf. It's what happens as you get old.'

She laughed. 'I don't believe it.'

'Don't believe what? About the deafness or about the getting old?'

'Neither. If you're old, then I must be well on the way – and I'm not! Nor have I any intention of ever getting old. As for the deafness, it's just your old trick. You listen to yourself – so hard you can't hear anything else.'

'Or anyone else?'

She nodded. '*Ipse dixit*,' she said smiling, faintly mocking.

They sat in silence for a while. She was staring into the fire, and he was looking at her, admiring her warm colouring, her dark, glowing eyes, and the vivacity of her face even when, as now, it bore a thoughtful expression.

Suddenly he burst out laughing.

'You're the only thing in this room that doesn't look shabby,' he exclaimed. 'You look absolutely great. That dark green's a fabulous colour. And the velvet makes you look positively regal.'

Regretfully he had let go of this pleasant memory and relinquished the daydream that went with it. No point living in the past, he told himself. The present had plenty to offer – the house I was brought up in, leisure, a comfortable income, time to read, time to walk about the countryside, good health. I'm really very lucky.

He looked about him for confirmation of his good fortune, and remembered his words to Alicia about the shabbiness of the place. And that had been a year ago. Things had hardly improved since then. They don't, if you do nothing about them, he told himself. And the shabbiness, he knew, was beginning to extend to the owner of the house as well. And it wasn't so easy to do anything about that. Dye his hair, perhaps?

He had realized some time ago that it could no longer be classified as dark.

He had a good look in the mirror. Pretty well white, really, especially at the front. It made a striking contrast with his dark skin and eyes, and he was aware of this, and not altogether displeased by it. But the fact remained that the white hair and the wrinkles round the eyes were all signs of ageing. Growing older is all very well if you're maturing at the same time, he thought. But am I? Suddenly it seemed to him that he'd got stuck in some sort of limbo, neither advancing nor retreating. In suspension. And growing older all the time. Getting nowhere, mentally, morally, spiritually. On the way to being an elderly drop-out.

It was a depressing prospect. To shake himself out of his gloomy mood Peter decided that some form of action was called for. He must get out of the house a bit more. He would go on one of those long walks he had frequently taken when he had first come here after his father's death. It meant going through the village to reach the high ground beyond. Perhaps that was why he had stopped going that way, just to avoid the village. And he remembered the feeling of annoyance he so often experienced when out walking if he saw another human figure. Perhaps he really had become a bit of a misanthrope!

He prepared a sandwich, put it in his pocket and set off.

On the outskirts of the village he came across two little girls picking wild raspberries. He was quite close to them before one of them saw him. She gazed at him with panic-stricken eyes, then turned and fled back to the village.

'Run, Mary, run!' she cried. 'It's the hermit.'

The other little girl followed her in a mad, terrified stampede. On the road lay two little polythene bags with raspberries spilling out of them. Like blood, he thought. He felt a shiver run down his spine, and turned and went back to the house.

He left his unneeded sandwich on the kitchen table and wondered what to do next. He needed some occupation to drive from his mind the scene of the two little girls running from him in terror – but what? That was the trouble with leisure. It lacked the power to drive out unwelcome thoughts. So now he knew what people thought of him.

The hermit.

But why this terror? Was there something frightening in his appearance, in his very self? Or was it simply that the mere idea of a hermit was in itself frightening?

But then, there had been all sorts of holy men, saints even, who had been hermits. Evidently he didn't qualify for that category, he thought with a wry smile. And there seemed to be nothing between that and the other, terrifying extreme. Not in the popular mind, at any rate. But in reality? Could one not be an ordinary, middle of the road, harmless sort of a hermit? He tried to think of examples of this type, but could not.

And if only the two extremes were possible and since there was no question of his belonging to the upper crust, what then? He found it as hard to believe in his own complete wickedness as in his own supreme goodness. He had committed no crimes, he hadn't even wished to commit any. Perhaps he wasn't doing much good in his present way of life, but he certainly wasn't doing any harm. The worst that could be said of him was that he had cut himself off . . . no, that was too strong an expression, it implied too much deliberate choice – he had allowed himself to drift away from his fellow men. Was that a crime?

His restlessness drove him from room to room, looking for an answer. At one point he found himself staring at a large bookcase full of his father's books. He put out his hand and picked one out at random. *The Meditations* of Marcus Aurelius. His father had often spoken of it, almost with veneration. Perhaps for that reason Peter had always avoided it, knowing how different his father's tastes were from his own. Perhaps it's time I changed my mind about this chap, he thought. Perhaps he's not really such an old bore as I've always assumed. He felt so thoroughly disoriented that he decided to let himself be guided by chance and this unknown philosopher. He would open the book at random and just read till he found something, anything at all, that could apply to his present situation, and then he would try to put that idea into practice.

Even if it meant selling all his wordly goods and giving to the poor? Was that the sort of thing Marcus Aurelius was likely to recommend?

Peter knew the Roman was a Stoic, so he was prepared for some pretty harsh measures. But his need of some kind of direction in his life had suddenly become so great that he was prepared to try anything.

He opened the book and read:

A branch severed from an adjoining branch necessarily becomes severed from the whole tree. A man, likewise, who has been divided from any of his fellows has thereby fallen away from the whole community. But whereas the branch is lopped by some other hand, the man, by his feelings of hatred or aversion, brings about his own estrangement from his neighbour and does not see that at the same time he has cut himself off from the whole framework of society.

Pure coincidence, he told himself. Still, it was rather extraordinary that he had lighted on such an appropriate passage, tailor-made for his requirements. Bull's-eye, Marcus Aurelius, he admitted grudgingly.

So, I'm a severed branch, he told himself. And I seem to have done it myself through my feelings of 'hatred and aversion'. Hatred? Perhaps not as bad as that. But aversion, yes, certainly, more and more aversion, towards more and more people. And where had it started, this aversion?

Perhaps when he'd started having problems with his partner. Instead of clearing the matter up, he'd turned away – an aversion in the literal, etymological sense. It seemed to him now that he had founded his present way of life on a piece of unfinished business. And, according to this analysis, it only needed one example, one estrangement from his neighbour to bring about the whole thing, to cut himself off from the whole framework of society.

He had known for some time that he was cut off in this way, and it hadn't worried him. He could get along without society. But now, meditating on this passage, he saw that the whole thing had gone much further, that it necessarily had to do so. For society, the community, was as much a part of the natural world as the individual is a part of the community. He had now progressed to the final stage, he had cut himself off from the natural world, and that was why he could no longer feel its joy. For he acknowledged now that his life had been rather joyless for some time past.

Nevertheless, he read on, *it is in our power, by grace of Zeus, the author of all fellowship, to grow back and become one with our neighbour again, so playing our part once more in the integration of the whole.*

To grow back, he mused. Not go back, but grow back. A lengthy process, and a painful one. Growth means change and change means suffering. But the reward would be 'playing our part once more in the integration of the whole'. And suddenly he saw the whole process not as a painful necessity, but as a challenge and a promise. The idea of playing his part, not merely for his own sake, but for the sake of the whole, seemed to lift the huge weight of purposelessness from his shoulders. He knew what he had to do. The difficult bit was deciding how to do it, where to start in his quest for some sort of human relationship.

He decided against trying to revive any of his old friendships. The task in hand would be difficult enough without the memory of all his past failures. And it wouldn't do to try here in the village, either. His reputation as a hermit would make the task doubly difficult. Again he thought of the two little girls who had fled from him. He imagined what the encounter could have been like if they hadn't recognized him as 'the hermit'. The little dark one, who looked about eight years old, might have smiled shyly when he greeted them.

(Query: *would* he have greeted them? Well, yes, now he would.)

Her companion, with fair curly hair, a little bit older, less timid, would have answered. She might even have come over and offered him some of her fruit. 'One raspberry,' he would have said, thinking of Cyrano's one grape. And she would have picked the biggest raspberry from her bag, and held it out to him with red-stained fingers. And then the little one would have come forward, holding out a raspberry for him, and he would have taken it and thanked them gravely, and they would all have played their part in the integration of the whole.

But because he was 'the hermit' it had all turned out quite different, and the peaceful tableau of the two little fruit-pickers had turned into a frantic scamper of blue-jeaned legs and cries of fear, and two pathetic little bags of spilled raspberries lying in the dust.

No, he would have to go somewhere new, where he had no reputation to live down, and start from scratch. Where he was going he didn't know. He would just set off and let chance find a place for him.

13

Peter set off that very day, and chance found a place for him – several, in fact, during the course of the next few months; none of them particularly satisfactory. He had decided to look for some kind of work, as this would inevitably bring him into contact with other people. It did, of course, but perhaps not the most promising kind of contact on which to build a relationship.

The main problem was that there are no engineering jobs available to the casual worker. All he could hope for were unskilled jobs, where his fellow workers would have nothing in common with him. In the next eight months he worked as a hotel porter, night watchman, book salesman, gardener, window cleaner and assistant at a small sawmill. Most of the jobs were dreary, some were physically demanding, and none of them was much good from the point of view of establishing new relationships. The job as night watchman he found relatively pleasant, since it catered for his habitual love of solitude. But for that very reason it was the least suited to his present purpose, and he decided he'd better look for something else. When he gave in his notice the owner of the factory asked him why he was leaving.

'It's too quiet,' he explained. 'I never see anyone to talk to.'

The man sighed. 'Yes,' he said. 'That's why they all leave.'

Peter felt that perhaps he was beginning to get somewhere. At least he now had a reaction in common with his fellow men. True, his desire for more company arose from his convictions rather than from his tastes. He hadn't actually felt lonely. Still, he seemed to be moving in the right direction. And he hadn't taken the easy way out, staying on in an undemanding job. He was facing up to his problem.

It wasn't till he found the job in the sawmill that he began to feel he was in the right place. It was just a small outfit, run by the owner with the help of a few part-timers. After three weeks Andrew Coggan offered him a full-time job and got rid of the other part-timers, so the two of them worked together all day, saying little but getting on well. Peter had the use of a caravan a few hundred yards from the sawmill, and sometimes Andrew would come round in the evening with a couple of cans of beer and they would chat – if you could call it that. Just the odd remark, surrounded by silence.

Andrew said very little about himself. All Peter knew was that he came from somewhere in the central belt of Scotland, some small village with a big sawmill, where he had learned his trade. But that was quite enough for Peter. The fact that Andrew said so little about himself exonerated him from having to be explicit about his own circumstances. For once he felt he wasn't holding back expected information, and as a result felt more at ease with Andrew than with anyone else for a long time back.

Andrew too apparently enjoyed his 'wee crack' as he called it, for he took to coming round more often and staying longer. Then he would get up, saying, 'Aye man, Peter, it's time to get away home. There's work to do the morn.' In moments of relaxation he would slip back into the speech of his Scottish background.

It wasn't much of a social life, but Peter was well satisfied. He felt he was coming nearer to a good relationship with another human being, and that, after all, was the job in hand. That he and Andrew knew so little about each other mattered not a whit. They understood each other. What more could you ask?

Peter had been working in the sawmill for quite a few months when a disturbing little incident occurred. It was a hot day in late spring, and they had broken off for a few minutes' rest, sitting on a log by the side of the road. A car drew up and the driver asked how far it was to the nearest filling station.

'Just a mile down the road,' said Andrew.

'Hey!' shouted a voice from the back of the car, and a man leapt out. 'If that isn't Andrew Docherty's voice! What you doing here, Andrew? I thought you were in New Zealand.' The man advanced, beaming.

Andrew sat stiffly on the log, without moving. He had turned rather pale.

'Sorry, mate,' he said. 'Wrong number. My name's not Docherty. I'm Andrew Coggan.'

'Oh, come on,' insisted the stranger, 'of course you're Andrew Docherty. I've known you since we were both at school together.'

Andrew shook his head. 'Not me. Never seen you before.' Then he got up and tapped Peter on the shoulder. 'Come on,' he said, 'there's work to do.'

Peter could see that Andrew was upset, so he asked no questions. But he was convinced that it wasn't a simple case of mistaken identity.

From then on Andrew was a changed man. He looked worried, spoke even less than before, and stopped coming round for his 'wee crack'. Peter wished there was some way of letting him know that he didn't mean to ask questions, as he suspected that this was what was keeping Andrew away, the fear of having to explain the unpleasant incident.

This uneasy situation continued for some ten days. Then,

one morning, when Peter turned up at the sawmill he found a police car parked outside. In the little office he found Andrew standing between two policemen.

'Sorry, Peter,' said Andrew. 'You've lost your job. And so have I. It's curtains, I'm afraid.'

'And the sawmill?'

'Kaput. No sawmill. Nothing. The law is stepping in, taking everything over.'

One of the policemen moved towards the door. 'Come on then,' he said. 'You've seen him. Now let's go.'

As he approached the door Andrew stopped and turned towards Peter.

'Come and see me, will you? If you're still around.'

'Where?'

'Inside, of course. Where else would I be going with this lot?'

Peter stood for a long time in the doorway after they had gone. He had no idea what to do. No point in working, no point in doing anything here. The business didn't belong to Andrew any more – if it ever had. He then wondered about his tenure of the caravan. He supposed he'd better get out, before that was taken over too. And the sooner the better, he thought. For the first time it occurred to him that his rootless way of life might give rise to doubts about his honesty. The police might well take him for a vagrant.

And then it struck him that Andrew, with his history, whatever it was, had perhaps assumed that there was something equally shady in his employee's past. Not bloody likely, he thought. I've never had the initiative to risk breaking the law. But then, he added, as if to excuse himself for this law-abiding weakness, I've never really been tempted to, have I? Always had plenty of everything.

Before leaving he decided that the best thing to do for the time being was to pretend he was on holiday and move into a boarding house. Somewhere in the area, where he could go and see Andrew. After that he could start looking for another job, preferably near where whatever prison Andrew was to be sent to after the trial.

It was midday when he got to the little town he had decided on, and he had some difficulty in finding a room. In the end he found a Mrs Barnes who admitted to having a vacancy, and he settled down for an indefinite stay.

He felt some misgivings when he went to see Andrew. He had never before gone to a police station on such an errand, and he found the prospect rather alarming. But what worried him even more was the fear of finding Andrew in a state of deep depression.

Andrew, however, looked much the same as ever, and was more talkative than he had ever known him to be. Was it perhaps because he now had no fear of incriminating himself by saying too much? Whatever the cause, he was eager to talk, and started off by telling Peter that the least he could do was tell him the whole story, since its unhappy outcome had cost Peter his job.

'You did know that chap in the car, then?' asked Peter.

'Yes, of course. And he knew me, and I'd a pretty good idea that meant the game was up. I suppose I'd better start at the beginning.'

14

I told you (*said Andrew*) I worked in this big mill back home, learning the trade and sweating my guts out for a pittance. The one thing I wanted was to be able to own my own little business, and be shot of that fat bastard who was exploiting us all. So I saved and saved, but I never had quite enough. Inflation, that was the trouble. And then one day the money was handed to me on a plate. Or that's what it seemed like. It had never occurred to me to steal anything, not one miserable quid, and then suddenly this seven thousand was handed to me on a plate, like I said.

This is how it happened. I used to spend a couple of evenings a week working in the office, doing the books, just to earn a little more. It was tiring, working all day and then slogging away at the books all evening. Well, I was in there working one day, late evening, in summer. It was hot and I was tired and I fell asleep. I woke up when it was already dark, hearing voices in the next room – the boss's room, that is. It was him and his fancy woman, and I could hear every word they said, because the door wasn't quite shut. They couldn't see me, and they didn't think of looking, either, as I should have been home long before that time. Well, the fat pig was boasting about how much money he had. In the bank, at home, and even in the office. Pretty drunk, he was.

"See this," he said. "I've got seven grand in this bag. Need it for tomorrow."

She said why didn't he keep it in the bank and write a cheque.

He laughed. "No way," he said, "not this little lot. I'm not letting this go through the bank. Don't want our dear friends at the tax office to find out about this lot. No thanks. So it's seven thou in cash going into this drawer, see, and I lock it, see, and put the key in my pocket. Safe as houses."

Well, they went on and on and stayed for ages, and I didn't dare move, because I knew what sort of trouble I'd be in if they found out I was there. But by the time they'd gone I knew exactly what to do. It didn't take me long to find the one locked drawer in the desk. I still don't know why he didn't put the money in the safe. Probably too drunk to remember the combination. Or too drunk to remember he even had a safe. Anyway, I forced the drawer and found the bag. I had a quick look inside and, sure enough, there was the lolly. I waited till I got home to count it, and there it was, a clean seven thousand, just like that. Mostly in tens, and a few fifties. No idea where it had all come from. Better not to know, I should think.

So there I was, the proud possessor of enough to start up a little business, what with what I'd already saved, that is. But I was clever. I didn't run off and get started right away. Oh no, sir. Not Andrew. Too canny for that, was Andrew. I decided I'd wait for a year before making a move. There was a stink, of course, when he found the money had gone. But the only person who knew about it was the girlfriend, and she'd spent the whole night with him, so she was in the clear. No, it was just one of those unsolved mysteries. All the workers were under suspicion for a while, as we all had access to the building. But they had no reason to suspect me in particular, and I got away with it.

A year later, when they'd forgotten all about it, I said I was going to join my uncle in New Zealand, and left the village. I wandered about different bits of England for a while, looking for the right place, and then I found it and set up my own business. And that's why I'm here and why you're out of a job.

'It's a pity you fell asleep that night in the office,' was Peter's comment. 'If you hadn't known about the money, you wouldn't be here.'

'Oh, I dunno,' Andrew replied. 'You win some, you lose some. My big mistake was pretending to be someone else when that chap turned up. If I'd only had the presence of mind to say I hadn't liked it in New Zealand and had come back here he'd never have smelled a rat. He'd never have remembered about the robbery, and how I was one of the people under suspicion at the time. I simply handed it to him.'

'On a plate?' suggested Peter.

'Yes, that's it. On a plate,' agreed Andrew ruefully. 'All the same,' he went on, 'I've really enjoyed these last few years with my own little business.'

Peter was shocked. He had expected some sort of expression of regret from the man. Perhaps not actual contrition, but surely some regret over the fact that the whole thing had gone wrong?

'You mean you would do it again?'

'Like a shot.'

'But, the stealing, I mean?'

'From that fat slug? Or his likes? Like a shot, I would. Where did he get it all? That's what I'd like to know. Exploiting his workers, at best. And I think his money was a lot dirtier than that. Theft! Property is theft. Believe you me, that man had a lot less right to the money than his workers. It was us that did the work.'

'You sound very Marxist.'

'God, no, I'm no Marxist. I'm against the whole bloody lot of them. A fat lot of good Marx did the workers. Look at

Russia. How would you like to work on one of their collective farms? All those bloody isms. I'm against them all. And we're hardly any better off here, with that damn Thatcher woman. Wanted to help the small businessman, she said. You'll see, she'll have us all out of business in another year or two. Well,' he added ruefully, 'not me. I'm out of it already.'

'And what happens now?' asked Peter.

'They'll send me back to Scotland for trial, as that's where the offence took place.'

Peter gave Andrew his new address and told him to let him know where he could be contacted, once his fate was settled.

'Some prison or other, I suppose. They've plenty of circumstantial evidence.'

Peter was deeply disturbed by his visit to Andrew. He tried to take comfort in the fact that Andrew seemed to be bearing up remarkably well under his misfortunes. But this, in fact, was part of the problem. He couldn't help feeling that some indication of repentance, or at least regret, would have been in order. Then he told himself not to be such a prig. After all, if you looked at things the way Andrew evidently saw them, all he had done was try to redress the balance, albeit in his own favour, rather than for the good of society as a whole. And why shouldn't the fat slug lose some of his ill-gotten gains?

What had he done to earn them?

He had exploited his workers, and it was only fair that one of them should get his share of the spoils. Andrew's position was perfectly tenable.

And yet . . . It was a dangerous thing for the individual to take the law into his own hands, however well argued his case might be. Besides, Peter had come to feel intensely suspicious of any argument based on general principles when it was wielded by the very person who stood to profit by its application. If he and Andrew had been discussing the rights and wrongs of property sitting quietly in the caravan, examining an abstract problem, he would no doubt have agreed more readily with Andrew's conclusions. But as things were he wondered how much of Andrew's conviction was *a posteriori*. Had he worked out the whole argument as a justification of his actions?

After all, Andrew had stated that it had never occurred to him to steal anything in his life before. The more he thought about it the more convinced he became that Andrew had acted against his own principles, thrown off balance by the unexpected possibility of all this money, handed to him 'on a plate'. And that being so, he felt sure that sooner or later Andrew would regret his action. The prospect of having his own little business, then the satisfaction of running it, had perhaps kept him from having to face the facts. And now, with the collapse of his dream and his feeling that the fates had been against him in sending his old schoolfellow to cross his path, he was bent on justifying himself.

But afterwards?

Would he come to see things in a different light?

Peter didn't know whether to hope for this or not. Remorse is not a pleasant experience to wish on anyone. And yet he felt, or at least he wanted to think, that deep down Andrew was a man of integrity, and would therefore have to come to terms with his own actions.

Meanwhile, what line was he himself to take in all this? He had promised Andrew he would keep in touch. So far he had been able to take a very noncommittal attitude, having been called upon to listen rather than to speak on this occasion. But what about the future? He could hardly pretend to agree with Andrew's view of the matter. On the other hand, he was afraid of what might happen if he showed his disapproval. He simply had no idea of how vulnerable the man might be. In his unhappy circumstances, criticism from the person who appeared to be his only friend might be really damaging. He didn't want to hurt Andrew and, for his own sake, he was reluctant to lose this one relationship that he had been able to forge.

Still perplexed and uneasy, he took himself off for a long walk that evening, right out of the town into a part of the country he hadn't been in before. The scenery was hardly spectacular, but it was pleasant and the early summer leaves and blossoms transfigured the trees and hedges. Peter decided to try to put the problem aside for the moment and concentrate on the beauty and peace round about him. He thought of the previous summer spent at home; of the few walks he had taken and of the little satisfaction that even the beauty of the surrounding countryside had given him.

Now, at least things were rather better. During the first months of his exile, joy had still eluded him. But since his settling down to work beside Andrew he had begun to feel his love of the natural world once again. He felt pretty certain that this was what followed from his renewed relationship with a member of the human race. He was beginning to play his part in the integration of the whole, as Marcus Aurelius put it. The price you had to pay, of course, for getting involved with someone else was, well, the sort of problem he had on his hands with Andrew.

But no, he decided, he wasn't going to think about that at the moment. He was going to concentrate on the world about him for the present. He was going to give himself up to the enjoyment of all this beauty. That hedge, for instance. He hurried towards the magnificent hawthorn hedge at the side of the road, ready to take in its message.

15

The hospital staff soon noticed that Peter was retreating into his shell again. It never occurred to them that this was a reaction to being in the big ward, and they became quite worried. They assumed he must be feeling depressed because he had so few visitors and hadn't received a single get-well card. They thought they'd better find out more about him. Had he no family – wife, children, parents, brothers or sisters?

No, there was no-one.

Never been married?

Yes, but divorced and out of touch with each other.

No friends, then?

Yes, one. Peter nearly added, 'But he's under arrest,' then thought better of it and said, 'But he's in New Zealand.' After all, it might have been true. For years people had thought that Andrew was in fact there.

On her next visit Mrs Barnes brought a letter from Andrew – just a note giving the address of the remand centre he'd been sent to near Glasgow. It occurred to Peter that Andrew would be expecting another visit, and that it would be many weeks before he was able to get about. He ought to write. But that posed problems of a practical nature. First of all was the business of getting hold of writing materials. After his years of solitary independence he found it very irksome to have to depend on other people for even such a simple thing as writing a letter. In the end he discovered that there was a shop in the hospital, and one of the nurses bought a pad and some envelopes for him. Luckily his right hand and arm were uninjured, enabling him to write:

Dear Andrew,

I'm sorry I can't come and see you. I'm in hospital with multiple injuries – knocked down by a car. It'll be weeks at least before I can get about.

Write. Yours, Peter.

Then the question of Andrew's name? Should he address the letter to Coggan or Docherty – or Doherty, or Dogherty? There seemed to be endless variants as far as the spelling went. He opted for Coggan/Docherty and left the prison authorities to cope with it. After all, the situation was probably not unknown to them.

The final difficulty was getting the thing posted without letting anyone see the address. He found he was most reluctant to let it be known he was writing to someone in jail. He didn't know whether to put this reluctance down to bourgeois prejudice or to his awareness that his apparent rootlessness left him in a rather vulnerable position. Would they not leap to the conclusion that he was a jailbird himself, hence abandoned by friends and relations alike? So he tried to devise some scheme to get the letter posted in secret. Try slipping it in beside his neighbour's correspondence, for instance.

But none of his neighbours seemed to do any writing. Give it to one of the cleaning ladies, who seemed to have less to do with the patients than the nurses? But he felt sure that such a titbit would be shared instantly with the whole ward. Bribe someone to post the thing without looking at the address, or at least to promise not to pass on the information? Drop it out of the window in the hope that someone would find it and post it?

At this point the absurdity of the whole thing struck him so forcibly that he was overcome by a fit of helpless giggling. He felt so weak and worn out with his problem that he simply hadn't the strength to stop himself.

One of the nurses was passing at the time and came to a sudden halt by his bed. 'My, you're surely in a good mood today!' she exclaimed in amazement. 'What's the joke?'

Peter couldn't tell her, and couldn't stop his giggling. He felt annoyed and embarrassed, and a bit shaken by his uncharacteristic behaviour.

But at least he was spared having to come to a decision about the letter. Seeing it lying on his bed the nurse picked it up.

'Want this posted?' she said, and made off with it before he could reply. Peter just had to hope she wouldn't look at the address.

The following morning his mood was even worse than before. He was apprehensive in case the letter's destination had been observed and passed on, and eyed all the staff with suspicion, from the cleaning ladies to the doctors. Had they classified him as undesirable? In addition he was still upset over his fit of giggles the previous day. It wasn't like him to lose control like that. And he was worried that he had been so anxious about the whole business. After seeing Andrew at the police station he had thought his chief concern was with his friend's moral position. Now he realized that one of the problems was going to be his own reaction to having a friend in jail.

He felt intensely depressed about the whole enterprise he had embarked on. Here he was, with a human relationship at last, and look at the mess it had landed him in! Had it not been for his friendship with Andrew, and for having agreed to going and seeing him in jail, he would have left the district as soon as the job folded up and he wouldn't have been on that piece of road when that idiot came careering along. And 'idiot' was the most charitable designation he could think of for the hit-and-run driver who had injured him. His present predicament was the direct outcome of his attempt to play his part in the integration of the whole.

Damn Marcus Aurelius, he thought. Look at the mess he's got me into.

He knew he was being childish. After all, he had only left his home in the first place because his life there had become intolerable and Marcus Aurelius seemed to offer a way out. He decided that he just wasn't well enough to cope with any of the problems in his life at that moment.

A vision of the white hawthorn hedge floated into his consciousness. It no longer brought with it a sense of unmixed peace and beauty, as it had at first. Now it was also linked to the shock and pain of the accident. But he tried to dismiss this aspect, and think only of the beauty and serenity of the wall of blossom. He pictured the little dark marks at the centre of each floret, and suddenly remembered that this was what was occupying him when the car came along. He wanted to find out whether the dark bits were in fact markings on the petals or whether they were stamens. The car had hit him before he'd been able to find out.

Must look it up somewhere, he thought.

Then he realized that there were no books here to look things up in, and that even if there were a library in the hospital he wouldn't be able to get to it. He felt so helpless and frustrated that the previous day's attack of giggles was nearly repeated with sobs instead.

By the next day he felt so sorry for himself, and so utterly incapable of helping himself in any way, that he decided he must contact Alicia. He was reluctant, though, to do this – and for a variety of reasons. For one thing, he had made up his mind when he set out on his enterprise that he was going to tread new ground, not repeat past mistakes. So old acquaintances were definitely out.

Besides, he felt at a disadvantage with regard to Alicia. It was thanks to his lack of commitment that the relationship had ended – or, at least, been interrupted. To come to her now for help was definitely tantamount to admitting his own weakness. It was also asking a lot of her generosity, given that it was he who had broken the bond.

But generosity, he reminded himself, was a quality Alicia had in abundance. He felt little doubt that she would respond positively. It was now nearly two years since he had seen her, and he wasn't sure whether she was still working in York. Besides, he couldn't remember either her number or her address. But he did remember the number of her parents' house in Auchentoull, where they had spent some weekends together. Her family had always been very friendly to him. If she was away from home he was sure he could leave a message.

He waited till the Saturday, in the hope that Alicia might be home for the weekend. Then he asked one of the nurses to bring him the phone and dialled the familiar number. It was a man's voice that answered. Presumably one of the brothers, but he couldn't tell which. He asked to speak to Alicia.

'Just a sec, I'll get her.'

He heard the receiver being put down, then the voice calling out:

'Lisha, Lisha! Telephone.'

In a minute he heard the tapping of high heels on the polished floor, and Alicia's voice said:

'Hello?'

'I'd forgotten they called you Lisha at home,' he said.

'Peter! Where are you?'

'In hospital. Can you come?'

'Yes, of course. Where?'

So that was it. He had capitulated and Alicia was coming. He could forget about his plans and his theories and his problems, and let Alicia take over. He closed his eyes and fell asleep.

By evening she was there. He became aware of a stir in the ward and looked up. Accompanied by a nurse, Alicia was advancing towards him. She seemed to light up the dreary surroundings with her colour and vitality. Every eye in the ward was on her. Suddenly he felt that the pity, or perhaps even contempt, that they had felt for him was turning to envy. That'll show them, he thought.

She sat down on the bed and took his right hand in both hers. Then she leaned forward and kissed him gently on the cheek, between two of the scratches.

'You don't need to explain,' she said. 'Nurse has told me about the accident. What I want to know is, what on earth were you doing in this part of the world?'

'Working in a sawmill.'

'You mean, sawing wood, and all that?'

'Yes. I know it sounds odd. It's a long story. I'll explain it later. Or you can ask Marcus Aurelius.'

Alicia nodded. 'You're tired now, aren't you? I'll leave you to rest, and I'll go and have a word with the staff nurse or someone about getting you away.'

'Where to?'

'Home. Back to Galloway.'

'But, Alicia, are you sure your parents can cope?'

'You forget Mum was a nurse. And Dad is still a doctor. Couldn't find a better household for the purpose.'

'But what will they say? I can't inflict myself on them.'

'They've already settled it all. I was given instructions to bring you back, as soon as you can travel. Now I'm going to see the nurse.'

'Wait. There's something I want to know. Perhaps you can tell me.'

'Well, what is it?'

'Hawthorn blossom,' he said. 'You know the little dark marks in the centre of each floret? What are they? Markings on the petal or stamens?'

'Stamens. Or rather, the anther on the stamen. The filament is white. Why?'

'Tell you later.'

'But it's important?'

'Yes, very. Thanks.'

Lisha went off to see the staff nurse and Peter closed his eyes. He should have known Alicia would be able to give him the information. He remembered now her interest in botany – she had done some illustrations for a book on wild flowers. Now that he'd got the exact picture of the hawthorn flower in his mind he was able to lie back and contemplate it in peace. He felt as if he'd spent a long, troubling time trying to see the thing properly. Since before the accident, in fact. It seemed like centuries. But Alicia had settled that problem for him, as she would settle the others. For the time being he was content to hand himself and his problems over to her entirely.

16

When Melville got back home after Alan's wedding he found most of the family gathered in the sitting room.

'Well, dear, how did it go?' asked his mother.

'Ghastly as always. That's the essence of a wedding.'

'Yes,' she agreed. 'Weddings are traumatic. I hated mine. But it has to be gone through.'

'Can't think why,' grumbled Melville.

'Glum aren't we,' remarked one of his sisters.

'"The wedding guest, he beat his breast",' quoted another.

'I wasn't a guest. I was best man. Much worse. That makes me an accomplice.'

'Are we to take it that you don't approve of Sheila?' asked Lisha.

'Oh no, it's not that. Not that at all. Sheila's lovely.'

'In that case he's jealous, and sorry he can't marry her himself,' put in the youngest.

'What's wrong, then?' asked Mrs Wilson with some concern. Alan was popular with all the family, and they hoped he hadn't made an unwise marriage.

'Sheila's a sweet, pretty, delicate-looking little thing, with about as much initiative as a wilting daisy, I should say. Just not the right girl for Alan.'

'Too like him, in fact?' suggested Lisha.

'Exactly. I think he needs someone with a bit more impact.'

'Like Lisha, for instance.'

'Exactly,' repeated Melville. 'It's a great pity you didn't snap him up, Lisha. I'm sure you could have done it.'

'No doubt I could have secured him, as Jane Austen puts it, if I'd had a mind to. But I didn't.'

'Why ever not, Lisha? I think he's super,' sighed one of the younger girls.

'Not my kind. I want someone to bully me.'

This raised a roar of laughter.

'God help the man who tries,' was her mother's remark.

Melville was still disgruntled. 'You'd think the institution of marriage would have died a natural death by now,' he muttered.

'Yes, dear, we know you don't approve,' said his mother, smiling at her husband, who had just come in and was standing behind Melville.

'And no wonder,' put in the doctor, 'with such a horrifying example before you,' and he gave his son's ear a tweak. Then, turning to his wife, he shouted:

'Wife, is that meal not ready yet?'

Mrs Wilson looked up from her sewing. 'Husband,' she said placidly, 'you'll get your meal at the usual time.'

'Usual! In this house!' exploded Melville. 'I wonder what time that means?'

'It means when your father comes in hungry, of course.' Mrs Wilson gathered up her sewing and stood up. 'I'll go and hurry things on in the kitchen,' she said.

If Melville had had his misgivings about his friend's marriage at the time of the wedding, he was by no means reassured when he made his first visit to the couple in their new home. Alan was already hating the business of schoolteaching, and was talking about trying to get a job in a polytechnic. Not as good as university lecturing, but surely better than his present job. Sheila looked sad and worried, and felt desperately homesick so far from Scotland.

And Melville could see that in addition to these troubles Alan and Sheila were not happy with each other. He understood why when Alan explained to him about the miscarriage and his feeling that he'd been trapped into an unnecessary marriage, which had forced him to give up his studies and take a job unworthy of him. He also got the impression that Alan was very aware of the educational difference between Sheila and himself, and had even made a few ambiguous observations in her presence that could be interpreted as a criticism of her standards. At first Melville wasn't sure whether she was sufficiently on the ball to get the allusions. But he was left in no doubt on the morning of his departure. He was to accompany Alan as far as the school, then go back and collect his things before taking the train back to London.

The prospect of another week's teaching had put Alan into a filthy mood. At breakfast they were discussing a new novel that had come out recently. Melville turned to Sheila and asked whether she'd read it.

'Don't bother asking her,' Alan put in scornfully before Sheila could reply. 'She doesn't read.'

Sheila blushed deeply, got up and left the room, muttering something about getting the tea.

'Tea!' said Alan with contempt. 'You'd think she'd know by now that it's coffee one drinks at breakfast.'

Melville was upset by the incident, and felt tempted to speak to Alan, on their way to the school, about his attitude to Sheila. But by the time the two of them were out of the house his pity for Alan had convinced him that it was better not to say anything. Poor Alan was so manifestly miserable. But he wondered whether he should say something to try and comfort Sheila when he got back.

He found Sheila red-eyed and confused, and before he had

decided whether to speak or not the decision was made for him when she suddenly burst into tears and fled to the kitchen.

He followed her there and sat on the stool next to her, while she sobbed into her apron.

'It isn't fair,' she wailed, 'it's just not fair. He knew before we were married that I'm stupid and ignorant and working-class. Why does he hate me for it now? I can't help being stupid, I can't help being ignorant, I can't help . . . '

'Hang on, hang on,' he said, tapping her gently on the shoulder. 'You're not stupid, you're not ignorant. You just don't know as much as he does about the things that matter to him. You haven't had his chances.'

Gradually she stopped crying and eventually managed to speak. 'Thanks, Melville. It's kind of you. But, like you said, I haven't had his chances, and there's nothing I can do about it. He should never have married me if that's the way he feels.'

Melville felt he ought to come to Alan's defence at this point. 'Well, there seemed to be a pretty good reason for marrying. But what's done's done. You can either make the best or the worst of it.'

'And you think I'm making the worst?'

'I think you're both making heavy weather of it.'

'Then what do you suggest I do? I can hardly go back to school now, can I?'

'Well, you can, in a way. There are lots of adult education classes. In a town this size there must be somewhere you could do an A level English course, for instance. It would give you some of the confidence you need.'

'Do you really think I could do it?' She looked at him in surprise.

'Of course you could. And then you could get on with the reading. Look,' he said, his enthusiasm rising, 'it's not only that it would put you on a better footing with Alan – educationally, I mean – but reading opens so many doors to you. You can live a completely different life when you're immersed in a book. And it helps you to see things in a different light. Being able to read is a wonderful tool. Being able to read with ease and enjoyment, I mean,' he added hastily, afraid she might think he was accusing her of total illiteracy.

Suddenly a little smile broke through her woebegone expression. 'It's easy to see you're a publisher,' she said. 'Looking for new customers, that's what it is.'

They both laughed.

'But seriously, Sheila, think about it.'

She nodded. 'I'll think about it,' she promised.

She thought about it and felt very tempted to go ahead. She remembered her initial intention of bettering herself, back in the early days, before the clouds had gathered. If it hadn't been for Melville she would probably have forgotten all about it, lost in her self-pity and resentment. Now she found that merely thinking of the possibility had helped ease her depression. The chief difficulty was the question of whether she should tell Alan or not. If she told him, she felt sure, he would treat the whole matter with contempt. But if she didn't, well, that would be hiding something from him, and she didn't like doing that.

Alan was still her God, albeit a hostile one now. She didn't dare to deceive him or withhold any information from him. She had done that once, over the miscarriage, and had paid for it bitterly, not only by having incurred Alan's wrath, but because she was now convinced that it had been an unworthy thing to do. She had, in effect, cheated Alan into marriage in her panic at the thought of losing him if the wedding were put off. Now she was paying for it with his displeasure, and she had promised herself she would never conceal anything from him again.

So she plucked up courage and told him one evening what she was planning to do.

Alan looked at her sceptically and said, 'Please yourself.'

Pathetic, he thought. As if an English A level could bridge the gap. The he noticed her crestfallen expression and told himself he was a brute. But he couldn't quite bring himself to say something encouraging about her plan. He compromised by asking in a kinder tone than usual whether she'd heard from her mother lately.

It was five years before the first child arrived. By that time they had moved to Manchester, where Alan had got a job teaching in a polytechnic. He was no happier there than he had been in the school, and still longed for a university post. There, surely, he would have had time to get started on his writing. For Sheila the change was an improvement. Manchester seemed less remote from Scotland, in distance and in the way of life. By now she had got her English A level and a few others as well. Alan seemed totally unimpressed, but having the certificates gave Sheila a little more confidence, and she found that Melville was right – the new worlds which her reading disclosed to her made her own world more bearable.

And then the children came, and life was too busy for her to be totally miserable. Alan was not the most devoted of fathers – though he was fond of the children – and he certainly wasn't the most supportive of husbands; but the children did draw them together a bit. So life went on; uneventful, disappointing on the whole, but bearable. Until the business of the headship of the department. That, for Alan, had started a downward spiral that nothing seemed able to stop.

17

It wasn't till the day after the appointment had been announced that Alan came face to face with Scratchley. He had seen him in the staffroom the previous day, surrounded by other members of staff, receiving their congratulations, and had been intensely annoyed by the unassuming manner in which Scratchley had conducted himself. Bloody hypocrite, he thought. Bet he'll go home and grin at himself in the mirror for half an hour – thinking, that's one up on old Hodges, and Parrott and Dawe, *et al*, and about twenty up on that pathetic failure of an Alan Morley. But he had promised himself he would behave with due dignity when the dreaded meeting should take place. He would congratulate his rival without letting a trace of resentment show in his voice or manner. He would be impeccable.

So, when he got to the college the following morning he had steeled himself for the ordeal. In the staffroom he found Scratchley standing beside the fireplace, talking to Mabel Martin, who was looking up at him with innocent blue eyes. I'll do it now, thought Alan, before anything can happen to upset me and make me bungle it. So he went up to the couple and waited for a pause in the conversation. Mabel had embarked on a long description of a classroom confrontation she had endured the previous day, and was too excited to notice the waiting Alan.

Scratchley saw him, but was held captive by Mabel's

exposition. Alan felt increasingly awkward, standing there waiting for attention. He knew Scratchley had seen him. Why didn't he interrupt the stupid girl and turn to the waiting Alan, who was, after all, a senior member of staff? But then, Mabel was the youngest, and undoubtedly the prettiest member of staff. His resentment simmered with growing violence.

At last Mabel noticed him, or allowed herself to notice him, he wasn't quite sure which. 'Oh, I'm sorry, Alan, I'm sure you have more important things to say to Dr Scratchley than my dreary little tale.'

'Oh no, nothing important, that is . . . just well . . . I just wanted to congratulate . . . er . . . ' He suddenly found he didn't know how to address the man. By his surname as usual? Seemed a bit casual to the man who was now virtually his boss. Dr Scratchley? None of the men had ever addressed him as that, and he was afraid it might sound like irony – or toadying. And if he now called him by his first name it would hardly do either. After all, as the superior, it was for Scratchley to initiate any increase in familiarity.

His voice trailed away and he didn't know whether to shake hands. He made a vague gesture in that direction, then decided against it, and was withdrawing his hand when Scratchley made a movement as if to take it. Hastily he held out his hand again just as Scratchley was beginning to withdraw his. Mabel turned away suddenly, trying to smother a burst of giggles, and the two men finally managed to shake hands, looking at each other with intense hatred. Alan turned away, leaving Scratchley standing there in a rather purposeless manner. As soon as the little incident was over Alan realized how he should have tackled the situation. The conversation between Scratchley and Mabel would in fact have been a good opportunity for getting the thing done quickly and easily. He should just have gone up to them and said, 'Sorry to butt in, I just wanted to offer my congratulations,' and then gone off.

And I think of it now, he reproached himself, with my usual brilliant *esprit d'escalier*. What a clown I am!

He couldn't get the awkward little incident out of his mind. It made his morning's teaching even more displeasing than usual. He knew he was bored, and felt sure he was boring the class. This is not what I was meant for, he kept telling himself. If only he didn't have a wife and children to support! If only he could give up teaching and concentrate on writing! He was sure he could manage to keep himself for a year or two, till the money from his writing started coming in. He realized that as a teacher he was no good at all, never had been. In fact, it was almost a moral obligation to give up the whole farcical endeavour.

But of course he couldn't, not with Sheila and the girls to support.

If only Sheila had a little more initiative, she could be supporting the family by now and he could get on with his writing. But no, he had to plod on with these dolts, teaching them little and boring them stiff.

He was still suffering badly from his sense of the ridiculous part he had played in the morning and, what was worse, his awareness that Scratchley must have felt acutely foolish too by the time they had finished their dumbshow, when he went into the staffroom at lunchtime.

Scratchley was pontificating, surrounded by a group of the others.

' . . . and what's more,' he was saying, 'there are ways and means of getting rid of the dead wood. We're not going to put up with that sort of thing in future, I can assure you . . . ' Scratchley looked up and their eyes met. Alan turned on his heel and went back to his classroom. He means me, he thought. I'm the dead wood. And how right he is. Only he's not going to get rid of me that easily. I need the bloody job.

If it weren't for Sheila and the children I'd soon tell him what to do with it.

He started reading the paper to try and calm down before his next class.

Fifteen miles city centre, small cottage
in delightful surroundings. Fully furnished,
all mod cons. Immediate entry . . .

Alan began to weave a daydream about this cottage. He could take it and move in. They could just about manage to run two establishments if the second one was very modest. Then he'd have time to get down to his writing, without the constant interruptions of family life. It was not for nothing that so many of the great writers had remained unmarried.

He would have to keep on with his teaching, certainly, at least to begin with. Not only because of the money, but because he wasn't going to give Scratchley the satisfaction of getting rid of him. He knew, and Scratchley must know, that you couldn't really be sacked from a teaching post unless you'd done something utterly outrageous. And he knew, and Scratchley must know, that this wasn't going to happen. I'm much too ineffective to do anything of the sort, he told himself. No chance.

So by his *ways and means* I take it he intends to make life so unpleasant for me that I resign. Well, just you wait, Dr Scratchley, I'll resign when I'm good and ready for it, with another nice little income to live on. And doing the sort of work I'm really meant to do, what's more.

On his way out of the classroom at the end of the afternoon's teaching he saw Scratchley again, standing in the corridor talking to the Principal. The two men were joking and laughing, and neither saw Alan. Or at least, neither of them *seemed* to see him.

On an impulse he went along to the phone booth and rang Sheila. He would be late, didn't know how late. Something had turned up. Just to let her know not to wait for him.

He got into his car and drove straight to the estate agents. A quarter of an hour later he was in his car on the way to High Midbury, feeling the excitement of going somewhere new, of having to find his way through unknown country.

18

By the end of the teaching day Herbert Scratchley had come to realize that he had a problem on his hands as far as Alan Morley was concerned. He had been furious with him in the morning over the shared awkwardness that Alan's attempts at congratulating him had created. If there was anything Herbert hated, it was being made to feel foolish. But he soon forgot all about the incident. He was a hard man, with a high opinion of himself, but not given to cherishing resentment.

But the little incident at lunchtime had bothered him quite a lot. He could see from Alan's expression that his reference to dead wood had been misunderstood. As it happened, he had been referring to the two trouble-making students who had disrupted Mabel's class. But he felt sure that Alan had thought the reference was to him. And, as if that weren't enough, he had in fact seen Alan in the corridor later on. But precisely because he was feeling awkward over the two previous incidents, and also because he was talking to the Principal, who apparently hadn't seen Alan, or hadn't wished to see him, Herbert had looked the other way. But after Alan had passed, Herbert saw his retreating back, and felt sure from the stiffness of his carriage that Alan had once again taken offence.

After the Principal had gone, Herbert went back to the staffroom in the hope of seeing Alan. The one thing he wanted to avoid was starting off on the wrong foot. He meant to introduce a number of changes that he knew perfectly well would be unpopular, and he couldn't afford to start off with any unnecessary ill-will on his hands. He realized that Alan was the person most likely to get in his way, because of his seniority and because of his tendency to feel put upon, and, above all, because he had been passed over in favour of so much younger a man. So Herbert felt the onus was on him to extend the olive branch. Besides, he thought, it must be pretty miserable for the poor sod, being passed over like this.

He hung around the staffroom for some time in the hope of seeing Alan, and in the end he made the heroic decision to go and see him at his house.

'Isn't Daddy home yet?' Jane wanted to know when she got back after her violin lesson.

'No, he phoned to say he'd be late. Something turned up.'

'What?'

'He didn't say. Work, I suppose.'

Eight-year-old Beth, the dreamy one, had one of her moments of total presence and put in:

'Daddy's always working. Last night when we went to say good night he sent us off right away because he'd got work to do.'

Sheila gazed at the small, reproachful replica of herself and sighed.

'But he'd gone out for a long walk before that,' pointed out Jane. 'He could have spent that time with us.'

Sheila sighed again. 'I suppose he's got a meeting,' she said.

'A meeting!' Tessa burst in. 'A meeting with a millionaire and he's going to give Daddy lots of money and we'll buy a house with a swimming pool and go riding every day.'

'Oh, don't be so silly, Tessa,' snapped Jane. 'These things don't happen in real life.'

'Well, she's only four,' pointed out Sheila. 'You can't expect much realism at that age.'

Just then the bell rang and all four of them went to the front door. Herbert Scratchley looked a bit taken aback by the reception committee that greeted him. Sheila had met him once at some college reception, but she showed such surprise at seeing him that he assumed she hadn't recognized him.

'I think we met once before,' he said. 'I'm Herbert Scratchley.'

Three of the four pairs of eyes fixed upon him suddenly acquired an expression of open hostility. The girls had all heard of him from their father, and had no hesitation in casting him as the villain of the piece. Sheila managed to keep her expression a little more noncommittal. She was embarrassed by the visit and by the girls' obvious hostility, and was afraid she wouldn't cope well with the situation. She was also bothered by the fact that she knew her make-up was in need of repair, and that she was wearing a rather dirty old apron. It wasn't long since she had read *Kipps*, and she felt like Ann when the posh callers take her for her own servant. Somehow she managed to get this particular caller into the sitting room and the girls back into the kitchen, as she explained that Alan wasn't home yet.

'Oh, I suppose he'll be back quite soon, though,' said Herbert.

'Well, no, I don't think so. He phoned to say he would be late. Some meeting . . . '

Herbert looked surprised. 'Really! Then perhaps I shouldn't stay. I just wanted a word with him about . . . ' It was now his turn to look rather disconcerted.

Sheila didn't know what to make of it. 'Oh, do stay. I mean, since you've come . . . to see him, that is.'

'Well, you see, Mrs Morley, it's about . . . The fact is, I think there seems to be some sort of misunderstanding between your husband and myself. That is . . . I know it must be a difficult situation for him, and I should greatly regret if any misunderstanding were to make things awkward between us. After all, we're going to have to work together, aren't we?'

Sheila admitted this.

Herbert was beginning to feel glad that Alan was out. Sheila seemed a much easier person to get on with than her husband. She was sitting looking at him with big, attentive eyes, free from the slightly mocking quality he always sensed in Alan.

'And as things stand, well, the fact is . . . ' He cleared his throat and began again. 'The fact is, I was in the staffroom talking to some of my staff – if you'll forgive the prolepsis, that is – I mean, I know it's not exactly my staff yet, but we were talking about next term, when it will be, and I was speaking in fairly strong terms about a couple of young louts among the students who've been making things difficult, and your husband came in in the middle of the conversation and, somehow, it's most unfortunate, but I got the impression he thought I was talking about him.'

How like him, thought Sheila. Loyalty to Alan kept her from saying it. Instead she said:

'I'm sure he wouldn't suspect you of . . . of anything . . . ' She was saved from having to think of a suitable end to her sentence by screams from the kitchen. She excused herself and dashed out.

'Sorry about that,' she said when she came back. 'It happens all the time with children.'

There was a pause during which both wondered whether to revert to the subject of the misunderstanding or to let it die a natural death. Opting for the latter, Sheila said:

'Have you any?'

'Oh, children! No, oh no. Not married! I've been too busy with my career so far to allow myself that pleasure.' Then, thinking that this might be taken as an oblique swipe at Alan and his unfinished thesis, he added gallantly:

'I'm afraid I've not been lucky enough to meet anyone to tempt me away from my studies.'

Sheila had taken advantage of the incident in the kitchen to remove her apron and comb her hair, and now felt sufficiently in control of the situation to offer him some sherry. He accepted, and they chatted amicably for half an hour, after which he said he really must go, and went. By that time there had been a number of interruptions from the girls, who ended up agreeing among themselves that he was really very nice.

Sheila thought so too.

While Herbert Scratchley was talking to Sheila and making a favourable impression on the girls, Alan was falling in love with a small, shabby, isolated cottage. It consisted of a small living room and smaller bedroom, a thin slice of bathroom, mainly occupied by the bath, and a kitchen just big enough to eat your meals in, provided there was never more than one of you.

Fine, thought Alan, just fine. A one-man cottage. Just what I want. One of the things that appealed to him was the rather primitive nature of the mod cons referred to in the advertisement. All his life he had lived in comfort – a West End flat in London, college accommodation, and, since his marriage, suburbia. Even though he and Sheila had been relatively hard up during the first years of their marriage, they had never had to do without the gadgets and comforts which the professional classes take for granted. In fact, it was largely because of these that they were hard up. It wasn't a thing Alan had ever thought about. He had always assumed that these things were necessary.

Now, looking at the chipped porcelain sink and the worn vinyl on the floor, he discovered in himself a great nostalgia for an austerity he had never known. He had an intimate but totally vicarious knowledge of poverty. He had skimped and scraped with his favourite heroes and heroines, but the reality of this interesting phenomenon had so far escaped him.

This place would help him to identify more completely with the dispossessed, without the faint suspicion of voyeurism that his awareness of his own material comfort sometimes awakened in him. He had never been able to assess how important this material comfort was to him, never having had to do without it. This place would put it to the test.

He stood in the kitchen looking out over the chipped sink to the line of trees along the horizon on the other side of the little valley. The ground dipped gently down to what was probably a small river or stream, then rose again more steeply. To the right the valley flattened out, giving a distant view of rolling countryside. There were trees of different varieties scattered about, and untrimmed hedges. And lots and lots of green fields. Green fields and untamed trees, he thought, remembering his longing for those things the previous evening, during his suburban walk. He felt an overwhelming conviction that this was what he needed. Space and silence, and no Sheila and no children. Here he would be able to fulfil himself and find his voice.

He left the cottage with regret, as if leaving a long-loved home, not knowing whether he would ever see it again. He simply didn't think he would ever find the courage to suggest this separation to Sheila. It struck him that his only hope was to act without consultation – go in to the estate agent's tomorrow before work and commit himself to taking the place. It he tried discussing it with Sheila beforehand he knew her tears would win the day. But he didn't really think he would ever have the courage to act unilaterally in the matter.

As soon as he got home the girls fell upon him in a state of great excitement.

'We've just had a visit from Herbert and he's nice, he's nice, he's nice,' they chorused.

'Herbert who?' At first he couldn't think who it could be. Then suddenly it dawned on him. 'You don't mean Scratchley?'

'Yes, Daddy, and he's nice and he said . . . '

He looked at Sheila for confirmation. 'Is this true?'

'Yes. He left just a little while ago.'

'What was he doing here? And why are they calling him Herbert?'

'Because he said we were to, so there!' Jane was evidently as excited about it as her younger sisters.

Again Alan turned to Sheila. She too was looking more animated than usual.

'Is this true?' he asked again.

'Well, yes, he was very friendly – with the children, I mean. And he wants them to call him Herbert. And actually he said he wants all the staff to be on first name terms – in the English Department, at least.'

'We all are, except for him,' Alan pointed out acidly. 'And anyway, what on earth was he doing here – apart from reducing the children to screaming idiocy?'

Sheila gave a sigh of exasperation and walked back to the kitchen. 'I might have known you would take it like this,' she remarked.

Alan followed her into the kitchen. 'I'm not taking it like anything. I just want to know what on earth he was doing here.'

'There you are, you see! "What on earth!" That shows what you think of his visit. "What on earth" reeks of disapproval. That's how you're taking it and how you could be counted on to take it.'

'"What on earth" is intended to convey surprise, not disapproval.'

'Same thing,' snorted Sheila.

'Really, Sheila, if your A level English hasn't taught you the difference between surprise and disapproval . . . '

'In this case there's no difference. Just like you to use an ambiguous term so you can shelter behind the other meaning.'

A hit, he thought. A very palpable hit. He was aware of this tendency in himself, and resented having it pointed out. 'I suppose I should congratulate you,' he sneered, 'on your use of the word "ambiguous". That proves your A level did teach you something after all.'

'Nothing to do with A levels. No one could be married to you for fifteen years without knowing the meaning of that word.'

Alan decided to move back to his original question. 'You still haven't told me what he came here for.'

'To speak to you. He thought you had misunderstood something he said, and he wanted to put matters right. Rather sensible, I thought.'

Sheila told him what Herbert had said about the students. Alan wasn't altogether satisfied that Scratchley had been talking about them and not him, but had to admit – to himself, that is – that his having taken the trouble to come and try to explain things seemed to indicate a willingness to be reasonable. And if, by the end of the evening, he felt a little less ill disposed towards his new superior the net result of Herbert Scratchley's visit had been to set Alan and Sheila at odds. Even his relationship with the girls had not escaped, as they knew of the antagonism between their father and their new hero. The thought of the cottage came back to him like a breath of cool, sweet air, and he decided that, come what may, he was going there. And because of this decision he took care to say nothing about the cottage to Sheila.

Next morning he felt his determination was wavering. He

wasn't sure it was quite fair to leave Sheila with the children on her own – even if he was, naturally, going to continue to support them. In the end he decided to leave the decision to chance. If there was anywhere to park near the estate agent's he would go in and take the cottage. If not, he would drive on and try to forget about this possible paradise.

He felt a mixture of relief and disappointment as he approached the office – the whole street was lined with parked cars. Well, that was it. The decision, it seemed, had been made for him. But just as he was driving past, slowly and regretfully, he saw a parked car in front of him signal to pull out and move off. Without waiting to see whether there was anything close behind him, Alan jammed on his brakes and flashed his lights. The car moved out, he moved in, and ten minutes later he came out of the office.

The cottage was his, for the next six months at least.

19

Dear Melville,

I'm writing to you because you're the only person who can perhaps help me to understand what is happening. As Alan's best friend you may know something about his plans. To me this has come as a complete and utter surprise. Last week he announced that he intends to move into a little cottage fifteen miles out into the country, to live there on his own. He says it's because that's the only way he can get enough peace to get started on his writing, and that he only thought of it when he read the ad in the paper last week, and that he just acted on impulse.

Ever since we met he's been talking about wanting to write, so I realize it's important to him. But, can he not write at home? And he'll still have to do all the work for the college even if he's living in the country. I don't see that he'll have that much extra time, do you?

Please tell me if you have any idea of what's in his mind. Needless to say I have a few nasty little suspicions nagging at me. Is the writing just an excuse? Has he met someone else? Or is he just fed up with the lot of us?

What worries me most is that I don't think it will do any good. I think he's too tied up with his work – which he hates – to be able to do any writing. I wish he could give up the job but what would we live on? If only I could earn some money instead. Then he could have time to write and stay with us. But there's really nothing I can do, stuck in the house looking after the girls.

I'm sorry to bother you with my problem, but I just don't know where to turn. If anyone knows what's in his mind it must be you.

Perhaps the biggest fear I have is that what's wrong is that he's having some sort of nervous breakdown. Do you think this is likely? He really does seem most unhappy and difficult all the time now. What do you think? Do please write.

Yours affectionately,
Sheila.

Dear Sheila,

No, I had no idea about the country cottage business. And I don't think there's another woman, and I don't think Alan's having a nervous breakdown. If he's really got anything to write about, this is his chance. Let him try. I think the real problem is that he's unhappy mainly because he belongs to the vast majority – that is, people who have to do work they hate. If going off and living in the country is going to give him satisfaction, so much the better for all of you. Let him feel you are co-operating, not fighting the idea.

Now that you've got over your panic about the written word, would you be interested in doing a little hack work for my firm? Nothing exciting, but the pay's not bad.

My love to you all,
Melville.

20

Alan left for the cottage as soon as the summer term was over. It was exactly two weeks since he had first seen it. To his surprise Sheila's resistance to the idea seemed to crumble at the last minute. He left behind him three tearful children, but a serene Sheila. The girls, he hoped, would soon settle down. No doubt Sheila would remind them that he had promised to have them out at the cottage every Saturday.

It was a relief that Sheila hadn't insisted on coming to see the place and help him move in. He had no doubt that she would be more competent in solving all sorts of practical problems, but he wanted to do everything himself. For once in his life he didn't want his living done for him.

By the time he reached the cottage with his carload of personal possessions he had got over the upset of the parting and its corresponding feelings of guilt, and was thoroughly absorbed in his new surroundings. Before turning the key in the lock he stood outside the front door and listened to the silence. Silence? It was lovely, but far from silent. Birds were singing, bees buzzing, small things rustling in the hedge on the other side the road. But no cars, buses or lorries to be heard. Wonderful!

Some sort of gesture, he felt, was needed before actually taking possession. Something in Latin would be ideal, but he could think of nothing appropriate. Well then, something from opera? How about *Salut demeure chaste et pure*? But that was perhaps taking rather too much for granted. Besides, he wasn't fond of Gounod. Then he got it, and walked into the house humming the stately opening bars of Beethoven's 'Consecration of the House'.

He decided not to try and write anything for the first week or two. Just settle in, get the feel of the place, be totally relaxed. Then he would be in a fit state to produce something worthwhile. Meantime it was like being on holiday. He had never felt so free, so aware of his surroundings before – except perhaps during the blissful weeks in Galloway with Melville and his family. He had to admit that the scenery here was humbler and less picturesque.

But it would do. Everyday scenery, but of a high standard. At present it had all the delight of the unknown to recommend it; later it would have the equally desirable virtue of familiarity. He sat down in the sitting room and looked out of the window. He could see a bit of hedge, a piece of green field, half a tree and a generous proportion of blue sky. He got up whistling 'Blue Skies' and went out to the car to start bringing things in.

By the end of the month he decided it was time to start writing. No idea had come to him so far, but then, he wasn't really trying, was he? The thing to do was just sit down and start writing. So he sat down at the table, armed with paper and pen, and waited for inspiration. None came. Perhaps, he thought, I really ought to have chosen my subject first. What do I really know about?

The answer that came to him immediately was – English grammar. Well, that's a non-starter anyway, he thought. You can't really write a novel about English grammar. He had taken it for granted all along that what he was going to write was a novel. English grammar wouldn't do, so what next? What else did he know about? English literature, of course. Hardly promising either, was it? Then it occurred to him that the only other subject he really knew intimately was himself. But that would mean autobiography, straight or concealed. And he knew that this was where most beginners started. Well, he didn't want to begin like a beginner. He'd have to think of something else.

After an hour or two spent, at one moment contemplating the difficulties of free composition and at the next moment gazing out of the window, simply enjoying the view and the quietness, he decided that the most important thing in his life at that particular moment was his developing relationship with his surroundings, and that this was what he ought to be writing about. But he didn't really know enough about it just yet. He'd be well advised to spend the summer concentrating on learning what was going on in the fields and the trees and the hedges.

He'd already bought himself a book about birds and another about wild flowers, and had spent many happy hours trying to identify the various specimens. All he needed now was a book about trees. Then he could devote the rest of the summer to mastering his material. After that it would be time to start writing. He visualized a sort of *Wind in the Willows*, only for adults. Or a sort of *Walden* with no axe to grind. What he wanted to do was share with the reader his delight in the humble and entrancing world about him.

If there were no readers so far to share his delight in the natural world, there were at least his three daughters, who took a great liking to the place from the start. Usually Sheila would bring them on a Saturday morning, stay for a while, and then leave them with Alan for the rest of the day. Sheila obviously was not impressed by the cottage. She found its shabbiness depressing, and its loneliness unnerving. She was a city dweller who had always been content to be surrounded by concrete and traffic. Even suburbia seemed a bit on the wild side for her. A flat in the West End was nearer her ideal.

But the girls were thrilled by their father's bucolic surroundings. Alan was struck once again by the odd distribution of companions. You would have thought that Beth, the middle one, would team up with either the elder or the younger sister. But instead Beth was usually on her own, while the other two, in spite of the six-year gap between them, were nearly always together. The two of them would set off, roaming the nearby fields and hedges, Jane anxious to explore and understand all she saw, Tessa equally anxious not to be left out. She tackled life with gusto, Jane with enquiring precision.

As for Beth, she didn't tackle life at all, but drifted through it in a sort of ecstatic dream. Alan often found her sitting alone in the remains of the little garden behind the house, gazing into nothingness, a rapt expression on her face. While the other two were closely in touch with the world about them – Jane intellectually, Tessa in a more visceral way – Beth appeared in touch with something quite different, but he had no idea what it was.

The differences in character and appearance that his daughters displayed had always been a great puzzle to him. Jane showed some physical resemblance to her father, and had inherited his primarily intellectual outlook on life. And Beth, as far as appearance went, was a small edition of Sheila. But where the other-worldly streak in Beth had come from was difficult to determine. Well, he thought at times, we don't really know each other, any of us, do we? Perhaps there was a spiritual and introspective side to Sheila's nature that had never developed. As for Tessa, she seemed to bear no resemblance to either of her parents, with her gutsy zest for life and her unstoppable determination to go everywhere and do everything.

Now that he had made his two big decisions – first, that he was going to get down to his writing at last, and second, that he wasn't going to put pen to paper till the end of the

115

summer – Alan felt easier in himself than he had for many years. He could spend all day pottering about the garden, wandering about the fields and woods, or experimenting in the kitchen without feeling that he should be doing something else. Above all, he didn't have the guilty feeling that he should be getting on with his writing. He *was* getting on with his writing, merely by living like this. Collecting material, that's what he was doing. And for the first time he was able to enjoy the company of the girls freely and without nagging doubts about the profitability of time spent in this way. With them and through them he felt he was learning more about the world he was going to write about.

The summer went by peacefully.

Then came September and with it the realization that term would soon be upon him. He would have to spend all day in college, and part of the evenings would have to be given to preparing work and marking exercises and essays. Still, it should leave a few hours every evening for his writing. The important thing, he told himself, was to keep going once he'd got started, even if some days it was no more than a sentence or two. *Nulla dies sine linea*, that was to be his motto.

He knew from his long-abandoned research how difficult it was to get started again after a gap. There were to be no gaps. Confident in his work plan, he set off for his first day of term without too much trepidation. It wouldn't be easy, of course, with Scratchley – sorry, Herbert – in charge, but still, he had the refuge of the cottage to go back to. Nothing could change that. And in winter it would be dark by the time he got back, so there would be no temptation to spend an hour or two wandering about looking at birds and seeing whether the dog roses were out on the hedge beside the bridge yet. No, he was sure it would be all right. Just a case of establishing a routine and keeping to it.

The routine established itself right from the start, remorse-lessly. Herbert had had the sense not to change the whole syllabus right away. But he now made it clear that by the following session there was to be a complete 'redirection of aims', and this they were to start working towards right from the first day of this new term. Alan realized he was going to have to work up a vast amount of new material for the following session; in addition, he was going to have to reorient his present lectures towards this change, bringing in as much of the new material as was compatible with the old format. In other words, there was not one single lecture he could give without first spending a long time grooming it to fit the new requirements.

At first he was filled with despair. Even if he forgot all about his own writing he didn't see how he could possibly find time in one evening to prepare all the following day's classes. After all, at home he had spent most of each evening working; how on earth was he to find time for this additional burden? Gradually it dawned on him that most of the time spent ostensibly working at home had in fact been spent day-dreaming. His 'preparation' had in fact been a respectable excuse for opting out of family life. He had spent very few hours actually doing the work he thought he was engaged in. This meant that, by devoting the same amount of time to the work, and actually doing it instead of dreaming about having enough time to write, he was able to get through the workload.

But it also meant that finding an hour or two for writing in the evening was out of the question. After a few weeks of intense rebellion he came to the conclusion that he had better leave the writing to the vacations. Plenty of time then. Perhaps he should really have got down to the actual writing this summer. Then he would at least have made a start. But no, he couldn't regret his idle summer spent collecting material.

117

It had given him the happiest months he had known for many years. The actual getting things down on paper would have to wait, but its time would come.

Meanwhile, he found to his surprise that he didn't dislike the new work as much as he had intended to. I suppose I needed a challege, he told himself. In other words, I'd got into a rut. Getting out of it was hard work, but at least it wasn't boring.

One day in mid December Alan sat down at his desk with paper and pen in front of him. It was the first day of the Christmas vacation, and the time had come at last. He was now going to begin his novel – to begin actually writing, that is. He had thought about it a bit, and knew vaguely what it was about. Now all he had to do was choose the words.

He paused, pen in hand, wondering where he should begin. Chronological order, of course, would be the simplest. But would it be the most telling? Besides, how far back do you go? The more he thought about it the more difficult he found it to discover the point at which relevance began. More than an hour later he still hadn't written anything. To his annoyance he suddenly remembered Joseph Grand in *La Peste*, who spent years wrestling with the first sentence of his novel. And I haven't even got that far, he thought ruefully. I don't even know what my first sentence is supposed to be about. He got up and put coal on the fire.

As he returned to the desk by the window he noticed a figure approaching the cottage. It seemed rather an improbable sight. For one thing, he wasn't used to having callers. For another, the figure turned out to be that of a well dressed woman, advancing along the country road in wobbly high-heeled shoes.

Alan went to the door and opened it just as the woman reached the doorstep.

21

'Oh!' she exclaimed, surprised. 'I was just going to ring.'

'I thought I'd save you the bother.'

'How kind!' The high-heeled woman was smiling in a mocking, provocative sort of way. Then, looking more serious, she said:

'I wonder if you can help me.'

'I'd love to.' Alan made the statement in all sincerity. She was a remarkably good-looking female. Not too young, forty-ish perhaps, but elegant and sure of herself. She was wearing a suede jacket with a scarlet silk scarf tied round her neck. Her face was framed by a mass of red curls, her eyes heavily made up, her lips even redder than the scarf. Altogether very striking, Alan thought.

'My car's broken down a little way along the road. Could I use your phone, and can you tell me the name of the nearest garage?'

'Yes, of course. But aren't you in one of the motoring organizations?'

'I'm afraid not.' The woman smiled teasingly. 'I'm rather improvident.' She smiled appealingly. 'And there's always a good Samaritan about when I'm in trouble.'

'I'm sure there is,' Alan replied with conviction. 'Let me have a look first, before we try the garage, shall we?'

'Oh, if you would be so good. It's probably something terribly simple, like a loose lead, whatever that is.'

Alan had little confidence in his ability as a motor mechanic, but was eager to try. On their way to the car she told him she had just moved in to the cottage half a mile along the road.

'So, you see, we're neighbours,' she said, smiling. 'Half a mile's nothing in the country, isn't it?'

'Nothing at all.'

'Close neighbours, even, by country standards, don't you think?'

Alan was too busy trying to remember all he knew about the inside of a car to be able to find a suitable reply to this insinuation. But he registered it, and was not displeased.

Round the first bend they found a blue sports car. Alan approached the subject of his mechanical prowess with some misgiving. Remembering what the owner had said about a loose lead he thought he might as well try that first, before getting into deep water with solenoids and carburettors.

'Let's see,' he said. 'Better look inside the bonnet. How do you open it?'

'That I do know!' The woman dived into the front of the car and Alan was able to lift the bonnet.

'Here we are!' he said almost at once. 'A loose lead. You must be psychic.'

'Oh, I am, I am. It's really quite useful at times.'

'Funny,' he said as he lowered the bonnet. 'I can't think how the thing got loose. It seems to fit remarkably well. All the better, of course. It's not likely to happen again in a hurry.'

The woman looked at him out of big, innocent eyes. 'I'm sure it won't,' she said.

Alan suspected that the owner of the eyes wasn't all that innocent. He had a vague idea that he was missing something, some sort of a joke that the woman had seen and he hadn't. What did it matter, anyway? She was a most attractive woman, and he was enjoying himself. He couldn't let her go without offering her a cup of coffee first, and she accepted. They got on so well that she even stayed on for an impromptu lunch.

When at last she left he was delighted to think that he had her as a neighbour.

He thought about this happy proximity for some time, then decided to get back to the task in hand. But if he had found it difficult to get started before the woman's visit, he found it even more impossible now.

Rachel, she said was her name. Rachel Miller. Nice name, Rachel. It seemed to suit her, though he couldn't think why. If anyone had asked him a few hours before what sort of a picture the name Rachel conjured up in his mind he'd have been at a loss to answer. All the same, he was convinced that it was just the right name. He wondered what an exotic-looking female like her was doing in the heart of the country. Admittedly, her cottage looked a far more comfortable and stylish affair than his, but still . . .

He would have loved to know what had brought such a woman away from the city lights. No doubt if they got to know each other a little better he would find out in time. From their conversation he gathered that she had been around quite a bit – London, Paris, Vienna. He supposed she ought to make him feel like a country cousin beside her, but somehow she didn't. There was a warmth and welcoming quality about her that made him feel at ease in her company in spite of the obvious differences of background. At work and with Sheila he was used to the feeling that he was the one that came from the better background. But he certainly had nothing of the cosmopolitan aura that surrounded this woman.

Two evenings later he was sitting by the fire reading, when he heard the doorbell ring. His heart gave a great leap. Could it be Rachel?

She was standing in the doorway, looking more dramatic

than ever, with a long black scarf wound round her head, hiding all her curls. No lipstick, but lots of dark eye-shadow. All very black and white and very intense. He was so impressed by her appearance and her silence that he said nothing, only opening the door and stepping aside to let her pass. When he turned round after closing the door he found her standing just a few inches from him.

'I need a man,' she said.

His habitual caution prompted him to play for time. He wanted to be sure he wasn't misunderstanding her. After all, she might just be teasing him. He remembered the mocking tone so frequent in her voice. He'd better not commit himself and then be made to look foolish.

'For the car?' he asked.

'For me.' She put her arms round his neck, and soon he was fully convinced.

After that they spent most nights together, either in her cottage or in his. Most of the evenings, too. It was fatal for his writing, of course, but that didn't matter. Once again he decided that real life must take priority. Once again he gave himself wholeheartedly to the collection of material.

And what material!

Life had never been so full before. He thought of his Don Juan days at Cambridge and it all seemed a pathetic sham. What he had taken to be the heights of sensual passion now seemed to him nothing more than a superficial titillation. And none of the liberated young women he had known then could hold a candle to Rachel as far as personality was concerned. They all seemed empty and characterless. Perhaps it wasn't entirely their fault, poor things. They were too young, they were unripe. They had done too little, seen and felt too little. Rachel was older (she never specified how much older), and she had been around, had seen the world and, above all, had lived her life fully – as she still did. Everything she did, whether it was making love, preparing a sandwich, or telling one of her outrageous stories, she did *con passione*.

Although they spent long hours talking together, he never really found out much about her. This was the result of a fixed determination on her part.

'I'm not going to tell you anything about my past,' she announced early on in their relationship. 'My past doesn't matter. It's finished. I'm not interested in my past.'

'But *I* am.'

'Then you shouldn't be. My past is dead, my past *me* is dead. There's only the living me, in the present now. And that you have. Isn't it enough?'

'Yes, of course. Never in my life have I been given so much. And yet I want the past you too, to throw light on the present one.'

'It throws no light. Life is discontinuous. The present Rachel has nothing to do with past Rachels. Or with any future ones. There is only the present.'

'But the present is modified by the past. It has to be.'

Rachel stood up suddenly and walked over to the window. Alan couldn't see her face, but he heard the sudden tension in her voice.

'No, I won't have it. I refuse to be modified by the past. That cancels out free will, and I will not give up my free will, no matter what you say.'

After a moment's silence she spoke again – in a quieter, almost pathetic tone. 'I am what I want to be. Always, every moment of my life. My own creation. I can't bear the thought of being circumscribed and hindered and . . . and damaged by memories of the past or fears of the future. Life is what you make it, always at any given moment.'

Alan came and stood beside her at the window. 'Perhaps you're right,' he said. He couldn't make up his mind whether her words contained great wisdom or sheer folly.

'Perhaps you're right,' he said again. 'Up till recently I can see I've lived my life mainly in the past and the future, very little in the present. And I see why you've asked so few questions. You don't really want to know about me.'

'No. I don't want to know *about* you. That involves the past. I think you're carrying a heavy enough burden of past as it is,' she added with a smile. 'I know you have a wife and children and are very anxious for me not to be around on Saturdays. And so I have kept clear, and intend to continue to keep clear, till such time as . . . ' Here she paused and gave him a mischievous smile.

'Till such time as . . . ?' he prompted.

'Till such time as you show signs of being mature enough to be able to cope with any situation that might arise.'

'Isn't that looking into the future?' he suggested in the gently mocking tone he had acquired from her.

She laughed. 'Getting dangerously near it,' she admitted. 'We'd better concentrate on the present.'

'*Carpe diem*,' he said.

'Yes, but not in the usual sense. Most people mean you've got to grab what you can in the present because the future won't be so good. That seems to me a mean and calculating way of looking at life. I say, take the present, whatever it may be like. That's what we're offered. It's here. That's all we know.'

'*That is all*

'*Ye know on earth, and all ye need to know*,' Alan quoted.

After this conversation he tried hard to stop wondering about her history and her circumstances. It was clear that she was used to having far more money to spend than he had. Her clothes were expensive, her housekeeping extravagant. She had obviously travelled extensively, and was full of amusing stories about what she had seen in Bucharest or someone she had met in Rio. But she never said what she was doing in those places, why she went there or why she left. When he asked why a woman like her had buried herself in a small cottage in the heart of the country, she merely said she could think of no explanation that didn't involve her past history. Any explanation was therefore irrelevant. He found this trait in her annoying but was always silenced by the sheer magnitude of her impudence.

They sometimes went rambling together and she proved an acute observer, often noticing things he himself had missed, in spite of all his enthusiasm. She seemed to possess the quality of unlimited enjoyment characteristic of children. Indeed, she reminded him of Jane, with her keen observation and passionate desire to know, to classify, and of Tessa, with her impetuous enthusiasm for whatever the moment held.

22

One day in late spring Alan's daughters arrived in a state
of great excitement. 'We've just seen the most wonderful
woman,' they shrieked as they got out of the car.

'Really? Where?'

'At that cottage along the road. She was wearing skin-tight
leopard trousers and—'

'Not real leopard, silly.'

'I didn't say it was real—'

'And a bright red blouse—'

'Also skin-tight,' put in Sheila.

'And her hair was bright red, and her lipstick and her nails.'

Beth intervened for the first time:

'She looked like a flame. She was lovely.'

'And she smiled and waved to us. Wasn't that nice?'

'What was she doing?'

'She was just standing at the door. And after we'd gone she
turned and went into the house.'

'As if she'd been waiting for us,' added Jane thoughtfully.

'Do you know her, Alan?' asked Sheila.

'Yes, sort of. She's my nearest neighbour, you know. But I
don't know much about her,' he added, happy to think he was
being moderately truthful with this statement.

'But what on earth is an exotic flower like that doing in
a cottage in the country?' Sheila evidently wanted to pursue
the matter.

'I don't know. She hasn't confided the reason to me.' Alan hoped that a flippant answer would convince Sheila that the matter was of no importance.

But the girls had been too impressed by Rachel's flamboyant appearance to drop the subject so easily, and he had to give several more answers of various degrees of evasiveness before he was able to direct their attention elsewhere.

That evening, after he had taken the girls home, he stopped at Rachel's cottage on the way back.

'You created quite an impression this morning,' he remarked.

Rachel laughed. 'I just took a fancy to seeing your family. And I don't believe in peeping out from behind the curtains. When I'm looking at someone I like to be seen.'

'Rest assured, you were. Seen and admired.'

'By all?'

'By all the children. Sheila is less outspoken.'

'And didn't admire me, anyway.'

'How do you know?'

'I saw her. A woman who looks like that couldn't possibly admire a woman who looks like me.'

Alan was stung into a defence of his wife. 'Sheila's still very pretty, in the English-rose tradition.'

'Exactly. And English roses don't mix well with the more exotic blooms.'

'That's funny, that's exactly how she described you, as an exotic flower.'

'How discerning of her!'

Alan felt a bit annoyed. Rachel was obviously laughing at Sheila. It made him feel slightly uncomfortable. He would rather have kept these two parts of his life completely apart. Or else he would have liked to discuss the whole matter seriously, trying to be as fair as possible to all concerned. But to have Rachel laughing at Sheila while refusing to learn anything about her seemed a bit unfair. He got up to leave, prepared to take his resentment home with him. But Rachel disarmed him with an unexpected apology.

'I'm sorry,' she said. 'I should have curbed my curiosity. I had no right to interfere. And merely letting them see me was a form of interference.'

'It certainly made an impression,' he replied, mollified. After all, Rachel was Rachel, spontaneous and unpredictable. She had taken a fancy to see his family and had acted on it as one could have expected. And now she had apologized with characteristic generosity.

'And I think your little girls look sweet,' she added. 'What a pity we are so . . . so incompatible.'

Not long after this there was a long spell of bad weather. It rained nearly every day, and when it wasn't raining a cold wind blew endless clouds across the sky. Alan and Rachel were disappointed. This was the season they had been looking forward to. They had planned picnics and long excursions into unknown territory, hoping to widen their knowledge of the local flora and fauna.

It wasn't till one day in May that the sun broke through. Alan was in the college, and suddenly realized he could get away early that day. The afternoon was to be devoted to revision, so he didn't need to teach. With a great sense of liberation he got into the car and set off for the cottage. He would stop at Rachel's, help her to make up some sandwiches, and they would set off to explore the higher reaches of the river.

On his way home he noticed that the hawthorn hedge beside the turn-off from the main road was at last in full bloom. He remembered that there was an equally imposing hedge just before the river. He would be able to admire it with Rachel, who claimed she had never seen hawthorn blossom close up. 'That's the penalty for having spent all my life in cities,' she had explained. 'My natural education has been sadly neglected.'

Alan reflected with satisfaction on the part he was playing in putting right this omission.

When he got to her cottage he was surprised to see her car in front of the door with the hatch-back open. The car was filled with an array of large pigskin cases. Rachel emerged from the door at the moment carrying yet another case.

He got out of his car in mystified silence. As soon as she saw him Rachel dropped the case she was carrying and looked at him in obvious chagrin. For once she seemed not quite equal to the situation.

'I thought you were at the college,' was all she managed to say.

'I was.'

They looked at each other for a while in silence. Then Alan said:

'Pardon me for stating the obvious, but I take it you're going away?'

She nodded.

'Where?'

'I don't know.'

'Oh, come off it, Rachel. You're not going to tell me you're just going to get into the car and give it its head.'

'More or less just that.'

'When are you coming back?'

'I'm not coming back.'

'Never?'

'Never. You know I never go back. That's not the way I live.'

'And you were going away without saying a word, thinking I would know nothing about it till you'd gone? You weren't even going to leave me a note?'

'No, nothing. I thought that was the best way. I still

think it would have been the best way. Parting is always difficult, painful. And I was right, as you see. This is painful, isn't it?'

'Yes, but how do you think I'd have felt if I'd come back and found you gone, with no explanation?'

'Any worse than this? After all, you're getting no explanation this way either. There's nothing to explain. I'm just going, that's all.'

'Sometimes I wonder if you're right in the head,' he exclaimed. 'How can you talk such nonsense? You can't just walk out without offering any explanation after all we've meant to each other. For we have meant a lot to each other, you can't deny that.'

'I'm not denying it. But you've just explained it yourself. We're talking about what we *have* meant to each other. Past tense.'

'Perfect,' he corrected, the grammarian in him still at work even in the midst of this emotional crisis.

'You needn't be so sarcastic.'

'Perfect tense,' he said icily. 'Grammar, not sarcasm.'

For a moment she looked discountenanced. Then she brought out the word 'Pedant!' and turned to lock the cottage. After that she pocketed the key, picked up the last case and made for her car.

Before she could get in Alan seized her arm and made her turn to face him.

'I'm not going to let you go off like this, without even a parting kiss.'

'What's the use of a kiss given and received in hate?'

'But I don't hate you. I'm angry and . . . and desperate, but I don't hate you. And why should you hate me? Merely because you've decided that I'm now a bit of the past, is that it?'

'Yes, partly that. And partly because of this hideous,

unnecessary scene. You should have let us part with dignity at least.'

This rebuke silenced Alan. He turned away and got into his car as she got into hers. A moment later both cars drove away, in opposite directions.

23

As soon as she started at Art College Lisha decided she was now to be known by the correct version of her name, in order to prove to the world at large, herself included, that she was now completely grown up. The family, of course, didn't see it that way, and would never change, and at home it didn't really matter. But she felt sure that in the outside world the name Alicia commanded more respect than the nursery version she had lived with up till then.

Going to Art College was a big thrill, and leaving it was an even bigger one, for she was now a working woman. She found it exciting to think that she was contributing with her work and her specialized knowledge to the business of keeping the world going. She felt she was earning her place in society. Helping to catalogue an obscure collection of paintings in a provincial museum was perhaps not the most adventurous of occupations but she derived considerable satisfaction from dealing with these objects which had already stood the test of time, and which would still be looked at, perhaps even admired, a hundred years later. And she got on well with her colleagues, especially her immediate boss, Susan.

So life was going along very nicely when she met Peter Eward and fell in love with him, that very day. She knew from the start that this was the most wonderful man she had ever met. Part of the wonderfulness consisted, precisely, in the manner of their meeting. She was at a swinging party and enjoying it greatly, when she was nearly knocked off her feet by an unexpectedly exuberant piece of dancing behind her. She felt herself falling and thought she was going to end up on the floor, under the feet of the dancers.

But suddenly her arm was seized from the right, holding her steady. Her balance regained, she turned to find a tall man releasing her arm and looking at her in some concern.

'Are you all right?' he asked.

'Yes, thanks to you,' she answered. 'I really thought I was going to be trampled underfoot. Thank you so much.'

The man smiled. 'Not at all,' he said, then added with a twinkle, 'Any time.'

As soon as he had gone she turned to one of her colleagues and asked:

'Who is that?'

'Peter Eward.'

'Not . . . not Susan's husband, surely?'

'Yes, why not? You look quite amazed.'

'No, I'm just . . . I mean, he's wonderful, isn't he?'

'Why shouldn't Susan have a wonderful husband? She's a nice person, and very attractive.'

'Oh yes, I agree. I think Susan's great. It's just . . . well, if I had a husband like that I'd be telling the world.'

'Well, they've been married quite a few years. I expect some of the excitement rubs off in the course of time.'

Lisha was convinced that the excitement would never rub off for her, if she were married to Peter. She made for a quiet corner and sat down to think about this momentous change in her life. For she had no doubt at all of the importance of the encounter. She knew she was in love – for good, of course. And the fact that the man was married, and married to a woman she knew and liked, meant that there was no hope for her. Suddenly the situation had become breathtaking and

133

tragic at the same time. She was now committed to a lifetime of unrequited love.

She was still sitting quietly, thinking over this enormous change in her life, when she saw Susan and Peter standing in front of her.

'Are you all right?' Susan asked.

'Yes. Fine, thank you.'

'Peter told me you'd just had a narrow escape. Then he saw you sitting still and he came to ask me if that was like you. And it isn't. So are you sure . . . ?'

'I'm fine, really. It's just . . . well, perhaps I was just a little shaken,' Lisha admitted, unable to give the real reason for seeming so withdrawn. 'But I'm quite all right now,' she added.

'Right then, let's prove it,' said Peter. 'Come and dance.'

After that dance Lisha spent the rest of the evening dancing with other young men and thinking of Peter. Not one of them danced, or looked, or spoke as well as he did. From now on, she realized, all her contemporaries would seem nothing but callow boys to her.

She went to bed very late that night and cried for a long time out of sheer thankfulness. In spite of her usual *joie de vivre* and her positive approach to life, she had for years been troubled by the fear that she might miss out on what seemed to her the most important of all experiences, that of being in love. Now at least she knew that this aspect of her life would not be sterile. It was a hopeless love, of course. Even if he were free, how could she hope that the wonderful Peter would ever think of anyone so unimportant and manifestly imperfect as little Lisha – no, Alicia.

Even the name 'Alicia' could do nothing to raise her into the requisite category, but all this was in any case secondary. The marvellous thing was that she had at last met the perfect man, that her emotions were no longer running wild, without an object. She fell asleep awed by the feeling that she had at last found her emotional centre.

During the following year Lisha saw Peter occasionally at concerts, parties or other social gatherings – often enough to keep her passion alive, not often enough to upset her state of equilibrium. But then an Italian scholar wrote to say he was interested in a collection of paintings by a minor Venetian master and wished to come and study the examples of his work in their collection. It so happened that they hadn't yet got round to doing anything about these paintings, which were stored with a large number of other non-urgent material. This meant a lot of extra work for Susan and Alicia. Sometimes they would work in the evening in Susan's flat, and meetings with Peter became more frequent and more intimate. Seeing Peter bringing in a tray with coffee for the working women, or making toast by the fire, made him somehow seem less inaccessible, and Lisha found it hard to maintain her attitude of hopeless but contented love.

The Italian scholar appeared and threw the department into a flutter. He had melting brown eyes, exquisite manners and a delightful interest in everything he saw. During the week he spent with them most of the girls in the department would have happily worked till midnight every night to provide all the information he needed. But as head of the department it was Susan who was most involved, with, of course, her personal assistant, Alicia.

When the day of Signor Rollo's departure came there was considerable gloom in the department. Lisha felt a certain amount of mild contempt for the obvious adoration all the others seemed to feel for the man. But then, she reflected, perhaps she too would have succumbed to Signor Rollo's Latin charm if she hadn't been so engrossed in her love of Peter.

Susan was to drive the departing idol to the station to catch the train for London. Just before leaving she came up to Lisha with an envelope in her hand.

'Alicia dear, could I ask you to do me a great favour? I'd forgotten that I won't be home till late tonight – I've to go to a meeting in Sheffield. I forgot to tell Peter, and the phone's out of order, so I can't ring him up and tell him. Could I possibly ask you to hand this in to him on your way home tonight?'

'Of course. No problem.' Lisha was delighted at the prospect of seeing Peter, but felt that perhaps there *was* a bit of a problem. She had never been alone with him before, and wondered how well her studied indifference would stand up to the situation. The best thing would be just to hand over the envelope and refuse to go in.

But when Peter opened the door she was startled to find him looking utterly ashen, and hesitated before handing over the envelope.

'Is something wrong, Peter?' she asked. 'You look terrible.'

'Come in,' he said.

She hesitated, and he added:

'Everyone will know soon enough anyway, so why not you?'

This was more than her curiosity could resist, and she forgot her previous resolve and went into the flat, holding out the envelope.

'And I can guess what's in that,' he said as he took it.

'A meeting in Sheffield. She forgot . . . '

'Fiddlesticks!' he interrupted her as he opened the envelope.

Startled by this uncharacteristic rudeness, Lisha drew back a couple of paces.

'I think I'd better go,' she said. 'I suspect I'm *de trop* here.'

'It seems I'm the one that's *de trop* here,' he replied. 'As you can see, you've landed in the middle of a marital drama. And everyone's going to know tomorrow when she doesn't turn up at her work. So you might as well stay and let me blow my top.'

He read the letter and put it down in silence. Then he walked over to the window and stared out of it, apparently oblivious to Alicia's presence. She stood awkwardly near the door, beginning to suspect what had happened, but unsure what she ought to do. Peter stood by the window for a long time, and Lisha couldn't make out whether he was struggling against grief or anger. When he turned round it seemed to her that anger was the dominant emotion.

He looked at her and shrugged his shoulders. 'Well, that's that,' he said. 'End of marriage.'

'Has she . . . gone off with—?'

'Yes. The little dancing master.'

'You mean Signor Rollo?'

'Who else?'

For a while neither of them said anything. Then Lisha decided she'd better break the silence:

'What I don't understand is, how did you know before opening the envelope?'

'Because of the state the bedroom's in. You may have noticed that Susan's a very tidy person. Well, there are clothes lying all over the place, and three of her cases are missing. She must have had to pack in a great hurry, after I'd gone off to work.'

Alicia's indignation exploded. 'But how could she! How could she leave you and go off with a man she'd only just met!'

'She'd known him for a year. She met him at that conference in Rome last year and they've been corresponding ever since. I didn't think it was important. I thought it

137

was just about work. Never thought she'd run off with him.'

'But . . . but . . . '

'But what?'

'Oh, nothing.'

'But what?' he insisted.

'She told us all she'd never met him. I remember it so clearly because before he arrived we were all guessing what he would look like. Susan said she thought he would be short and fat and smelling of garlic.'

'Well, he's not quite that bad. But it's still pretty humiliating, having your wife run off with a little popinjay like that. For he is a popinjay, don't tell me he isn't. I suppose she must have been desperately bored with me.'

'Oh Peter, don't be ridiculous! How can you say such a thing!'

'Well, she's gone, hasn't she? Must be a reason for it.'

'But I thought you were both so happy!'

'We both put up quite a good show. But we knew it wasn't the perfect marriage. After all, there's no such thing, is there?'

'A perfect marriage, you mean?'

'Yes. Or even a moderately happy one. Do you know of any?'

Alicia was shocked. 'Oh yes, lots.'

'Name one.'

'Well, my parents, for one. And . . . oh well, lots of others.'

'My dear Alicia, most marriages are a perfect disaster. You don't want to admit this, of course, because you no doubt are hoping, or even confidently expecting, to make one of those happy marriages of which you see so many examples.'

Lisha told herself it wasn't surprising that Peter should speak disparagingly of marriage just at this point. She was about to renew her defence of the institution when it struck her that right now it was important for him to believe in the impossibility of a happy marriage. It was bound to lessen his sense of failure, she supposed. So she said nothing about her own expectations in the matter. Besides, they were too tied up with his own situation, which had now, suddenly, become very fluid.

'Perhaps you're right,' she conceded. 'Perhaps all the happy marriages are only so in appearance. Like yours, it seems.'

'Right,' he said.

'I suppose it's a consolation, in a way.'

'You mean, I haven't lost all that much in reality?'

'So perhaps you won't be as heartbroken as . . . '

'As I ought, in all decency, to be?' After a pause Peter added, 'No, I don't think I'm heartbroken. I'm angry and disoriented and humiliated. But I'll get over it.'

Lisha took this statement as her cue for leaving, and stood up. 'I'd better go,' she said. 'I expect you've got quite a lot of things to think out.' And so have I, she nearly added.

At the door she paused. 'I'm sorry I was the bearer of bad tidings.'

'Not really. I knew already. All you brought was confirmation. All the same, in olden days you'd probably have had your head chopped off.'

'Something to be said for living in the twentieth century,' she said. It was only after he had closed the door that she realized that the whole framework within which their meetings took place had now disappeared. No more evenings working in the flat with Susan, no more casual encounters in the museum when he came to pick Susan up. If they were to meet again it would have to be through the initiative of one or the other. Yes, she reflected, she certainly had a lot of things to think over.

Lisha was shocked and distressed by Susan's behaviour.

While admitting that there were sometimes grounds for the breakdown of a marriage, she found it impossible to believe that any woman married to Peter could be justified in leaving him. There was also the prospect of some difficult moments at work. Luckily none of the others knew that she was to go to the flat, so there was no fear of being grilled by them. The last thing she wanted was to discuss the matter with anyone else.

Her own position in the museum would also be greatly changed by Susan's absence. However indignant she felt against Susan now, working with her had been a great joy, and she would miss her.

And above all, there was the problem of seeing Peter again. If he didn't look her up – and why should he? – then she would have to take the initiative herself. But would she ever have the courage to do so? The gap between them seemed enormous. After all, he was eleven years older, well established in his profession, and the husband of her former boss.

But Peter was free! That was the wonderful thought that kept floating above all her worries and misgivings. She was no longer bound by loyalty to his wife, and no longer in danger of putting someone else's marriage in jeopardy. There was a lot of emotional readjustment to be done. She need no longer think of herself as bound to a love that must for ever remain silent and unrequited. Just as suddenly as she had found herself bound to a hopeless love, she now found herself freed from this fate. Suddenly the impossible dream had entered the realm of the possible.

By the time she went to bed Lisha had decided that she would make the first move if she hadn't heard from Peter within the next few days. She would cook up some excuse or other and go and see him. Then it struck her that she would be better to go without an excuse. Don't be so grudging, she told herself, don't be so cowardly. You're going because you want to see him. Why shouldn't you let him know?

Three days later he phoned her at the museum.

'Look,' he said, 'there's a lot of stuff here that Susan left in the flat that belongs to the Museum. For obvious reasons I don't really feel like making a personal appearance. Could I possibly ask you to come and collect it? Or I could bring it round to your place.'

'I'll come,' she said. 'What about this evening?'

They were standing in the kitchen, making a cup of coffee, when Lisha said:

'If you hadn't phoned, I'd have come round anyway some time this week.'

'For the stuff?'

'Oh no, I'd forgotten there was anything left here. No. No excuse. Just to see you.'

'Alicia,' he said, 'you're a great girl. I wanted to see you too, but I wasn't honest enough to make the move without an excuse.'

24

They soon settled into a comfortable routine.

Lisha went round to Peter's flat two or three times a week to help him get things more or less the way he used to have them in his bachelor days. She helped him move furniture, empty out cupboards, put all Susan's things into the spare bedroom, reorganize the kitchen.

'No more fancy stuff,' announced Peter. 'I won't be going in for *cordon bleu* cookery or massive entertaining. My guests will be lucky if they get a mug of coffee.'

'But it will be an excellent mug of coffee!'

'And what more can hospitality offer?'

Their relationship was comfortable and comradely. Peter was glad of her undemanding and cheerful company, and she had a practical streak which was a big help for his domestic readjustments. He still found it very difficult to face people, and Alicia's presence during the dramatic first hours of Susan's desertion meant that he could feel at ease with her, without the need to give or withhold explanations.

He realized, of course, that there was a danger in the relationship. Alicia might well take things too seriously. Consequently he was careful never to overstep the limits of affectionate camaraderie. They joked and laughed and discussed the merits of Peter doing his own cooking as opposed to eating out, and other such matters. And when she left to go home she was given a friendly peck on the cheek. Nothing there, surely, on which she could found any unwarranted expectations.

After all the readjustment in the flat had been completed they continued to see each other, though less frequently. Sometimes they would go to a concert or a play, or else they would just sit in the flat and talk.

It was on one of these occasions that Lisha surprised him by asking:

'Would you like to make love to me, Peter?'

After a startled pause he countered with:

'Would you like me to?'

'That's not fair. You should answer my question first. And anyway, you must know the answer to yours. Of course I would. But what about you?'

'And the answer to that question is the same. Of course I would. But . . . '

'I don't see how there can be any buts, if that's what we both want.'

'There's a difference between what you would like to do and what you want to do.'

'I don't see it.'

'It's like this. I'd *like* to make love to you, of course I would. But I don't *want* to – because I know we should both regret the emotional consequences.'

'You mean you think I'd expect more involvement from you than you're prepared to give?'

'Well, don't you think there's a danger of that? You're eleven years younger than I am, you're full of idealistic and romantic notions. For you it would be a total commitment. I know it would. You're not the promiscuous sort.'

'And you're not prepared to give a total commitment, I can see that. And you think that would spoil it for me. Is that it?'

'Well, it would, wouldn't it?'

'Not in the least.'

'Alicia, you don't know what you're talking about.'

'Yes I do. I've been in love with you since the day we met – that evening at the dance, remember? I've known since then that you were the only man I could ever love. And I knew from the start that I could never have you – or that's what it seemed like then. And I accepted that and loved you at a distance, and never even hoped for anything else. And I was contented and thankful I'd met you, even if I could never have you. So you see: I know what I'm talking about.'

Peter came over and sat beside her, taking her hand in his. 'How I wish things were different, my dear. How I wish *I* were different, so that I could give you the love you deserve. But I know my own limitations. And I know how you would suffer.'

But in spite of his firm resolve, or perhaps because of hers, they ended up making love, and Lisha spent the night in the flat with him.

After his initial self-reproach Peter allowed himself to forget his misgivings. Lisha was so glowingly happy that he found it hard to persuade himself that he was doing her a wrong. And who knows, perhaps he would change. Perhaps in time he too would want a more complete commitment. But after a few months, when Lisha suggested she should move in with him, he realized things weren't going to work out as simply as he had hoped. For his immediate reaction to the suggestion was one of fear – a sudden, paralysing fear that his life was being invaded, that he was being asked to give more than he wanted to give. He was meditating his reply, wondering how to answer without hurting her, when she broke the silence.

'I'm sorry,' she said. 'I shouldn't have suggested that. It shows that you were right in the first place, doesn't it? It shows that I've not been content with the looser sort of relationship you want. Please forget I said it. Please, let's go back to where we were before I spoke.'

'Yes darling, we'll try,' he said, knowing only too well that there was no going back.

From that moment something was lost from their relationship. Each felt guilty, and neither could go back to their earlier spontaneous freedom. The carefree innocence of the first months was gone. Peter blamed himself. Why could he not give himself as completely as Alicia did? Was it sheer selfishness? He now began to wonder whether this was what had gone wrong with his marriage. Were Susan's estrangement and final desertion due to the same sort of frustration? Susan had none of Alicia's spontaneity and humility. It would have been terribly difficult for her to ask for a greater share of his life. Perhaps the little Italian was more generous with his inner self. He knew there had been many things wrong with the marriage; but perhaps this possibility that he was only now beginning to see had a lot to do with its ultimate failure.

He began to realize that he had no close personal relationship except with Alicia. And even that wasn't as close as she would like it. He had been very attached to his mother, but she had died many years before. And since her death he had certainly not been in close touch with his father. You could hardly say that the relationship had deteriorated; there had been no quarrel, no break. It had just evaporated, apart from the most infrequent and brief of contacts. His father lived alone in the big house in North Yorkshire where the family had lived for generations. When he went to visit him Peter always felt that he was more in touch with the house than with its occupant.

He had a few friends, none of them very close. And then there was his partner in the engineering firm they had set up some ten years ago. They had always got on very well, and seen quite a lot of each other even outside working hours.

But somehow, now, things weren't going so well there either. They seemed to be getting on each other's nerves, he couldn't quite tell why.

So many things seemed to be wrong, or at least unsatisfactory. He couldn't help noticing that the one common element was himself.

The situation at the office had degenerated still further when the news of his father's sudden death seemed to offer at least a temporary distraction, as he would have to go into the country to attend to things. And soon he saw that the new situation could perhaps offer a permanent solution to two of his problems. He could sell his share of the business and thus be rid of the constant disagreements with his partner. And that would leave him free to go and live in the family home, which might ease the situation with Alicia. They would, of course, go on seeing each other, but less often. He hoped that absence would make her heart grow not fonder, but stronger and more independent.

When he told her his idea, Alicia was appalled.

'But you can't go and bury yourself in the wilderness like that!'

'Why not? I've just spent ten days there clearing up my father's affairs, and I felt I could live there very happily. Don't forget, that's where I was brought up.'

'Yes, but how long is it since you left? Do you know anybody, but anybody, there now?'

'Not really. But I'll still be in touch with you and all my friends here. You could all come and stay with me. You would, at least, surely?'

'Yes, of course. You know I'd go to the ends of the earth to see you.'

'Well, that won't be necessary, it's not quite as far as that. In fact it's really very accessible. I don't see what the big problem is.'

'But what would you *do?* You can't sit and contemplate your navel all day.'

'There's lots of things I can do. All the things I've always wanted more time for. Reading, hill walking, gardening . . . '

'And concerts and plays and shopping and exhibitions and good restaurants,' she went on ironically.

'And I'll have television to let me know how the world is getting on without me,' he went on. 'And, above all, I'll have time. Masses of gorgeous, glorious time! Tell you what, let's both go and spend the weekend there. Then you'll know what I'm talking about.'

'I know what we're talking about. You forget I was brought up in the country. I know what rural life is. But my rural life is filled with lovely brothers and sisters, my parents, all my childhood friends. I've gone back so often since I left home that I haven't lost touch with any of them. Besides, we live in the village. Your place seems to be out in the wilds. But I'll come and spend a weekend in your wilderness if you come and spend one in mine. Then you'll see the difference.'

At first Lisha was rather put off by the austere Yorkshire scenery. But by the end of the weekend she had to concede that it had its attractions.

'But just wait till you see my dear little Galloway hills, and the lovely bays and the sea, oh the sea! There's nothing like it. It's a warm, happy, friendly landscape – not like this.'

Peter saw, and was convinced. It was all utterly delightful: house, family and scenery. However, as he pointed out, the choice was not between living in her family home or his, but between city life and country life in his own rather gaunt family house, with no family thrown in.

He stuck to his plan, gave up his share of the business, and moved out to the country. Lisha had done her best to dissuade him, with a few more visits to Galloway. He became very fond of her home and her constantly changing family. You never knew which of the brothers and sisters would be at home at any given weekend.

'It's lovely,' he told Lisha. 'I enjoy it immensely here, and I hope we'll keep on coming for the odd weekend once I'm settled in my wilderness. But it hasn't made me change my mind. In fact, it's reinforced my position. Life here makes city life seem all the more unacceptable.'

'Hoist with my own petard,' she exclaimed, laughing. 'Yes, of course we'll come back here once your exile has started.'

But in fact none of those weekends materialized, largely because Peter settled in to his new life so well that he felt no need to get away. At first Lisha came to stay with him frequently, then at increasingly long intervals. Peter's new way of life put a certain emotional distance between them. Now that he was more satisfied with his daily life, he felt the need of Lisha's presence less than before. He hoped the lengthening intervals between her visits meant that she felt more independent and was finding other things to fill her life with. He spoke of this to her one day.

'Yes,' she said, 'I'm definitely more independent and I've found plenty of things to fill my life. But you know why, don't you?'

He gave her a troubled look. This was not what he had hoped for:

'Oh, I'm not reproaching you,' she exclaimed. 'But since you've raised the subject I want to make it clear that I never wanted these alternatives in my life. All I wanted was you. I know I said I would take as much as you could give and be satisfied with that. But in the long run it wasn't enough. I found I couldn't live in an increasingly large vacuum. So I had to take steps to fill it, that's all.'

Peter didn't ask whether she was satisfied with her present alternatives. He was afraid he knew the answer.

* * *

Some time later Lisha went home for the weekend and was delighted to find that her visit coincided with one of Melville's somewhat rarer trips to Scotland. On the Sunday morning the two of them went for a walk, following the stream they had known and loved all their lives. After a mile or so they sat down on the raised, grassy bank and Lisha threw a twig into the water. Melville followed suit, and they watched the two twigs as they floated downstream.

'We're not competing,' said Melville as he threw another one in. 'Pity, for I seem to be winning.'

'I wouldn't be too sure,' said Lisha as she threw in her second twig. 'Your first one's caught in an eddy. Mine's going to catch up on it.'

Melville sighed. 'A terrible fate, getting caught in an eddy. Apropos, are you still seeing Peter?'

Lisha laughed ruefully. 'Hardly at all. I seem to have been released from that particular eddy. He doesn't need me any more.'

'Sorry?'

'Yes, of course. It's nice to be needed.'

'Not always. It can be a bit of a bind. But even when it's nice, it shouldn't be necessary. I hope you don't think it is.'

'Why ever not? What's wrong with being needed?'

'Nothing. It's when you need to be needed that the trouble starts.'

Lisha shook her head. 'I don't see what's wrong with that.'

'Just this: it turns you into a sort of parasite. You feed on someone else's need. There's nothing wrong with being needed, but there's even less wrong with not being needed. If you are now in that happy position, I'd say: get on with it and enjoy it.' After a pause he said:

'After all, that's what you're made for. You have a great

capacity for receiving and giving enjoyment. I think you should specialize in that.'

'But that's just what I was trying to do. With Peter, I mean.'

'I know. But I think you should be a bit more indiscriminate. Just enjoy anything and everything. With or without Peter.'

'I'll try. And I suppose I could start with being glad he doesn't need me any more.'

'Yes. After all, it was his need that brought you together. You really haven't all that much in common.'

'I can't agree there. We have a lot of tastes in common.'

'Tastes, yes, I agree. But your characters are so different. He's a loner and you're a social and sociable animal.'

Lisha sighed. 'I wonder if he's really happy in his wilderness.'

'I shouldn't worry about it. He'll let you know if he isn't.'

'You make him sound very selfish.'

'Most of us are. But that's not how I meant it. What I'm saying is that either he's happy, which should make you happy, or he isn't, in which case he'll want you back, and you can rejoice in that.'

'In other words, I can't lose?'

'Right.'

Lisha gave a little laugh. 'So it seems we really are living in the best of all possible worlds.'

'Indeed,' he answered. 'Where else could one find a Lisha?'

25

After that conversation with her brother, Lisha began to feel a sense of liberation that surprised her very much at first. For a while she even felt guilty about it. How could she possibly feel glad that Peter didn't need her any more? But as time went by she began to feel that her 'alternatives' were gradually sliding into first place in her life. She wondered whether she should write and tell Peter. After all, perhaps he was still blaming himself for having cast her off. It might be a kindness to write. On the other hand, it might seem almost like a gesture of defiance. She couldn't decide whether to write or not.

In the end inertia won, and she didn't write.

Life had recovered its flavour. She was enjoying her work again, going out with friends, even beginning to enjoy the company of men of her own age. Among these was Frank, whom she had known and liked for years, without ever considering him as a possible boyfriend. If it hadn't been for Peter she might have realized long before this that Frank was an eminently desirable admirer.

He was one of those people who just seem to be naturally good at living – rather like Lisha, in this respect. He was tall, fair and athletic, a keen sportsman, interested in everything, intelligent, friendly, lively . . . He was even comparatively well off, and was making a good career for himself as a sports commentator.

Lisha's life opened out in a number of directions when she

started going out with him. One of his enthusiasms was rock climbing. Lisha had done her share of hill walking, but had never seriously contemplated going up a cliff face. Frank soon convinced her that this was the only way to get any satisfaction out of climbing a mountain, and, in spite of some opposition from her family, she set off on her first ascent. She found it rather frightening and utterly irresistible. After that she was hooked.

Frank was duly taken home for a weekend, to be inspected by the family, and to convince them that rock climbing was the safest thing in the world. The parents remained somewhat sceptical, but all the younger members were convinced, and eager to set off with him right away. And all the family, parents included, agreed that Frank was a delightful young man who would always be welcome among them.

'That's a nice boy Lisha's got hold of this time. He seems to have a happy, friendly nature,' said her father after Frank's first visit.

'Yes,' replied his wife. 'He's at home in the world. Rather like Lisha, don't you think? No unnecessary agonizing.'

'Did you not think Lisha did a bit of agonizing over Peter?'

'Yes, but no more than was necessary. She seems to have got over it very well.'

'With some assistance from Frank. Let's just hope he doesn't drag her up too many rock faces.'

'Yes,' she agreed. 'That's the one thing I could wish different in him. In all other respects he's a perfect darling.' After a moment's pause she added, 'And I don't at all like this trip they're planning for next weekend.'

'Cairngorms? Needn't be too dangerous.'

'No, but Lisha's only a beginner.'

'Don't worry, they'll take that into account. After all, Frank's in charge of the party and he's obviously very fond of

Lisha. He'll make sure she's not exposed to any unnecessary danger. They won't be dragging her up the north face of Ben Nevis, you know.'

'No,' Mrs Wilson sighed. 'Not yet.'

The night before they set off for the Highlands, Lisha spoke to her mother on the phone, then wished she hadn't, for her mother seemed really uneasy about the expedition.

'Look, Mum, there are six of us going, and all the others are very experienced climbers. *And* we'll be staying in a cottage that belongs to somebody's uncle – can't remember whose, but one of the party – *and* it's only a few miles from where we'll be climbing . . . Yes, Mum, yes . . . of course I'll be careful . . . but there's nothing to worry about, really . . . '

By the end of the conversation Lisha felt uneasy too. She told herself it was only on account of her mother's worry, and that she herself felt perfectly confident about the whole thing. And yet, somehow, she just didn't feel right about the enterprise.

It's divided loyalties, she told herself. Wanting to live up to Frank's expectations and not wanting to do something that so obviously worries the family. If only I hadn't phoned. Mum's just as worried as she was, and now I'm all unhappy and divided about it.

This type of internal conflict was something Lisha had very seldom experienced, and she didn't know how to cope with it. When they set off the following morning she was still feeling uncertain and unsettled and she didn't enjoy the journey as much as she had expected. She knew the other two couples quite well by now, and as a rule all six of them had a hilarious time in the van on their outings. This time, however, they all noticed Lisha's subdued state, and asked her if she was all right.

'I seem to be getting a bit of a cold,' she admitted, shortly before they reached the cottage.

After a sleepless night, tormented by her divided loyalties, Lisha decided not to go on the climb, pleading a bad cold, whose symptoms she had exaggerated somewhat.

The rest of the party, free from the constraints of having a beginner among them, decided on a more serious climb. On their way back Frank was killed by a falling rock.

26

It took Lisha a long time to recover from the shock and sense of guilt caused by that accident. Besides, Frank's death meant more than the loss of a friend and lover. They had been on the point of announcing their engagement, so it meant her whole future must be changed. She accepted this, telling herself that there was nothing unusual in her situation. From time immemorial men and women had lost their loved ones and had to reshape their lives. What she found much harder to accept was her sense of guilt over the death, and of this she spoke little.

If I hadn't lost my nerve, she kept thinking, it would never have happened. If I hadn't pretended to be worse than I was, I'd have had to go with them, and they'd never have been near that cliff face when the rock fell down. If I'd put as much effort into concealing my cold as I put into magnifying it, Frank would still be here.

But it was not in Lisha's nature to revel in self-condemnation. After a while she began to look at the matter more objectively. Her guilt was no greater, and no less, than if the accident hadn't taken place. She hadn't even known they were going to do that particular climb till after they had left.

The decision had been taken in her absence.

In the end her natural buoyancy triumphed and, after a spell of sadness and guilt, Lisha was able to resume her normal life.

27

Rachel's departure plunged Alan into a raging sea of anger and frustration.

He was angry with her for going off, frustrated because she had told him so little about her life, and furious with himself for having let her take him over so completely. He now thought of her as an unscrupulous adventuress who had used him to while away the long hours that for some obscure, and probably discreditable reason, she had decided to spend in a country exile. Right from the start, he thought, she's done nothing but use me, from the very first day. From lover to motor mechanic, I've been there to fill her needs.

Suddenly the black waves of anger receded, leaving a clear space in which he saw what he had failed to see that very first day. It was all a put-up job. That car breakdown, the loose lead . . . She herself had pulled it off, to give her an excuse for enlisting his help. Psychic indeed! So she just happened to suggest the right thing! Any other man would have seen through her little ruse, and, what's more, she would have expected him to. But he had been guileless enough to swallow the whole story, psychic powers and all. No wonder she seemed to be mocking him.

His fury flooded back as he realized what an innocent he had been. How she must have laughed at him, again and again. The only consolation he could find in the whole sad story was the fact that she seemed to find he was all right in bed. It didn't say very much, of course, given the lack of competition. But still . . .

Two days later he was still seething with anger and humiliation when he received an unexpected visit from Mr Mott, who ran a good old-fashioned grocer's shop, the best in High Midbury. His prices were a bit above the average, but Alan loved going in there and seeing all the drawers lining the walls, all neatly labelled, with a variety of apparently unrelated commodities – almonds, cinnamon, baking soda, beans (haricot) cloves, splits (what on earth could they be?), dates . . . Alan and Rachel had pondered deeply on a possible system of classification for these varied delicacies, but had been unable to come up with anything more likely than Wont and Use. Some day, he told himself, he would ask Mr Mott. But the expression on the grocer's face as he stood on Alan's doorstep made it perfectly clear that this was not the moment for frivolous enquiry.

'I'm sorry to incommode you, Mr Morley,' the man began, 'but I just wonder if you could give me a little information about a matter of some importance to me, and to some of my fellow shopkeepers.'

'Certainly,' said Alan, unable to think of any relevant information he might possess.

'It's about your former neighbour, Miss Miller – or would I be more correct in designating her as *Mrs* Miller?'

Alan had often been struck by Mr Mott's addiction to formal phraseology and wondered whether it was a chronic characteristic of the man or whether it was induced by the knowledge that he was speaking to a member of the teaching profession. On this occasion, however, he was too nonplussed by the grocer's request to think about the terms in which it was couched.

'I honestly couldn't say.' He realized his answer could

apply to both Mr Mott's questions, and left the grocer to come to his own conclusions in the matter.

But Mr Mott was not to be put off. 'There are two points at issue,' he remarked. 'One, where has the lady gone? And two, how to address her?'

'I really don't know the answer to either question, I'm afraid.'

'Quite so, Mr Morley. Yet it is a matter of some importance to me, and to my fellow colleagues in High Midbury, to establish the lady's whereabouts. There are, it appears, considerable sums involved. As your good self has been seen so often in company with the lady, we thought, naturally . . . '

'You'd better come in.' Alan sighed, realizing he wasn't going to get off as easily as he could have wished. It was only too true that he and Rachel had often done their shopping together. He had realized that this was perhaps a bit imprudent, but only from the point of view of keeping Sheila and his colleagues out of the picture. He now began to see Rachel's departure in a much uglier light. It wasn't simply the caprice of an undisciplined spirit.

Before sitting down, Mr Mott surveyed the dingy little living room, and Alan was very conscious that his surroundings had been weighed up and found wanting. For the first time he felt ashamed of the mean little room, with its cheap, chipped furniture. Sheila's disapproval hadn't mattered – it was inevitable, given her tastes and ideals. And Rachel didn't seem to have noticed or cared, even though her own cottage was on quite a different level. But he squirmed at the sight of Mr Mott's pained expression.

'Well, Mr Morley, you no doubt are beginning to acquire some sort of an idea of what the trouble is. The situation, as I see it, is that Miss Miller – or *Mrs* Miller, as the case may be – appears to have left the area owing considerable sums to various establishments, myself included. I'm afraid some of us have been rather imprudent. She was such a charming lady, and always paid cash during her first weeks here, that many of us let her run up bills of considerable proportions. Now, after a certain amount of, shall we say, encouragement on the part of some of us, the lady settled quite a few accounts – more than one of which ran into the hundreds, I may say.'

'Good.' Alan felt that a monosyllable might seem a bit inadequate as a response to Mr Mott's flow of words, but that was really all he could rise to.

Mr Mott shook his head and sighed. 'Alas,' he declaimed, 'the lady paid by cheque. Need I say more?'

'They've bounced?'

Mr Mott looked even more pained, perhaps as much at the inelegant choice of words as at the situation they described.

'I'm terribly sorry to hear this,' Alan said, 'but I'm afraid there's nothing at all I can do about it. I have no idea where she's gone.'

The grocer was evidently trying to conceal his incredulity. 'No forwarding address?'

'No, I'm afraid not.'

'Then perhaps you can help us by facilitating some information as where the lady came from?'

'I'm sorry, I can't help you there either. I have no idea.' As he spoke Alan couldn't help seeing what a ridiculous situation he was in. Of course no one would believe he had none of this basic information about a woman in whose company he had been seen so often. At the same time he was beginning to feel some sympathy for his visitor, in spite of his pomposity. Several hundred pounds might indeed mean a lot to a small business.

And then he realized that he too was one of the victims. Some weeks previously Rachel had borrowed fifty pounds from him, which she was always about to return. Wretchedly he now wondered whether this might have been one of her reasons for wishing to avoid a farewell scene.

Mr Mott stood up. 'Well, Mr Morley, since you have no information to give me . . . We had thought, my colleagues and myself, that you would have been eager to help the innocent parties in this affair.'

'But I would like to help. I just can't. I've no idea where she is, or where she came from. Honestly. As a matter of fact, I don't mind confessing that she owes me money too.' *Actually, I do mind confessing*, he thought. *I mind terribly. But if it helps to convince the man* . . .

It didn't help. Unconvinced, Mr Mott moved towards the door in dignified silence. Before getting into his car he turned and faced Alan.

'I suppose,' he said, 'us shopkeepers can at least be thankful that all *we* have lost is money. Our integrity remains unsullied.'

Alan went back into the house seething with indignation. *Bloody cheek*, he thought. *Well, he's just lost himself a customer, that's for sure.* And then he realized that, even without Mr Mott's Parthian shot, shopping in High Midbury must be out of the question from now on. He would never be able to brave these shops again, knowing they must all think him a pathetic fool, turned into a figure of fun by an unscrupulous woman, or else an accomplice, prepared to let the innocent suffer in order to protect her. *As if that bitch needed any protecting!*

He looked around him at the humble surroundings in which he had been so happy, and hated everything he saw. *I must get out of this*, were the only words that came to his mind. *It may be a cliché*, he thought savagely, *but it's true. I simply can't stay on in this place. I can't shop in High Midbury any longer, I'm sick of this little slum, and what am I going to do here all summer, alone?*

160

He thought of all the hours he had hoped to spend with Rachel, wandering about the countryside, and felt overwhelmed by misery and emptiness. It never once occurred to him that he could spend all those long hours getting started on his writing.

I'm going home, he decided. That's the only thing to do. It's what I should have done long ago, before getting involved with that tigress. Sheila may be a bit difficult, and she's not exactly stimulating company, but, my God, she would never behave like that. I can't imagine her having an affair with another man, and she's not secretive. I can read her like a book.

He didn't pause to reflect that he hadn't derived much enjoyment from the reading. And all he wanted now was to go back home. He supposed he'd better discuss the matter with Sheila first, though he couldn't see how she could possibly object. Still, it might seem a bit offhand if he just turned up with all his stuff, unannounced. No, he would go and see her. This very afternoon would be ideal. The girls would still be at school, so he and Sheila would be able to talk in peace and quiet.

He set off right away.

28

There was no room to park in front of the house, so Alan drove round the corner. It was usually quieter there, but even so he had to drive quite a bit along before he was able to park. Not my day, he thought. Not my week, not my year, not my bloody life! He felt as if nothing had ever gone right for him. Here he was, planning to come back and live in the very house he had been so glad to get out of less than a year ago. And coming back with nothing achieved.

Not one word written.

Sheila was out. Probably gone round to the shops. He let himself in with his own key. It was funny how familiar the house seemed, even though it was months since he had been in it. On Saturdays he had got into the habit of driving the girls back after their day with him in the cottage and then going back again without coming in. Because of Rachel, of course.

He wondered about the house for a while, then went upstairs to his study. To his surprise he found a typewriter on his desk. Funny, he thought, mine's in the cottage. Why should Sheila want another? Quite a neat little job, actually. Then he remembered that she had used his typewriter for her A level essays. Perhaps she had embarked on another course. It hadn't occurred to him to ask.

Wondering what she might be studying now, he picked up the sheet of paper lying on the desk beside the typewriter. It was a letter, and he saw at once that it was signed by

Melville. There was no mistaking his flamboyant hand. What on earth could Melville be writing to Sheila about? And it was, indisputably, addressed to Sheila, not to both of them. 'Dear Sheila,' he read. Then he had a struggle with himself, knowing that he shouldn't read it uninvited. But then, when a man finds his wife and his best friend corresponding, is he not entitled to know what it's all about? He read on:

Thanks for the latest batch. Great stuff! Cheque enclosed. Keep on writing.
Yours aye,
Melville.

Sheila writing! And being paid for it! And earning Melville's praise for it! Melville, with his high literary standards! The whole idea was grotesque. To think that she had taken advantage of his absence to steal a march on him in this way, when it was he who was supposed to be doing the writing. And anyway, what on earth was Sheila capable of writing?

She could hardly even write a thank-you letter when they were married. Her style was so pathetically childish that he'd had to help her with a lot of the letters acknowledging wedding presents. But of course, that was sixteen years and several A levels ago. She must have learned something from her studies, after all. All the same, it was utterly outrageous. That she should be writing professionally when he had not even got started was a piece of treachery infinitely worse than marital infidelity. This was striking at the very roots of his self-image.

He was still standing with the letter in his hand when he heard the key turn in the lock downstairs. He felt too shocked and upset to face Sheila at this moment. He tiptoed out on to the landing, listening to hear where she went. It would probably be to the kitchen, to unload her shopping. Knowing how methodical she was about putting things away he felt certain this would give him long enough to slip quietly downstairs and out of the house while she emptied her bag. And at least she wouldn't have seen his car, parked in the side street. That was one thing in his favour, in the midst of the disastrous run of calamities that were afflicting him.

To his horror Sheila didn't make for the kitchen, but crossed the hall as if to start coming upstairs. Instinctively, without thinking of the consequences, he made for shelter. He was standing just beside a walk-in cupboard. The door had been left ajar, just enough for him to slip in. He heard Sheila coming up the stairs and going into the study. Then he heard her opening drawers and muttering, and realized she was probably looking for the letter, which he was still holding. After a while she seemed to give up and went downstairs again. In the semi-darkness of the cupboard he listened anxiously, trying to make out whether she had gone through to the kitchen. From the cupboard the sounds came to him muted, unidentifiable. She was probably in the kitchen. It might be all right to slip out. But he couldn't be sure.

By now he was cursing himself for his moment of panic, realizing he was now committed to a stay in the cupboard of unspecified duration, or else a confrontation with Sheila. The indignity of being caught hiding in a cupboard in his own house was more than he could face. When, in addition, there was the issue of Sheila's writing to be tackled, the whole thing was unthinkable. Better to stay hidden, even if it meant having to spend the night in the cupboard.

As he stood there in his solitary confinement he meditated on his capacity for getting into ridiculous situations and making a fool of himself. He remembered his attempts at getting back into the hotel on his wedding night. That had been bad enough, but this was worse. And then the whole

Rachel business. He'd certainly made a real fool of himself over her. And the opinion all the village shopkeepers must have of him by now! What demon in him forced him to behave like a particularly inept clown? He thought of his parents with their poise and somewhat pompous dignity. Why had he inherited none of their qualities?

A little dignity, even if allied to pomposity, would have made his life a lot easier. As for poise . . .

Realizing he might have a long wait ahead of him, Alan determined to make himself as comfortable as the situation permitted. He had had very little sleep over the past two nights. A little rest during his incarceration would be very welcome. Beside him stood a pile of large cardboard boxes. He lifted down the top box and in the dim light he could just make out the outline of an electronic typewriter on the outside. Of course, that would be the one on top, wouldn't it?

Probably the most recent acquisition. He hoped it was sufficiently full of packing to bear his weight, and put it down in the corner, behind the door. Then, rather gingerly, he sat down on it. It held. With a sigh of relief he leaned back against the wall. He laid the letter from Melville on the ground at his feet, not quite sure what to do with it when he ultimately got away.

His thoughts went back to his parents with a certain nostalgia for the uneventful and orderly life of their household. He tried to imagine how they would react to the sort of situation he had got himself into. It was difficult, because he couldn't imagine either of them playing the buffoon as their son so often seemed to do. But perhaps they too slipped up occasionally. After all, he didn't really know them all that well – not nowadays, at any rate. Contact with them since his marriage had been sporadic and, on the whole, uncomfortable. There seemed to be no way of bridging the gap between them and Sheila. They treated their daughter-in-law with bewildered courtesy, as if she were a being from another planet – for whom they felt no ill will, and with whom they had no means of establishing any meaningful relationship. Sheila in her turn was paralysed by fear, ashamed of her gaucherie, and unable to do anything about it.

Alan had always been saddened by the conviction that his parents would have loved to be on friendly terms with their daughter-in-law, while Sheila would have been thrilled to enjoy a taste of their sort of comfort and elegance. On one occasion, when the Morleys went to the Bahamas for a holiday, Alan and Sheila were given the run of the flat, and Sheila was happier than he had ever seen her before or since. For her it was sheer bliss to be in the midst of all this luxury and culture. If only there had been some means of communication between her and her in-laws, they could all have been so happy.

For the first time he reflected that perhaps he could have played a more active part. He should have been the bridge they needed to bring them together. Till now it had never occurred to him that he could be anything other than an agonized spectator. He had often accused Sheila of being supine, and had more than once recognized that fault in himself. Now he saw it in his parents too. Four adult human beings, all allowing the chance of a happy family life to slip away through passivity. It was pathetic. And as the man in the middle he was the one with the best chance of establishing a link. But he had muffed it, as he always did. Another failure to his credit.

The sound of the front door opening brought him back to the present. The girls had evidently come in, with their usual accompaniment of noise. Now there would be no chance of getting away unperceived for a long time. The girls must have their meal, then there would be the ritual of piano and violin practice. During all this time they were liable to be running about all over the house. He just hoped this was one of the days that Sheila took them swimming in the evening. That would get them out of the house and give him his chance.

Meanwhile, he was having difficulty in keeping awake; and yet he knew he couldn't afford to fall asleep. It could easily lead to detection. Suppose he snored? Or he might miss his chance and have to spend the night in the cupboard. Even if he waited till they were all asleep he might not get away undetected. Sheila was a light sleeper, and would probably hear the creaking stairs as he went down – three of them, and he couldn't quite remember which, so he would almost certainly step on at least one of them. No, he must stay awake and seize his chance when they went out – *if* they went out. He could only pray that they would.

And meanwhile he would have to occupy his mind in some way, just to keep awake. The pale rectangle of Melville's letter on the floor seemed to suggest an appropriate subject for meditation. Taken in conjunction with the picture of his wife he had been contemplating only moments before, the idea of her being a successful author was inconceivable. Alan could not deny that his violent reaction to the discovery stemmed to a great extent from jealousy; but sheer astonishment also played a part.

There must be more to Sheila than met the eye – or, at least, his eye. He tried to see her as competent and successful, but it was difficult. She had always been so subdued, such a dead loss with people. And then he remembered the wine and cheese party at the college which they had attended a few weeks before. It was a yearly event which the Principal gave for the staff and their spouses. Up till this year Sheila had always shown herself very reluctant to go. This year, however, it was she who brought the matter up, and said they'd better go, for the sake of appearances. Although his colleagues knew he was living in the country he had made it clear that it was in order to get on with his writing, and that there had been no break-up. Sheila pointed out that their appearance together would help to confirm this. He had gone, as he always went to these things, out of a sense of duty. Sheila, he presumed, was as reluctant as he was.

As soon as they arrived Herbert came up to them and greeted Sheila warmly. Doing his Head-of-Department-being-nice-to-spouses thing, thought Alan, as he slipped away to engage Mabel in conversation. Some time later he looked across the room and saw Herbert and Sheila still together. The amazing thing was that it was Sheila who was doing the talking. She looked quite animated, and Herbert was listening to her with keen attention. Alan had forgotten all about this little scene till now, when the image suddenly took on an unexpected relevance. It seemed that, during all those years he had been living beside Sheila, almost without noticing her, she had acquired one of the qualities in which she had been so sadly lacking, that of a certain social ease and poise.

And now it appeared that she had learned how to write. It was unbelievable, and utterly intolerable. His anger and humiliation rose to fever pitch as he thought about it. If the girls hadn't been in the house he would have been tempted to go right down and reproach her bitterly. But with what? Simply with succeeding where he had failed, that's what it came to.

He stifled a groan and tried to think of something else. Immediately the image of Rachel presented itself, mocking and alluring. How she must have laughed at his literary pretensions! For, whatever her history and her morals might be, there was no denying the fact that she was an intelligent, talented and well educated woman. She was also a very determined one. If she had wanted to write she would have gone ahead and done so, and made a good job of it too. His own ambitions and parallel futility must have seemed utterly pathetic to her.

Alan's mood of self-denigration changed to sheer self-pity as he thought of how unlucky he had been with the women in his life. Sheila, who had dragged him down all those years, only to shoot ahead of him without warning and beat him at his own game. Then Rachel, using him, laughing at him, and turning the whole village against him as a parting gift. He felt betrayed by both of them. And then he thought of Lisha, all those years ago in Galloway. He had admired her so much, had been ready to fall in love with her. But prudence had won the day. He must get his degree first, he must finish his thesis first. Later there would be plenty of time. And then he had met Sheila, and suddenly there was no more time left – not for thinking of Lisha, anyway.

His thoughts turned from the past to the future. What was he going to do now? How could he come back and live in this house now that he knew about Sheila's writing? Not only would the humiliation be too much for him, but there was also the question of Sheila's betrayal. For that's what he felt it to be. It was bad enough that she should make a success of her writing. But the indefensible thing was that she should hide the whole matter from him. The hypocrite, the whited sepulchre. And to think that she was earning money she had told him nothing about, just when he was finding it so hard to keep the two households going. He could never forgive her. Never, never.

He fell asleep hearing the word 'never' endlessly repeated in his exhausted mind. And the word pursued him as he struggled along a dark tunnel, up to his knees in water. As he neared the end of the tunnel he saw the water was suspiciously dark – mud? blood? – and another voice was superimposed on the everlasting 'never'.

They waded thro' red blude to the knee, intoned this other voice. He was Thomas the Rhymer and he was looking for his 'ferlie'.

And then he saw her standing at the end of the tunnel, and it was Rachel, holding out her arms to him. He reached out towards her and, as their hands touched, she turned into a huge pink jellyfish with streaming red hair. He tried to draw back, but he was already entangled in her tentacles, slimy and stinging, while the great, soft body pressed closer and closer into his face till he could hardly breathe. He woke up with a scream of anguish, which was answered by a multiple scream from downstairs.

At first Alan had no recollection of where he was. Then, as recollection came to him, he heard Sheila's voice on the stairs, faint and frightened.

'Who's that? For God's sake, who is it?'

He scrambled to his feet. 'It's all right, it's only me,' he said, emerging through the cupboard door.

Sheila called out to the girls, 'It's all right, it's only Daddy,' and all three appeared and stationed themselves behind her on the stairs.

'What on earth were you doing in the cupboard?' demanded Sheila.

'Sleeping.'

'Why?'

'Because I was tired. Why else?'

'But Daddy, why did you scream?' Jane had got over her fright and was, as usual, determined to get to the bottom of things.

'I had a nightmare.'

Tessa turned to her mother. 'Why was Daddy hiding in the cupboard?'

Sheila shook her head in perplexity. 'I don't know, dear. Can you explain, Alan?'

'No, I can't.'

'Alan, are you all right? What's the matter?'

'Nothing. Oh, nothing at all is the matter.' Alan spoke in tones of the heaviest irony.

Beth started to sob and flung herself into her mother' arms.

Sheila's voice was dangerously near to tears as she appealed to Alan:

'Please, please tell me what's the matter. What am I to think of this behaviour? Why were you hiding in the cupboard?'

Alan felt as if he'd wakened up from one nightmare only to find himself in the middle of another.

'I have no explanation to offer,' he said. Then he pushed past the four figures on the stairs and ran out of the house.

29

He drove like a maniac till he was clear of the town. Then he stopped in a lay-by and sat for a while with his hands pressed tightly round his temples, trying to calm the ferocious pain in his head.

All he wanted was to find some convenient cliff and drive over it. That seemed to him the only thing that life had left to offer. The trouble was, he could think of no suitable cliff anywhere near. Besides, he was too tired to think. He'd be better to go back to the cottage and get some sleep first. Then he could have a look at a map . . .

He drove off again – slowly at first, from utter weariness, then faster and more recklessly, as all the events of the past few days crowded in on him. He was so engrossed with his grievances that he nearly missed the turning off the main road. He jammed on the brakes and pulled the wheel round violently. The car swung round, screaming, and zig-zagged wildly as he struggled to get it under control. He saw the figure of a man in front of him, and felt sure he was going to run him over. By a miracle the car swung round again in time to miss the tall figure. But as they passed he felt a sickening thud as the side of the car lurched into the man. Before he could see anything in the rear window the car had got round the next corner and was racing along, away from the accident. He knew he ought to stop, but his courage failed him.

Ten minutes later he got out at the cottage, sick and faint

with shock. He could hardly believe what he had done. All his previous disasters faded into insignificance beside the thought that he had knocked someone down and failed to stop. It seemed like a cruel and senseless prolongation of the nightmare he had been living for days.

He spent the night wandering about the house, feverish, delirious, almost hysterical, trying to think how to find out whether he had killed his victim. The one thing he could not face was the possibility of compromising himself. His sense of guilt was great, but his fear was greater. He simply had not the strength to face the consequences of his action.

By morning he had worked out a plan. It was Saturday, so all he had to do was phone Sheila and tell her not to bring the girls and then he would have the weekend to himself. He phoned, and got the impression that Sheila was perhaps relieved at not having to come over. She sounded concerned about him. He was all right, he assured her, just this terrible headache. That was what had been wrong yesterday. He would explain all about it when he saw her.

After that it was a case of waiting for the local paper to be delivered. It arrived mid-morning, and he had no difficulty in finding what he was looking for. As he expected, it was under 'Hit and Run'. At least I'm not a murderer, he thought, after reading the paragraph. Not unless he's died since. He phoned the hospital and asked about Mr Peter Eward's condition. Mr Eward, it appeared, had spent a comfortable night. Alan thought this was highly improbable but he knew it was the standard formula. Yes, Mr Eward was suffering from a number of fractures, but no, his life was not in danger.

'Who shall I say called?' asked the voice.

'Lord Jim,' he replied and hung up.

Well, that was it. He was not a murderer, he had been spared that. But he seemed to have been spared little else. His life lay in ruins about him, his self-esteem gone for ever. He felt so ill that he had little difficulty in believing that all he had to do was go to bed and just never get up again. Death would bring its release. The experiment was over. It had ended, predictably, in failure.

After the girls had gone to bed Sheila went into the cupboard Alan had been hiding in, to see if she could find some clue as to what he had been doing there. The first thing she saw was Melville's letter lying on the floor. She realized she had found her clue, and had no difficulty in reconstructing events more or less accurately. This was the very thing she would have done a great deal to avoid. She had discussed the matter with Melville when he had first suggested she should do some writing for his firm. Both had realized it was a tricky situation, and agreed to say nothing of the matter to Alan, not till he had produced some writing of his own. Then it would be easy to establish his was was serious writing, whereas Sheila's was mere hackwork, supplying the flesh for the mass-produced bones of some hackneyed love story.

The trouble was, Alan's masterpiece had not been forth-coming. Both Sheila and Melville felt sure that anything he wrote would be infinitely superior to Sheila's made-to-measure instalments. But even Sheila's work was better than no writing at all. And it was at least bringing in some cash. So the moment of revelation had to be put off, and put off again, while they waited for something from Alan.

And now he had found out, and would never believe it was delicacy that had kept her from telling him. Besides, given Alan's suspicious mind, it was even conceivable that he might think there was something more than mere friendship and business going on between her and Melville. There were, she knew, no grounds for such a suspicion. She had come to the conclusion years ago that Melville just wasn't interested in women, except as human beings. The mere fact of existence seemed to be a claim on Melville's friendship and generosity.

But that was as far as it seemed to go.

Which, she had always felt, was perhaps just as well. The loneliness of her marriage, with the unbridgeable intellectual gap that Alan seemed so constantly aware of, might have disposed Sheila to look with favour on the advances of another man, especially one who had always showed her such consideration and friendship. As it was, he filled the place of a brother, both for her and for Alan, who had no other close friends. How she wished Melville's work didn't keep him so far away from them. At this particular moment she would have given anything to be able to appeal to him for help. But since Alan had seen the letter and was probably seething with suspicion, Melville was the last person on whom she could call.

She spent an anxious weekend, wondering what was really the matter with Alan. A headache, however bad, could hardly account for his erratic behaviour. Time and again she was on the point of phoning him, but restrained herself, fearing a violent reaction to her 'fussing', as he called more or less any action on her part that involved taking an interest in his affairs. She reflected that it was very difficult to get it right. On the one hand she was constantly being accused of being supine; on the other, her fault lay in 'fussing'.

On Monday morning she vowed she would phone in the evening. No point in phoning during the day, he would be in college. And then, halfway through the morning, the phone rang. It was Herbert, wondering if she could give him any information about Alan. He hadn't turned up for work, but didn't seem to be at the cottage either, as the secretary had phoned repeatedly without getting a reply. Herbert wondered whether perhaps he wasn't well and had gone home to be looked after.

'No, he's not here, and I've no idea where he is. I assumed he was at the college. It's rather worrying. He was here on Friday and didn't seem at all well. And on Saturday he phoned to say not to take the girls, as he wasn't well enough to cope with them.'

'Do you think he might be too unwell to answer the phone?' Herbert suggested.

'I don't know. I think I'd better go and see.'

'I'll come with you. I can't have you going there on your own. Just in case there really is something seriously wrong, I mean.'

'Oh, how kind of you. Shall we meet at the cottage?'

'No. I'll come for you. I'll be with you in twenty minutes.'

Sheila put the phone down with a sense of relief.

Herbert arrived exactly twenty minutes later. Sheila had been undecided as to how much she should tell him. He was, after all, Alan's boss, and she didn't want to give the impression that Alan was unable to cope with his work. But her hesitation was short-lived, for Herbert soon made it clear he had a shrewd idea of how bad things were.

'There's been something the matter with Alan for a long time,' he began. 'He's just not himself, just not coping.'

Sheila felt tempted to say, then that means that he *is* himself, but refrained. This was hardly the time for frivolity.

'You don't know what's wrong, do you?' asked Herbert.

Sheila shook her head. 'I don't know, I just don't know.'

'How's his writing getting on?'

'I don't think it's getting on at all. He doesn't seem to have actually written anything down yet.'

'But isn't that what he's supposed to be doing, out there in the wilderness?'

'Yes, but he's not reached that stage yet.'

Herbert gave a snort of disbelief. 'Well then what stage *has* he reached?'

'He's collecting material.'

'Collecting material? What on earth's he writing? Some sort of learned treatise?'

'No. A novel.'

'For God's sake, you don't need to collect material for a novel. We're all brimming over with the stuff. What on earth does he want more for?'

Sheila managed to stop herself from saying once again that she didn't know. Instead she said she thought Alan wanted to write about the world of nature, and felt he didn't know enough about it yet.

'But a novel? *The Worm's Revenge*, an action packed hard-hitting exposé of life below the topsoil – something like that?'

Sheila felt a ripple of annoyance. 'I think what he intends is something about a sensitive person's reaction to the natural world.'

'*Touché*,' said Herbert. 'I'm sorry. I shouldn't joke about it. But you must admit it doesn't sound like very promising material for a bestseller.'

Sheila was still a little offended on Alan's behalf. 'No, but then, that's hardly what he'd want to write, is it?'

'Not what Alan would want to write, I agree. Wouldn't at all mind writing one myself, if I knew how. All that lovely money.'

'Turn left here,' she said, 'at that hawthorn hedge.' She still spoke rather drily, feeling that perhaps she was beginning to understand Alan's aversion to Herbert. There certainly was a touch of brashness.

Herbert changed the subject. Evidence, Sheila thought, of a certain sensitivity. By the time they reached the cottage she was feeling too apprehensive about what they might find, or the reception they might get, to think of anything else. Alan had always been very jealous of his privacy at the cottage, and had made it clear he didn't want her turning up unexpectedly. Now she was about to do so, in the company of the very man he most disliked.

But if there was nothing wrong, why wasn't he answering the phone?

And why had he not turned up at work?

This time, she felt, she had a good excuse for her 'fussing'. Besides, she had the support of Alan's head of department. She felt glad she would be able to shelter behind Herbert, should there be an outburst from Alan. Perhaps a touch of brashness and insensitivity wasn't such a bad thing after all.

'Well, he must be at home. There's the car at the door,' remarked Herbert.

They got out and rang the bell. Nothing happened. They rang again several times, then tried the back door. They peered into the kitchen but saw no signs of life. Then they tried the front of the house once again and looked inside the living room. After that they tried the bedroom, but the curtains were drawn and the window was closed. They rang again, they called Alan's name, they knocked on the bedroom window.

'We'll have to break in,' Herbert decided. 'Not this room, though, that might give him too much of a fright.'

Once again Sheila registered the evidence of thoughtfulness on Herbert's part.

'The kitchen might be best,' he went on, 'let's try that.'

'But the kitchen's got the sink at the window. It won't be so easy to get in there.'

'No problem,' said Herbert confidently.

When they got back to the kitchen window Herbert found it unsnibbed at the top, and soon had it open enough to let him climb in. A moment later he had opened the kitchen door, and they were both in the house.

As Herbert made for the bedroom Sheila suggested:

'Shouldn't I go in first?'

'I don't think so, really. You don't know what you may find.'

'Still,' she insisted,' if he's very ill I think it will be less of a shock if he sees me first.'

'True. You go first, then. I'll come as soon as you call me.'

Sheila tiptoed into the room and found Alan lying on the bed, fully clad. He was very pale, and his hands were trembling. He looked at her with glazed eyes and whispered something she couldn't make out. She bent over him to hear better.

'Go away,' he whispered.

'Alan, you're ill. We must get a doctor.'

'No doctor. Go away.'

'But we must get a doctor. This may be serious.'

'I know. I hope it is.'

'Oh, Alan. Don't be so childish.'

Alan made no reply. Sheila turned towards the door and beckoned to Herbert, who came in.

'We'd better get a doctor, old man,' he said. 'I see you're far from well.'

'Leave me alone.'

'But look here – that's not on, you know. Must have medical attention. We can't just leave you here to die.'

Alan raised himself on one elbow and glared at Herbert. 'Fool!' he brought out with surprising venom. Then he lay back and turned over on his side with his back to the intruders. Just in case they hadn't got the message he put his hand on the wall, then let it slide slowly down.

Herbert moved towards the bedroom door. 'Where's the phone?' he asked. A minute later he came back and said:

'The ambulance should be here in a few minutes.'

They stood waiting awkwardly, ignored by the silent figure on the bed.

Sheila felt intensely apprehensive about what would happen when the ambulance crew appeared. Would Alan agree to go with them? Would he be well enough to get up, anyway? Would they need a stretcher – or a strait-jacket, if Alan fought them off? The thought of this last possibility affected her so much that she let out an anguished little gasp.

Herbert looked at her, then cleared a pile of clothes from the only chair in the room, dropping the garments on the ground.

'Sit down,' he commanded.

Sheila sat down gratefully. She was glad of the rest, and, above all, was thankful to have someone else there so manifestly in charge.

When at last the ambulance arrived Herbert said:

'I'll go. Stay where you are.'

In a moment he came back into the room, followed by the two ambulance men.

'Right then, Alan. Up you get.'

Herbert's tone was so assured that Alan (without so much as looking at any of his persecutors) got up and walked out to the ambulance.

30

Lisha came back into the ward and said it would probably be all right for Peter to leave in a day or two. They just wanted to take some more X-rays before discharging him. Meanwhile she would find herself a hotel and spend as much time as possible with him in the ward.

'I don't suppose either the patients or the staff know what to make of your visit,' said Peter. 'The only visitor I've had so far has been an elderly landlady – and now you appear! They must be guessing wildly.'

'Perhaps they think I'm a social worker.'

'Actually, I think you'd make a splendid social worker. You're good with people, and you're confident and efficient. I think you'd be much better doing that, instead of burying yourself in a museum all day.'

'Oh, didn't you know? That shows how long it is since we've been in touch. I gave that up last year, and now I'm working at home, doing flower illustrations. I love it, so the social services will have to wait for a while before I'm ready to join them.'

'So you're living at home now?'

'Well, yes and no. I'm in a little cottage in the village. So I still have my independence, and the family as well.'

'The best of both worlds, in fact. Trust you to find the way. Most of us can't manage to get the best out of even one world.'

'Well, we'll try to let you get the best of both while you're staying with us. You'll have to stay with my parents at first, of course. You'll need the medical staff. After that, we'll see. I did suggest moving in beside you once before, remember, and you weren't keen.'

'I was in my cut-loose-from-everything phase at the time. I'm more socially oriented now.'

'There's something you could do for me after we get back to Scotland,' Peter remarked later that day, 'only I think you might find it a bit strange.'

'What is it?'

'You could perhaps go and see a friend of mine in jail.'

Lisha looked surprised, but soon recovered her usual poise. 'Yes, why not?' she said, then added, 'Where did you meet?'

Peter laughed. 'Not there, anyway. Remember I mentioned a sawmill? Well, that's where we met. He was my boss. I suppose I ought to tell you why he's in jail, only I don't think I can without his permission.'

'That's all right. He's a friend of yours. That's enough guarantee. I don't suppose a jail is all that much worse than a hospital to visit, anyway.'

Two days later, before picking Peter up at the hospital, Lisha went round to Mrs Barnes to collect his things, and to thank her for her visits.

The door was opened by someone who appeared to be the cleaning lady, and who ushered her into what she called the lounge – a stiffly furnished room, most unsuitable for lounging. In a moment Mrs Barnes came in. Her expression was pleasant and expectant. Lisha told her she had come on behalf of Peter Eward, and was surprised to see her expression change immediately to one of hostility.

'Oh yes, Mr Eward. Quite so,' said Mrs Barnes, almost icily.

Lisha explained that she was taking him to convalesce in her parents' house, and would like to collect his things.

Mrs Barnes left Lisha in the room without even asking her to sit down. Her behaviour seemed hard to reconcile with that of a woman who had taken the trouble to visit Peter once a week since the accident. Perhaps she's taken a fancy to him, and looks on me as a rival, she thought. But it was difficult to imagine Mrs Barnes, with her straight grey hair and her angular figure, as likely to cherish tender thoughts about anyone.

In a few minutes Mrs Barnes came back carrying a case, which she handed over stiffly. Lisha was so angry at her manner that she almost decided against thanking her for the visits to her injured lodger. But Peter had entrusted her with the commission, and she felt she had to carry it out.

'Mr Eward charged me to thank you for visiting him in hospital,' she said, her voice completely devoid of its usual warmth.

'Oh yes, the visits. Quite so. I thought it was the Christian thing to do. But then, of course . . . '

'Of course what?'

'Well, I didn't know, did I?'

'Didn't know what? Are you accusing Mr Eward of something?'

'Oh, it's not for me to make accusations. I even meant to go and see him yesterday, and I'd even bought the grapes. But then, that was before I knew . . . ' She nodded with menacing significance.

'Before you knew *what?*' Lisha was so distressed by this innuendo that she added, 'Oh, please, Mrs Barnes, tell me what it is that you've got against my friend. I'm sure there must be some mistake.'

Hearing the appeal in Lisha's voice, Mrs Barnes unbent enough to ask her to sit down, and lowered herself rigidly on to the chair opposite. Her expression of disapproval had given way to a look of uncertainty and affliction.

'This is all very upsetting,' she began. 'It's terrible, just terrible to think . . . You see, it was all because of my next-door neighbour's daughter, she's a nurse at the hospital, and she came in yesterday to borrow some eggs, and she told me that a friend of hers, who's also a nurse in the hospital, only this one is in Mr Eward's ward, the friend, that is, not my neighbour's daughter – well, she posted a letter for him and it was addressed to someone in prison. And they're all saying . . . well, no one knew anything about Mr Eward, he never told me a thing, he never said anything about himself, and I didn't know where he'd come from or what he was doing here, or anything . . . And I've got my business to think of, and if word got around that I was harbouring criminals or undesirables . . . '

Mrs Barnes looked so upset at this point that Lisha began to feel quite sorry for her.

'I can quite see that,' she conceded. 'But I can assure you that this is Mr Eward's only connexion with . . . with that sort of thing. It's just a man he got to know in his travels and in whom he's taking a friendly interest. Mr Eward has worked as a civil engineer most of his life and has never had any problems with the law.'

'Well, I'm very pleased to hear that. It was terrible to think I'd had someone like that in the house, and him such a nice, quiet, well-spoken gentleman who never said a word. You won't tell him, will you, what I thought?'

Lisha laughed. 'Don't worry, he won't hold it against you.'

When Lisha was leaving a few minutes later, Mrs Barnes suddenly darted into the depths of the house and came back carrying a brown paper bag.

'The grapes,' she said. 'They'll do for the journey.'

As they were heading north, Lisha produced the brown paper bag and explained about Mrs Barnes's misgivings. Instead of laughing as she had expected, Peter sat silent for a little. Then he said:

'I can't blame her, really. I had much the same reaction myself. And I hadn't a business to take into consideration. And yet I had all sorts of problems about posting that letter, because I didn't want anyone to know it was going to a prison. And that's a problem that still has to be faced if I'm going to keep in touch with Andrew.'

'You're not thinking of casting him off, are you?' Lisha sounded shocked.

'Oh, no! I didn't mean that sort of *if*. But the problem is there. None of us wants to be implicated. Even when we want to help.'

Lisha couldn't see the problem. She said she would have no difficulty in acknowledging a friendship with a convict.

'Perhaps it's a matter of temperament,' suggested Peter. Then he added, 'But I think there's more to it than that. You're working from a position of security – total security, living at home, where you've been known all your life, with parents whose respectability is beyond question. You can afford a few disreputable friends. And I suppose I could have too – in the past.'

'Before you cut yourself off from all decent, right-thinking people?'

'Exactly. But once you've become a sort of tramp, once you lose your roots, it's a different matter. Poor Andrew. I wonder if he realizes what lies ahead, when he gets out.'

Lisha sighed. 'I'm afraid he won't get a great welcome from the Mrs Barneses of this world.'

Peter was still thinking of how the matter affected him. 'The irony is that Andrew was the first person I managed to get some sort of relationship with, and now he looks like being the stumbling block—'

'Not with the people that matter,' said Lisha firmly. So firmly that Peter let the subject drop.

31

It took Peter several days to recover from the journey, and he was left to himself quite a lot and not expected to mix in the daily life of the family. Lisha had explained how he had cut himself off from humanity and had been painfully trying to find his way back to some form of human contact when the accident had happened. They all saw this as an extra reason for letting him have all the rest and quiet he needed. But gradually Peter began to make it clear that he wanted to be considered as an ordinary member of the family, within the limitations imposed by his injuries.

A few days after Peter had arrived at Auchentoull Lisha went to see Andrew in prison, and was able to report back that he had now changed his mind and wasn't so sure he'd commit the robbery again if he got the chance. Peter took some comfort from this piece of news.

As his condition improved he began to get longer visits from Lisha and her parents, and any other members of the family who happened to be about began popping in for a word or two rather oftener. Two of Lisha's sisters and one brother had married and settled in the village, and they all had children. Peter encouraged them to visit him too, thinking of the two little girls who had fled from him that day near his home. The Wilson grandchildren were, on the whole, a lively bunch and didn't look as if they would flee easily from anyone. Peter had had little contact with children, and had always tended to feel ill at ease with them. Now he made a special effort to get to know them and, if at all possible, to like them. After the awkwardness of the first few days was over, he found to his surprise that he was positively enjoying their company.

In a way, he thought, they're easier to get on with than adults. Pity I wasn't able to start with them when I set off a year ago. It had never occurred to him and, besides, he realized that any stranger trying to make friends with unknown children is liable to arouse alarm and hostility.

One day he asked Lisha:

'Do you have a favourite among your nieces and nephews?'

'From which I gather,' she replied, 'that you have. Which is it?'

'Becky, without a doubt. And you?'

'An aunt isn't allowed to have favourites.'

'But it's Becky all the same, isn't it?'

'Yes. That is, *if* I had one, I think it would be Becky.'

'And why?'

'Perhaps because she's so quiet and gentle and doesn't seem to mind not being one of the dazzling ones. I find this very endearing. And you? Why is she your favourite?'

'Because she reminds me of a little girl called Mary.'

'And who is this Mary? You've never mentioned her before.'

'I don't know who she is. All I know is that she was picking wild raspberries near Castery one day last summer. And I owe her a great deal. She and her little friend acted as a mirror for me.'

Lisha smiled. 'You mean the two little girls who ran away from you, I presume?'

'Yes. That was the beginning of my . . . my conversion, I suppose you could call it. If it hadn't been for those little girls I expect I'd still be living alone in that house, in limbo.'

Lisha considered her companion for some time, then she said:

'And yet . . . and yet I can't help thinking there is a bit of a hermit in you.'

'Yes, I agree. But I think I was doing it the wrong way. I became a hermit by default, as it were, simply because I lost interest in everything about me. And that's not good enough. You need a more positive reason. The proof is that I was unhappy. I had, literally, nothing to live for.'

'And you feel you've something to live for now?'

'Oh yes. The first thing is to get better. Perhaps I ought to thank the unknown motorist for giving me such a clear-cut purpose in life.'

'But you already had one when he knocked you down. You were trying to get back into the human fraternity.'

'That's true. But it was a long slow business, and I had, if you remember, just struck quite a serious snag.'

'Andrew?'

'Yes, Andrew. So simply having to recover from an accident is a beautifully uncomplicated task instead.'

'I'm glad to know you have a due sense of gratitude towards your benefactor. Not everyone would be able to view him in that light.'

'I didn't at first, I can assure you. But now I can see how he's played into my hands. First of all by giving me a straightforward aim in life, that is, getting better, and secondly by giving me the ideal setting for getting back in touch with humanity through you and your family.'

'But you could have had that anyway, without the need of an accident. You could have phoned me at any time. In fact, since you told me about your quest, I've been wondering why you didn't contact me in the first place. Why go off and do it the hard way, with strangers, when you have friends to call upon?'

'Because I had already failed with these friends. That was, in fact, the cause of my isolation. I felt it would be more difficult to start where there were past failures to blot out before anything could be achieved.'

'Yes, I suppose so.' Lisha spoke reflectively. 'And yet,' she added, 'you seem to have managed to relate to us all pretty well, in spite of the past failures.'

'That's true. And there's another thing I didn't see at the time.'

'What was that?'

'Pride. I think my pride was keeping me from coming to you with a confession of my failure. It took the accident and the misery and depression of hospital to make me pocket my pride and turn to you. After all, it's a lot easier to say "I need help because I have been badly injured" than to say "I need help because I can't manage my life". So that idiot of a driver really did me a good turn. Quite apart from everything else, it's so good just being with you again, Lisha.'

Lisha seemed reluctant to pursue the conversation in this direction.

'Oh well,' she said lightly 'I see we'll have to put up a monument to the Unknown Motorist. It seems the least we can do, considering how much he's done for you.'

Peter said nothing more about his feelings for Lisha. He knew he was in grave danger of falling in love with her once again and realized that he had no right to renew their old relationship unless he felt sure that he could make the union a permanent one, or that this was no longer what Lisha wanted.

Lisha too felt she could very easily fall in love with Peter again, and was afraid the affair might end as it had before. She didn't know whether she could stand yet another emotional upheaval – first Peter, then Frank, and now, perhaps, Peter again? It would be safer to keep her emotions under strict control. This meant making sure that Peter understood that she was not hoping to get back to their old relationship. She was sorry she had suggested the possibility of Peter's moving in to her cottage, and hoped nothing more would be said about it. She simply hadn't thought of the emotional dangers this might involve when she made the suggestion. The best thing would be for Peter to stay on in her parents' house till he was well enough to go back to his own.

Dr Wilson poked his head round the sitting-room door. Seeing his wife sewing by the fire he came in and sat down beside her.

'Well, woman,' he said, 'you can start packing right away.'

His wife looked up smiling. 'Am I being dismissed?'

'No, not yet. Can't do without you just at present.'

'Then why am I to pack?'

'We're going on holiday. On Monday.'

'On holiday! But we never go on holiday.'

'Precisely. And it's time we did. So we're going on Monday. To France. For four weeks.'

'But what about the practice? You can't just leave that?'

'I'll have no trouble finding a locum. Lots of qualified men looking for a sinecure like this.'

'Sinecure! Eight in the morning till God knows when at night, and at least three night calls per week.'

'Well, go on, I'm waiting. What's the next but? Or have you run out of objections already?'

'Far from it. It's a lovely idea, but I've nothing to wear, for one thing.'

'That's all right. I've booked us in at a nudist camp.'

'I'll ignore that one. Just tell me, where are we supposed to be going, and why?'

'Where, is a very minor chateau on the Loire. Why, is because the Camerons have asked us to be their guests there for four weeks. They seem to think I saved their ewe-lamb's life after she was fished out of the river last summer, and feel this is the least they can do to thank us. Next objection!'

'Well, what are we going to do about Peter? He's not really well enough to go home and do for himself yet, you know.'

'He can stay here. Robert and Richard will be in the house. They can look after him.'

'God help him, they can't even look after themselves.'

'Then it'll do them a world of good to have to.'

'Yes, I agree. But it won't do for Peter.'

'Then he can go to Lisha's. She herself suggested something of the sort when he first came. Said he could go to the cottage once he was well enough not to need proper nursing. He's quite well enough for that now.'

Mrs Wilson looked doubtful. 'I wonder if it's wise,' she said.

'Good heavens, woman. They've shared a bed often enough before now. Why shouldn't they share a roof for a few weeks?'

'I don't know. I've a feeling Lisha doesn't want to get too involved again. And sharing a roof seems to me a recipe for involvement. And I suspect it would just end up the same way. Peter's a darling, but he's not the kind that will make a good husband.'

'His first wife didn't seem to think so, anyway. But do you think Lisha really wants to be the second? She's doing very well with her drawing at the moment. Must she have a husband as well?'

'Yes, I know, Dick. She *is* doing well, and that would be enough for some women. But it's not the life for Lisha, really. She would make such a lovely mother. And she's thirty-six, you know. If she doesn't marry soon . . . '

In spite of Mrs Wilson's doubts the matter was put to Lisha, who immediately said it would be all right for Peter to come to the cottage. She was so delighted to think of her parents getting a well-earned and long-overdue holiday that the problem of her relationship with Peter faded into the background.

Peter was pleased with the arrangement. He was beginning to feel that he shouldn't impose on the Wilsons any longer, and the move to Lisha's cottage seemed a good way of delaying the decision as to what he was going to do with his life once he was well enough to move on. Besides, the prospect of being in the cottage with Lisha was very appealing.

A few days after he had moved in they were sitting in the little attic room that Lisha had converted into a studio. Peter was reading and Lisha was getting on with her drawing. Suddenly she looked up and said:

'There's something I've been meaning to ask you for some time, and I never think of it when you're about. It's about the hawthorn blossom. Remember one of the first things you asked me when I went to see you in hospital was about hawthorn, what exactly the flower was like. And you said it was terribly important to you. Why?'

'I'm not quite sure that I can explain. But I'll try.' Peter thought for a little, then spoke again. 'It's symbolic, I suppose. Somehow, for some reason, the hawthorn blossom on that hedge I was thrown into had acquired a special meaning for me.'

'Even before you were thrown into it?'

'Oh yes. In a way you could say that was why the accident happened. If I hadn't stopped to stare at the blossom I'd probably have been well out of the way before that car came along. I'd just been to see Andrew, and I was very unhappy about it. About what he'd done, which he'd explained to me that afternoon, and about his attitude. Somehow it seemed wrong for that particular man – at least, for my idea of what he was like. I was sure that the man I thought he was couldn't hold that attitude for long without suffering for it. Either that, or else I'd been quite wrong about him, and that was important and disturbing, for he was my first human contact of any significance since I'd started to find my way back to humanity. So everything seemed cloudy and uncertain and threatening.

'And then I decided to go a step back, for the moment. Instead of trying to relate to people perhaps I'd be better to relate to the world of nature. I'd even lost contact with that when I was still at home, but that at least had come back to me during my travels, and I could delight in trees and fields and flowers once again. So I went for a long walk, but my mind was still the centre of attention, rather than the world about me. And then I looked up and saw this hedge, and that really got through to me. I thought I'd never seen anything so lovely before. I felt as if it had suddenly sprung up there to soothe and delight me, to reassure me that, on that level at least, I had made some progress, that I was in touch, no longer in limbo. There it was, this wall of white, like an emblem of purity and peace and hope. I wanted to absorb it in its entirety, every detail. So I crossed over to look at it closely. I was fascinated to see that each spray of blossom was white, and yet not an even, glaring white. There were these tiny dark specks on it, giving a depth and softness to the white, and I wanted to know what these little dark bits were.

'When I came to in hospital, the whole world seemed to have turned white. But it was a hard, glaring whiteness. It hurt me and frightened me. It seemed utterly implacable. And then, after a while, I began to remember the whiteness of the hedge. I would close my eyes and try to substitute the soft radiance of the hawthorn for the glaring walls about me. And the

194

hawthorn came to stand for everything that was warm and soft and welcoming. And I remembered how it had comforted me before the accident. So I came to think of it as the emblem of a manageable world, free from the complications and betrayals of the world of men.'

'And yet the hawthorn was capable of betrayal too. All those scratches on your poor face!'

'Well, my view was perhaps a bit of an over-simplification. But that type of scratch at least heals very quickly. I've already lost most of the scars, and I haven't lost my passion for hawthorn blossom. Pity I'll need to wait nearly a year before I see it again.'

Some days later, when Lisha brought him his breakfast, he found a large envelope lying on the tray. He was now so much better that breakfast in bed was the only concession to invalidism he allowed himself.

'Post's early today, surely,' he remarked, looking at the envelope.

'It didn't come by post,' Lisha said. 'It's from me.'

Peter sat up in bed and picked up the envelope. Inside he found a pen and ink drawing of a spray of hawthorn blossom. It had been drawn with the greatest care and delicacy. The detail and clarity of the drawing were worthy of a place among the botanical illustrations by which Lisha earned her living, and at the same time it was a work of art, an interpretation of what the hawthorn had meant to Peter.

'Oh Lisha, it's beautiful, absolutely right. And what a lovely idea. You've understood it so well. When on earth did you do it?'

'In secret, at night after you were in bed. I didn't want to say anything in case it didn't turn out right. I'm sorry I couldn't manage the whole hedge.'

'It's perfect, simply perfect. Every detail just right. And you've really caught the spirit of it. You've put down in pen and ink exactly what it means to me. You've created a small miracle.'

Lisha stood smiling, touched by his enthusiasm.

'I'm so glad you like it. I was afraid I might not have got it right.'

'You always get things right. You're one of those people who seem to be properly centred. You have to make an effort to get things wrong.'

'And you?'

'Oh, I'm the very opposite. I have to make an effort, a constant effort, to get things even moderately right. It's taken me a long time to realize this. And I think that's what was wrong with my life, right up till the time I set off on my travels. I thought all I had to do was avoid doing wrong. And for someone like you, who gets things right intuitively, it seems to be all that's required. For me it isn't. I just drifted off into limbo. I need to set myself a goal, and work towards it all the time. Constant vigilance is the only way.'

Lisha sat down on the bed. 'Poor Peter, it sounds very tiring,' she said, half mockingly, and took one of his hands in both of hers. Peter put his other arm round her shoulders, drew her to him and kissed her.

'That was the first proper kiss we've had for years,' she observed.

'Yes, I know. We've a lot of lost time to make up.' And he kissed her again.

Lisha didn't protest when he drew her into the bed. Beside them, on the bedside table, a neatly laid breakfast tray lay forgotten, its coffee getting colder and colder.

32

After waiting in the hospital for a few hours Sheila was told that they didn't really know what was the matter with her husband. They would keep him under observation and make tests. Sedation would be given, if necessary. That was all they could tell her so far, and she might as well go home. As Herbert drove her back to her house they discussed the matter. They were perhaps slightly less puzzled than the hospital staff, and felt sure that the trouble was more likely to be psychological than physical, given the peculiar state Alan had been in for some days. Sheila told him about the cupboard episode and its probable cause.

'I'm sure he must have read that letter,' she said. 'I can't think how else it could have got into the cupboard. And of course he would be very upset about that. I suppose I'd better tell you what was in it, or it won't make sense to you.'

'Well, you've already told me it was from his best friend, and addressed to you. That in itself might well be enough to upset him.'

'Oh, it was nothing like that!' Sheila sounded shocked.

'But in Alan's peculiar state of mind it might have seemed suspicious all the same.'

'Yes, I know. That did occur to me too. But I think the real situation is even worse than that – from Alan's point of view, that is.' She then explained about her writing and Melville's part in the business.

'Wow! I can see what that would do to the budding author. To be pipped at the post by his own wife!'

'And a wife he's always thought of as really pretty dim.'

'Wow!' Herbert repeated, and fell into silence. After a while he said, 'But why didn't you tell him?'

Sheila explained. 'We thought it would be less hurtful if we waited till he'd got something written. Whatever it was, it would be much better than the sort of rubbish I'm being paid to produce. Then a comparison would make it clear that his writing was obviously superior. But so far there's been nothing to compare.'

Herbert suddenly remarked, 'You really are an extraordinary woman, Sheila.'

'Me?' she said in such evident astonishment that he burst out laughing.

'Yes, you. Hiding your talents like that. And only worried about the danger of putting your husband in the shade.'

'But it doesn't take any talent to write that sort of rubbish. After all, it's the sort of stuff I was reading all the time till I met Alan. And I don't have to think out the plot, or anything like that, you know.'

'Oh, that's nothing,' he said airily. 'Plots are no problem. A computer could do that. I think it's clear that Alan has always undervalued you, and you've taken yourself at his valuation.'

Sheila felt that an important new idea was breaking into her consciousness. Later on she would have to think about this, when the immediate crisis was over. She turned the conversation back to the problem in hand.

'Well, anyway, the important thing is to try and find out what's wrong with Alan. You think that finding that letter would be enough to . . . to derange him to this extent?'

'I don't know. You've got to remember that he's been intensely unhappy about the work situation for some time. My fault, that, I suppose.'

'Only in part. He's hated teaching from the word go.'

'And I've made things worse. But what I want to know is, why has he not written anything? He's had nearly a year in that cottage with nothing else to do. Or has he had something else to do?'

'What do you mean?'

'I don't quite know. But there might just be something . . . I say, do you mind if I do a little quiet sleuthing on my own? I've just got a hunch that there may have been something connected with the cottage that's been keeping him otherwise engaged, shall we say?'

'You mean another woman?'

'Who knows? *Cherchez la femme* and all that. Might be worth following up. I know it sounds a bit sordid. But he won't get the right treatment till someone finds out the cause of the trouble. And it doesn't look as if he means to tell us very much.'

'Yes, I think you're right. But what can we do? Where do we start?'

'You don't start. I'm not having you playing the part of the jealous, suspicious wife. I'm the person to do it. After all, as his Head of Department I too have an interest in the matter. So, if you don't mind, I'll do a little gentle sleuthing on my own. If I find anything out, do you want to know?'

'Of course! Why ever not?'

'I'm sorry. I see I'll have to revise some of my ideas about you. You look like the little woman who needs protection, but perhaps the stereotype doesn't fit.'

'Not any longer.'

Herbert looked at her enquiringly. 'You mean you haven't had the protection you needed?'

'Well, I don't know if I actually needed it. Probably not, since I've survived without it. But I would have liked it. The trouble was, you see, that Alan needed it even more than I did. And I see I've failed him there.'

'It looks like you've failed each other.'

That evening Herbert went back to the cottage and spent some time driving around, looking for neighbours. He found none. There was only one cottage at all near Alan's, and that was evidently unoccupied. He felt very tempted to break into Alan's cottage as he had done in the morning and have a good snoop round, to see if he could find any letters, photographs or other evidence that might provide a clue. But he couldn't persuade himself that this would be justified. Instead he decided to go to the village during the day when the shops were open and see if he could gather any information there. Anything he learned *there* would at least be public property. Not at all the same thing as looking for clues among a man's private possessions.

The following afternoon he left the college as soon as he could get away and drove to High Midbury. He made a number of unwanted purchases, and engaged the assistants in general converse, trying to bring the conversation round to the cottage and its inhabitant. As he went from shop to shop he perfected his technique. Nice area, some nice cottages round about, a friend of his had been living in one of them lately, etc.

Sometimes he drew a complete blank. Sometimes it became clear that his friend was known to the assistant, but he learned no new facts. What he did get was a general impression among those who recognized Alan's description that all was not well. There seemed to be a certain coldness in the response that he couldn't quite understand. Alan, after all, was a pleasant chap, with an inoffensive manner. He wasn't exactly brimming over with *bonhomie*, but there was nothing about him to turn people off. And yet Herbert got a distinct impression of chilliness and lack of response as soon as Alan was identified.

Puzzled, he stood in front of Mr Mott's shop, and decided this one was not to be ignored. It had all the marks of the old-fashioned high-class grocery, and he was sure it was just the sort of place that Alan, with his aristocratic tastes, would frequent.

It was Mr Mott himself who came forward to serve him. Herbert asked for olive oil. His visits to France had taught him to appreciate a good oil, so this was something he knew a little about. He felt sure Mr Mott would be an authority.

'First pressing, if you have it.'

'Yes sir. Here we are – extra virgin.'

'Good,' said the wily Herbert. 'I thought this looked like the sort of place that would have it. You have a bigger bottle?'

'Oh yes sir, certainly.'

The purchase was completed in the most amicable manner, while the relative merits of French, Italian and Greek olives and olive oil were discussed.

'I expect this is the place where a member of my staff who lives near here gets his olive oil. I should think he always goes for the best. I wonder if you know him. Alan Morley is the name.'

Herbert was astonished at the change that took place in Mr Mott's expression at the mention of Alan's name.

'Yes sir, I do indeed know him.' There was a pause while Mr Mott evidently struggled with his reluctance to upset a promising new customer, and his intense sense of injury. The latter won. 'To my cost, I may say I know him. I would not go so far as to say that Mr Morley is directly implicated in the loss that myself and other fellow members of the trade have suffered. But he obstinately refused to give us any clues to the whereabouts of the lady.'

'The lady?'

'The lady, sir, who absconded leaving many unpaid bills

and a number of cheques which the banks have refused to honour.'

'But what had Mr Morley to do with the lady?'

'You may well ask, sir, you may well ask. All we know is that they were constantly in company together. My fellow colleagues and I have observed this fact on countless occasions. So therefore we have come to the conclusion that Mr Morley must positively have some knowledge of her whereabouts, past or present.'

Herbert was enjoying himself. He relished Mr Mott's verbose style and his gift for tautology. And, in addition, he had stumbled upon what was obviously a very important clue. Further enquiries about the lady elicited her name, and a description of her appearance.

'Very striking sir, very striking. A very handsome lady, with flaming red hair, always very well dressed. And well spoken, a well educated lady, with an excellent accent. So how were we to know? And always so pleasant. And very knowledgeable, sir, very knowledgeable. There wasn't much that lady didn't know about malt whisky, sir. And a big spender. Only . . . ' Mr Mott paused, shrugged his shoulders, and sighed.

Herbert chatted on till he was sure there was no new material forthcoming. Anyway, he had what he needed. He was sure that the scarlet lady's defection had something to do with Alan's distraught state of mind. And if Mr Mott and his fellow shopkeepers had been unable to trace the lady, there was not much point in his trying to. Besides, it seemed unnecessary. His hypothesis had been confirmed.

Anxious as he was to impart his discovery to Sheila, he put off his visit till quite late in the evening, in the hope that the girls would all be in bed.

33

'Oh, Herbert! Come on in,' said Sheila. 'I'm so glad to see you. Melville's here. I phoned and told him all about Alan yesterday and he arrived this afternoon, bless him.'

Herbert didn't feel at all inclined to bless him. In fact, he felt a distinct sense of grievance against Melville as he followed Sheila into the sitting-room to meet Alan's best friend. He tried not to show his annoyance as he shook the hand of the tall, burly man with the long red beard.

'Melville knows all about the situation,' Sheila explained, 'so you can tell him any discoveries you may have made.'

Herbert had convinced himself that his annoyance stemmed from not being able to divulge his discoveries in front of a third party; but Sheila's statement had completely removed this difficulty. Why then did his sense of chagrin remain just as strong?

He didn't have enough self-knowledge to work out the implications. And besides, Sheila and Melville were waiting to hear what he had to say. He had spent quite a few hours imagining himself telling Sheila the awful truth, comforting and reassuring her. Now he saw it would all have to be quite different. Instead of breaking the truth gently, as he had intended, he found himself saying quite bluntly, 'Yes, it was just as I had suspected. There was another woman in the case.'

He then proceeded to describe his investigations. As soon

as he mentioned where the other woman lived Sheila looked up and said, 'I think I can tell you what she looks like.'

'You saw her?'

'Once only. It was a few weeks ago, one Saturday morning, when I was taking the girls to the cottage, where they always spent the day with Alan. As we passed the other cottage we saw a woman standing outside it. She looked at us as we passed, then waved and smiled. And once we had passed she went back into her house. Just as if she'd been waiting to see us, one of the girls said. Now I know why. She was very good-looking, with flaming red hair and dressed, well, rather like a high-class tart, I would say. The girls thought she was marvellous. It seems that their father thought so too. The girls told him about the encounter, but he seemed very casual about the whole thing. He gave me the impression that he knew practically nothing about her, and wasn't interested. I might have known that any man would be interested in such a neighbour.'

'And presumably she was interested in him, which was why she wanted to have a look at his wife and children,' added Herbert.

They speculated for some time as to who this strange woman was and what she was doing in the heart of the country.

'Running up debts and then moving on, seems to sum it up,' suggested Melville.

'In fact, just a common adventuress,' put in Sheila.

'No, not really,' objected Herbert. 'Something more than that. Mr Mott said she was well educated, intelligent, knowledgeable. And that's what makes it so difficult to explain.'

'Yes, it makes it difficult to work out what kind of a woman she really is. But it does help to explain her fascination for Alan. He would hardly fall for a common tart,' said Melville. 'And it seems I was wrong, Sheila, when I answered your letter nearly a year ago.' He turned to Herbert to explain. 'Sheila wrote to me when Alan decided to move to the cottage. She was very puzzled about it, and thought I might have some explanation. And she suggested there might be another woman involved. I wrote back and said I was sure there wasn't. Now it looks as if I might have been wrong.'

'Oh, but wait a minute,' put in Herbert, 'this woman didn't turn up till nearly Christmas. Alan had been in the cottage for about six months by then.'

'Yes, but he might have known her before. Perhaps she went there just to be near him.' Melville seemed determined to prove that he had given Sheila the wrong answer.

'But if he already knew her, where on earth would they have met?' Sheila wanted to know. 'I mean, we led such a quiet life. He really spent all his time at home and in college.'

'You don't have any red-haired sirens floating about the college, do you?' asked Melville.

'No. I'm afraid not. We don't rise to that sort of thing.'

After some more discussion they decided to put together everything they knew that could have a bearing on Alan's state of mind.

'First of all,' said Herbert, force of habit prompting him to take the leading role, 'there's work. Sheila tells me he's never really liked teaching, and now it's all much worse because of me and my new-fangled ideas. I expect that, as his best friend, you've heard about how awful I am?'

Melville raise both hands in a deprecating geature. 'Well, yes, I have been given the odd inkling,' he admitted.

'Then there's this siren next door. The mere fact of having an . . . getting involved with another woman would be pretty stressful to a decent sort like Alan.'

Melville looked up with an expression of surprise and respect that spoke volumes. Herbert saw the look and took it in with some amusement. You didn't think I was capable of appreciating that, did you, he thought.

'Then the consideration that, two days before his collapse, she ditches him. For, knowing him, we have to assume that he was telling the truth when he told the grocer he had no idea of her whereabouts.'

'I'm sure you're right there,' put in Sheila, 'he wouldn't lie about a thing like that, when she owed all those people so much money.'

'And, as if all this wasn't bad enough, there's this letter, making it clear that Sheila is a successful author, or at least that's what it looks like, when *he* hasn't even got started.'

'And the worst of it is,' added Melville, 'that the letter gave no indication of what sort of writing Sheila is doing. If he knew what it was he would feel less threatened.'

Sheila agreed. 'Yes. I see now that we made a mistake in not telling him about it right away. But who would have thought he would take so long to get started, and that he would find that letter? He hadn't been in the house for months. He'd taken to bringing the girls back on a Saturday and hurrying off without even coming in. I think I now see why,' she added ruefully.

'Finally,' pursued Herbert,' there's the question of a possible misinterpretation of . . . ' he paused, looking for a tactful expression.

'Of what might have been going on between Melville and I . . . me, I mean.' Sheila blushed for her grammar. She hoped the men hadn't noticed her slip, and would attribute the blush to the subject-matter under discussion.

'Exactly. It all adds up to quite a lot, don't you think?'

'Enough to cause the sort of reaction we're talking about?' queried Melville.

Sheila nodded. 'Yes, I think it well might.'

'Yes, in a sensitive sort of a chap like Alan,' agreed Herbert.

It was clear from his tone that he had not used the word 'sensitive' as an encomium.

'So what do we do?' asked Melville. 'Send Sheila to tell the doctors they're barking up the wrong tree if they're still looking for a physical cause?'

'I think they may be beginning to look for something beyond that, by now,' put in Sheila. 'They wouldn't let me see him today, and explained that it was because he was so determined to see no one. They thought it might upset him too much if they insisted. And I could see they realized this was rather abnormal behaviour. So they might be quite receptive to anything we can tell them that might help to explain things.'

They agreed to give all the facts to the hospital staff, in the hope that this would help.

After that a silence ensued. All three felt rather ill at ease. Herbert didn't quite know what to make of the relationship between Sheila and Melville. Was Alan the only link between them? Was the evident affection they shared simply the result of a wife's regard for her husband's best friend, and that friend's regard for his friend's wife?

He was disconcerted by the discovery that the slight undercurrent of antagonism he felt towards Melville could easily be described as jealousy. It seemed perfectly natural that the man should admire Sheila. And, after all, why shouldn't Sheila reciprocate? He was now convinced that Sheila's marriage had brought her little happiness. It therefore stood to reason, according to Herbert's view of life, that she should look for solace in some other quarter.

Melville too was slightly disconcerted by Herbert's presence and the obvious familiarity that seemed to have sprung up between him and Sheila. He was sure this must be something recent. Nothing that Alan had ever said had given the slightest grounds for assuming anything but the most distant and formal relationship between them. Yet, when the two elder girls, disobeying orders, crept downstairs and into the sitting-room, the joy with which they greeted Herbert was at least as enthusiastic as their reception of Melville himself. So it was clear that there had been a certain amount of coming and going. He wondered whether he ought to be feeling something like vicarious jealousy on Alan's account as far as Sheila was concerned. As for the girls, he was fond of them and told himself he was entitled to some first-hand jealousy in that quarter.

He realized how useful a man like Herbert could be to a woman in Sheila's position, and felt he ought to be thankful that she had this help available, since his own work kept him too far away to offer the sort of assistance Sheila needed. And at the same time he couldn't help speculating about the pair. Could it be that this was yet another factor in Alan's breakdown?

Had he discovered a liaison?

Perhaps this had contributed to his allowing himself to get entangled with the red-haired siren. Or perhaps it all went back even further. Could Alan's longstanding dislike of the man have its origin in Herbert's admiration of Sheila? Or Sheila's liking for Herbert? Don't be absurd, he told himself. You're letting your imagination run away with you. It can't possibly go as far back as that. But at what point, he asked himself, did the impossible merge into the just possible?

As for Sheila, she sensed the hostility between the men, which even their earnest attempt at helping to straighten out the family's problems didn't quite manage to conceal, and she wondered about its source. Was it just a fundamental incompatibility? There was no denying that the two men could hardly have been more different. And yet this hardly seemed sufficient grounds. After all, Alan and Melville were incredibly different from each other and yet their friendship flourished in spite of this. Could it be on account of her?

She tried to dismiss the idea as absurd. After all, she was utterly convinced that Melville didn't really care about women. But might he suspect a relationship between her and Herbert, and resent it on Alan's account? That might be a fairly reasonable supposition in such circumstances, although a false one in this particular case.

There was no special relationship between her and Herbert. At least, not so far. But she couldn't convince herself that things weren't moving in that direction, certainly as far as Herbert was concerned. It was evident that he admired her. And if he were to offer more than mere friendship? How would she react? And then she thought of Alan and all he must be suffering at the moment, and she blamed herself bitterly for even letting her thought stray in such a direction.

'Can I offer you a lift?' Herbert's polite words hid a desire not to leave Melville in possession.

'Oh, thanks, it's not necessary. I came by car,' Melville smiled blandly, suspecting the frustration that this answer would produce.

Herbert left in a thoroughly dissatisfied mood, not knowing whether Melville intended to spend the night in the house. He had arrived elated with the news he had managed to ferret out about Alan's outrageous neighbour. Now it all seemed rather less important than his having to leave without knowing just how long, and on what terms, Melville was staying.

'Doesn't seem such a bad chap after all,' was Melville's verdict after Herbert had left. 'Certainly not such a villain as Alan had led me to expect.'

'I know.' Sheila stood still, shaking her head. 'Alan simply can't stand him. And I can't really believe it's all due to professional jealousy. Alan isn't as mad about his career as all that, is he?'

'Not really,' agreed Melville. 'I think there must be some sort of chemical basis for the dislike, don't you?'

Sheila didn't quite see what chemistry had to do with it. She merely said, 'The girls don't share Alan's dislike, anyway.'

'So I've noticed.' He nearly added that Sheila herself didn't seem to share the dislike either, but decided this was not the time for what might be taken as a flippant comment or an unjustified piece of prying. But he would dearly have liked to know what Sheila felt about Herbert. He dismissed the idea from his mind with the thought that Herbert was probably wondering exactly the same about him, and turned to another point that had to be settled.

'Have you told Alan's parents yet?' he asked.

Sheila sighed. 'No, not yet. I thought I'd wait till we had some sort of diagnosis. Or rather, I've used that as an excuse for putting off the evil hour. You know how they terrify me.'

'Would you like me to tell them?'

'I'd simply love it, Melville, and it's sweet of you to offer. But I think I really must tell them myself. If I left it to someone else, even an old friend like you, whom they know and like, it would seem almost like a declaration of hostilities on my part. I'm obviously the person to do it. The point is, when?'

'The sooner the better, I should say. I don't think we can kid ourselves that it's all going to blow over, and that he'll be all right in a few days. The longer you put it off, the more of a shock it will be for them.'

'And the more they will resent my negligence in not telling them before.'

'Oh Sheila, Sheila, could you not just stop looking for blame from them? Can't you see how much more difficult it makes everything? I know you haven't much in common, but it doesn't have to be an unbridgeable gap, unless you want it to be.'

'But I've never been the one to criticize! On the contrary, it's just because I realize how far above me they are in every respect that I can't cope with them.'

'But they're not far above you in every respect. All right, that's the way you felt when you first met them. And you were probably right, or nearly so. But think how you've changed, think of what you've achieved. You can meet them on their own level, or at least much nearer to it now. But not if you hang on to your old script.'

'I suppose you're right. Only I don't know how to start. Where do I find a new, appropriate script?'

'Forget about a script. You don't need one now.'

Sheila looked unconvinced.

'Look, just try to look at things from their point of view. They have an only son, who means the world to them, and they're about to be told that he is in hospital with a serious and so far undiagnosed illness. If you simply keep that fact in mind, your own compassion and common sense will tell you what to say.'

Sheila nodded slowly. 'Do you think it's too late to phone now?' she asked.

34

Neither Michael nor Georgina Morley had ever admitted to each other or to anyone else that their son's career had been a big disappointment. Each felt it to be so, and forbore to mention it, in the hope that the other partner might not have come to the same unhappy conclusion. So Alan's lack of success in life, after the dazzling triumph of his first at Cambridge, was a subject never mentioned in the family. Had they been able to discuss the matter they would have discovered that each had a different interpretation to put on the unfortunate affair.

Georgina would have maintained that Alan was utterly blameless – unless you could attribute his lack of success to an imprudent marriage which had forced him to give up his research and take up a job unworthy of him. And she was careful not to attach the blame for this marriage to Sheila. It was just one of those things. Young people would fall in love. She had done so herself, though at a rather later age. And, no doubt because of their youth, they had not been able to weigh the pros and cons of the situation with the dispassionate realism that had come to her aid when she had to make the big decision.

Michael, on the other hand, was inclined to take a much more personal view of the matter. He blamed Sheila to a certain extent; but he realized that, even if there had been no Sheila, there would almost certainly have been someone else. The real trouble, as he saw it, lay in Alan himself, and in his unfortunate decision to take up his research in Edinburgh. If only he had decided to pursue his studies in Cambridge or London – or even Oxford – things would have been very different. For he was convinced that the PhD was not going well, even before Sheila came on the scene. Now, if that had happened a bit nearer home – a little nearer the parental influence – he, Michael, would have been able to see what was wrong and done something towards putting it right.

Not that he considered himself an authority on Scott, or anything of the sort. It was just that he felt there was something wrong with Alan's attitude. It they had seen more of each other at this point he might have been able to encourage Alan over a difficult patch. Or perhaps guided him in another direction. Whatever the difficulties may have been, he was convinced that Alan's real problem lay in his own character, and felt that a helping hand, or a good old-fashioned parental shove in the right direction, might have saved Alan from the results of what his father saw as a certain spinelessness.

Because of the inability of both parents to admit the outstanding mediocrity of their son's achievements the couple found themselves unable to say very much about him to each other. He became, if not a tabu subject, at least one that was never discussed in depth. They spoke of the girls, of their regret that distance kept them from establishing any form of close contact with their grandchildren, and were careful never to specify what sort of a distance it was that imposed this barrier.

The words 'Poor Alan' were never spoken, but the concept seemed to hang in the air. The thought of their son brought to both husband and wife a sense of disappointment, of lost opportunity – lost to him, and therefore also to them. They would have been so happy to rejoice with him, had there been any reason for rejoicing in his life. That there was not hung over them like a cloud. And their love for him kept them silent.

Even after Michael retired the household routine remained unchanged.

He was writing a book on the particular aspect of law that most interested him, and spent exactly the same hours in various libraries that he had spent in his office and in the law courts. There was in both of them a strong resistance to change, and they were happy to keep to the domestic routine that had been established twenty years earlier, when Alan had left the home to go to university. For both of them the unexpected was the enemy, against which they were constantly on their guard.

Georgina had had a trying day. She had known from the start it would be so, and had consequently wakened up with the usual tension headache. It was one of those days when a number of non-routine things had to be slotted in, with rather inadequate time margins in between. The worst aspect of the affair was their feeling obliged to ask one of Michael's colleagues and his wife round for a meal in the evening. In earlier days Georgina had quite liked entertaining, at infrequent intervals. It was a challenge which she met with her usual perfectionism. But over the last few years she had lost her taste for challenges and for any sort of break in the established routine. Michael too prefered life to flow along the everyday channels.

I suppose we're getting old, she thought. It's only natural at our age to slow down and settle into a sensible routine. There's no point in going beyond one's limits. After all, she reflected, she herself was over seventy, and Michael was pushing eighty, though he certainly didn't look it.

When, on occasion, the sensible routine had to be broken, she found it a considerable strain. So she had set this day down from the start as a *jour néfaste*. And when, after their guests had gone and she and Michael were thinking about going to bed, they were both a little put out when they heard the phone ringing.

'Who can that be?' she said. 'It's a bit late for phone calls, don't you think?'

'Indeed I do,' replied Michael. 'After ten o'clock at night. Not very considerate, is it, my dear?'

Georgina, looking rather pained, picked up the receiver and answered.

'Yes? Oh, yes. Oh no, not at all . . . Yes. Yes . . . oh dear . . . oh dear . . . '

Michael was standing beside her by now, anxiously trying to make out what the conversation was about.

'It's Alan,' Georgina whispered above the sound of Sheila's voice, 'he's ill.'

'Doesn't sound like Alan,' retorted Michael.

'It's Sheila,' Georgina hissed back at him.

'Well, you said it was Alan.'

'Yes, yes Sheila dear, I *am* listening. I'm just trying to explain to Michael that it's you who are phoning and Alan who is ill. And they don't know what's the matter? Then how do you know he's ill?'

The following evening it was Georgina who phoned. Sheila had only just got back from an almost entirely fruitless visit to the hospital.

'Any news?' Georgina's voice sounded so tense that Sheila's heart sank. All the news she had was devastatingly bad.

'Not really,' she said. 'No change to speak of . . . yes, I did see him today. But he wouldn't look at me or speak to me at all. As if we'd never met. And he's like that with everyone except the nurses. Melville went too, and you know how much he thinks of Melville, but it was just the same. Absolute silence, and no sign of recognition. Do you think it could be amnesia? He told the nurses that his name isn't Alan Morley. He gave another name instead, a queer, foreign name.'

'What was it?'

'Gregor Samsa.'

'Oh, my God!'

Sheila was shocked at the horror in Georgina's voice. 'What is it? What's so terrible about that name? I suppose it's a character in a book. He's always identifying with characters in books, isn't he?'

'Have you heard of Kafka?'

'Ye-es, I've heard of him, but I haven't got round to reading him yet.'

'Well, don't.'

'And this Gregor Samsa, who was he?'

'A character in one of his stories – who was metamorphosed.'

'Into what?'

Georgina hesitated. 'Into an insect. A sort of beetle.'

A faint gasp came from the other end of the line.

'Sheila, are you there Sheila?'

'Yes, I'm here.' Sheila's voice sounded near to tears.

'Look my dear, would it help if we came?'

'I don't know. I just don't know. He wouldn't speak to me or to Melville. I don't dare take the girls to see him. I think it might shock them terribly, especially if he refused to speak to them. And yet he might just speak to them. Or to you. After all, he's got nothing against you.'

Georgina said nothing about the implications of this last statement. She had never known how well Alan and Sheila got on; the distance between the two families was so great that she had no means of knowing.

After a brief discussion with Michael, Georgina spoke again. 'We think we'd better come, just in case it can be any help. We'll travel by train – neither of us feels like such a long drive these days – and we'll put up at a hotel . . . no, really, it will be much simpler all round that way, thanks all the same . . . '

For the first time in her life Sheila felt grateful to her mother-in-law, and actually looked forward to seeing her. Since Melville's departure that afternoon she had felt rather bewilderingly on her own. She told herself that this was silly. After all, she had got used to coping without Alan during the past year. But she had had no crisis to deal with during that time. It now struck her that, apart from the ups and downs of their relationship, there had been no serious crisis to deal with in all their married life. She wondered how much help Alan would have been in a similar situation, and then got confused trying to work it all out, because you would really have needed two Alans to fit the situation, one ill in hospital and the other at home beside her. She couldn't help feeling that his mother, that determined lady, would be of more use in a crisis than her son could ever be.

One of her problems lay in trying to keep the girls from realizing how serious things were. The arrival of their grand-parents was so unusual an event that it would do nothing to reassure them. But that couldn't be helped. Alan was the main problem, and if the presence of his parents could help . . .

Herbert came round later in the evening. He entertained the girls for a while, then sent them off to bed in rec-ord time.

'I don't know how you do it,' sighed Sheila. 'It always takes me ages to get them off.'

'Authority,' he said, 'that's what they need. A man's authority.'

Sheila shook her head doubtfully. 'Depends what man,' she said.

'Oh, I've no doubt they can run rings round Alan when they feel like it. I have the advantage of being less familiar. Authority and familiarity don't go all that well together.'

'And talking about authority, I told you Alan's parents are coming tomorrow. How much do you think I should tell them?'

'Everything.'

'Including the bit about . . . ?'

'About the red-haired temptress? Of course. That's the most important clue we've got. Or at any rate, it's the most probable single cause. So you've got to tell them.'

'I'm afraid they will he pretty shocked.'

'That's their problem. And I gather you're not all that close to them anyway, so why worry?'

Once again Sheila was taken aback by his businesslike, almost brutal attitude.

'I know we've never been close, and I've always been scared stiff of them, but I'm sorry for them all the same. I don't want to make things any worse for them than is necessary.'

'Well, this *is* necessary,' he pointed out. 'So don't waste time worrying about it.'

The following day Sheila met her in-laws at the station and drove them to their hotel. In a quiet corner of the lounge they discussed Alan's case over a pot of tea. To her surprise Alan's parents took the news of their son's presumed infidelity without any signs of distress.

'I'm glad for your sake, Sheila, that you knew nothing about it while it was going on,' remarked Georgina. 'That would have been even more upsetting.'

'That's true. I hadn't thought of that, but you're right. I suppose that's something to be thankful for.'

The older woman rested her hand lightly on Sheila's for a moment. 'That's right, dear,' she said. 'You've got to look on the bright side. All the more so when things look as black as they do at present.'

Sheila was touched. For the first time she seemed to feel real warmth in her mother-in-law's words.

When she told them about her literary efforts she was amused at the two very different reactions this information evoked. Her father-in-law looked up with a sudden jerk of the head, and his eyes flashed approval.

'Good for you, Sheila,' he said. 'I didn't think you had it in you. You've certainly made great strides.'

His wife hastened to agree. But Sheila had caught the look of pained disapproval when the purely mercenary, hacklike nature of the writing had been revealed. She reminded herself that this woman had been a poet of some distinction, and must feel sullied by a family connexion with work of such mass-produced mediocrity.

Sheila had decided that, in spite of Herbert's advice, she would suppress one thing, the bit about the cupboard. It showed Alan in too humilating a light, and she wished to spare his parents this embarrassment. But when asked how Alan had got hold of the information about her writing she said:

'He found a letter from Melville about it. At least,' she confessed, 'I suppose that's what happened.'

Michael pounced at once. 'You suppose? On what grounds do you suppose?'

'Well, I found it in a cupboard, and I'd left it beside the typewriter in the study.'

'Couldn't one of the girls have left it there?'

'No, I'm sure it was Alan.'

'Why, what makes you so sure?'

Sheila suddenly broke down under this interrogation and burst into tears.

Georgina intervened. 'Now Michael, don't be so sharp. We're not in a court of law, you know.'

219

Michael patted Sheila on the shoulder. 'Sorry, my dear. But we really must have all the facts if we're going to get anywhere at all.'

After a little sniffing and tear-wiping, Sheila went on:

'I know it was Alan because he was hiding in the cupboard.'

'Hiding in a cupboard? In his own house? Whatever for?'

Sheila gave her conjectural explanation. 'The one thing I can't understand,' she added 'is why he came back that afternoon without any warning. It's not as if he had any motive for wanting to spy on me – not till he'd seen the letter, that is. After seeing that, well, goodness knows what he may have imagined.'

They all sat in silence for a while.

Then Michael summed up the situation:

'Whatever may be the matter, I think we've all got to face it: Alan appears to be in a very unsettled state mentally. None of his behaviour over the last few days seems to be in the least rational.'

Sheila nodded. 'The nurse this afternoon said they were thinking of transferring him to a mental hospital. They are as baffled as we are at present, and none of the tests seem to throw any light on the situation. He talks to the nurses, but it's all utter nonsense; and he refuses to speak to any of the visitors.'

'I wonder,' mused his mother,' I wonder if there isn't perhaps a certain amount of method in his madness. The nurses say he's talking nonsense, but that may simply be that they don't understand his literary references – Gregor Samsa, for instance. He speaks to them in a way he must know they can't possibly understand. And he keeps silent to those who would know what he's talking about. Does that make sense?'

Michael was nodding his approval. But Sheila broke in with:

'But why should he not want to be understood? Surely we all want to be understood?'

'Not always, my dear, not always. There are circumstances . . . Georgina, can you think of a reason?'

Georgina sat thoughtful for a while. 'Fear?' she suggested. 'Or what about guilt? A feeling of unworthiness?'

'Right. Hence Gregor Samsa, don't you think?'

'You mean the beetle? He thinks he's so unworthy that he feels like a beetle?' asked Sheila in a shocked voice.

'It could be that,' admitted Georgina. 'But the point about the Kafka story is that this horrible metamorphosis was something that happened out of the blue, for no known reason, to an innocent man. He is turned into the loathsome insect through no fault of his own. That might be the meaning of the reference. Or it might be a mixture of the two things, he may be swinging from feelings of guilt to a sense of innocent outrage. It's all guesswork. We have so little to go on. We'll just have to see how he reacts to our visit.'

'I think I'd better not go with you. He might be less hostile without my presence.'

'Yes,' said Michael grimly. 'With a bit of luck he might rank us with the nurses and actually speak to us.'

35

I suppose (*reflected Alan*) they think they've saved my life. Fools! Interfering idiots! All they've done is ruin my death. I'd got it all set up. A few more days, perhaps even a few more hours, and that would have been it. Imbeciles! Can't they see that it's in their best interests, in everybody's best interests, for me to disappear? And in mine, my God, in mine too! My only hope. Annihilation. And Scratchley, bloody Scratchley, what does he want to come interfering for? Can't he see how much better it would be for him if I weren't there? In the Department for one thing – get rid of the dead wood once and for all. Get rid of the dissatisfied old fogey who still believes in the value of literature. And in his private life, get me out of the way, leave him a clear field with Sheila. For I know he fancies Sheila, I can see that all right. Thick as thieves. And yet he spoils it all by bumbling in and saving my life for me. So much for the whiz-kid and his genius! Anyway, he needn't be all that sure of Sheila. There's always Melville to take into account. Melville, my best friend, courting my twit of a wife and getting her lined up for literary stardom. My one and only friend. So much for friendship and loyalty.

Et tu, Brute.

Scratchley and Melville and Sheila – my best friends, my worst friends, my best enemies, my saviours! Officious imbeciles!

> Thou shalt not kill; but needst not strive
> officiously to keep alive.

But then, you wouldn't expect Scratchley or Sheila to remember the lines. If they'd even heard of them, yes, that's it, if they'd even heard of them. And so they saved me. I suppose they thought it was their duty. Their regrettable duty. Very moral, oh, highly moral, they are. Rachel, damn her, at least wasn't moral. Far from it. She didn't give a tinker's curse whether I was alive or dead. Not now and not then either. She wouldn't have cared if I'd dropped dead at any moment. So long as I didn't do it while I was in bed with her. That would have been rather inconvenient. But she'd have coped, oh, I'm sure she'd have coped. She's a resourceful woman, is Rachel. And she'd have let me die, beautiful, holy Rachel, she'd have let me die in peace.

Peace . . .

His thoughts continued to dwell on Rachel with some satisfaction, till she turned again into the huge pink jellyfish, clinging to him, smothering him, as she had appeared to him in his dream while he was hiding in the cupboard. Resolutely he turned his thoughts away from the jellyfish, back to Sheila, back to Scratchley, back to Melville, like an automatic reverse cassette player that went on and on eternally. It was exhausting, it was mortifying, it was hideously depressing, but it was necessary. This round of anger and self-pity and resentment was the one thing that could keep the other idea out of his mind. The moment he stopped thinking of his grievances he saw a tall white hawthorn hedge rise up before his eyes, with a defenceless figure standing in front of it. And he dare not look, dare not try to imagine the scene as the victim was flung into the hedge and left bleeding on the ground.

So, back to Scratchley and the dead wood, and Sheila and

her iniquitous literary ambitions, and her secrecy and her success. That Sheila should be writing anything at all was inconceivable. That she should have found a publisher was outrageous. What was she writing? What in God's name could she be writing?

He tried to think of her in her best moments, trying to find a clue as to what she could be writing. But even thinking back to the young Sheila he had fallen in love with he could find nothing to suggest that she had either the originality or the maturity to provide her with anything to say. So it must be rubbish, he thought with savage satisfaction. Rubbish which she has somehow got Melville to publish for her. And why? Why is Melville prostituting his professional integrity by accepting the sort of crap she can be expected to write?

Only one answer to that. The thought of his wife's infidelity and his friend's treachery seemed easier to stomach than the thought that Sheila might actually have made a success of the sort of writing he had spent his life hoping to make his mark in.

Or perhaps it wasn't Sheila at all who was doing the writing. Perhaps it was Melville, and they'd decided to pass it off as Sheila's just to get at him. To be outwritten by my best friend would be hurtful enough, he thought; but for my twit of a wife to appear as the author would be ten times more hurtful. That's it, they've done it to get at me. It's a put-up job, carefully planned or should I say orchestrated – yes, that's the in word – carefully orchestrated to humiliate me to the utmost. This thought gave him a certain fierce pleasure, with its insistence on the ill-will directed at him by his loved ones, and its scornful use of one of the recent clichés that he most hated.

But then he remembered that the letter had explicitly referred to the work as Sheila's, and had to abandon that little fantasy. Pity! It brought him back to the stark reality that there was no way of depriving Sheila of her authorship. Whatever she had written, and whatever its value, there was no denying that she had written something. One up for Sheila, blast her!

And so the endless carousel went on, round and round, again and again; feeding his anger, feeding his resentment, wearing him out, but achieving its purpose of keeping out the one unendurable thought. But he knew all the time that the memory was waiting there, ready to pounce, inevitably bound to be faced sooner or later. Meanwhile the monologue continued, holding the dreaded recognition at bay till his state of shock had diminished enough to let him look his enemy in the eyes.

Then he would have to take in the full extent of his guilt and failure. And face it he must, since they hadn't allowed him to die. At first he had thought he could carry it through, even in hospital, by refusing to eat. But they had worn down his resistance with their professional obstinacy. Yet another failure to his credit, failure to die at the appropriate moment. And the heartbreak in his parents' eyes had broken his vow of silence. He had spoken, though to little purpose.

Soon after he was sent to the mental hospital his parents went back to London, feeling they could do nothing for him. Sheila took to visiting him once a week, while Alan sat and stared through her as if she weren't there. She would sit in the car for a few minutes and cry, before going home to face the girls. The most difficult bit was trying to sound encouraging to them. But the six solemn eyes that stared glumly at her left her in no doubt as to the result of her attempt.

36

When they got back from France, Dr and Mrs Wilson lost no time in assessing the situation between Lisha and Peter.

'I see it's a case of *Vive l'amour,*' remarked the doctor as soon as they were alone.

'So it appears. I just hope it won't end in heartbreak this time.'

'Oh well, if it does it's to be hoped she'll think it was worth it. They certainly look blissfully happy at present.'

'Yes,' agreed his wife, 'they certainly do look happy. And well. Peter looks so much better.'

'He certainly looks as if he needed no more recuperating. I think I'll tell him he's well enough to go home.'

'Oh, Dick! You wouldn't, would you?'

Her husband burst into a hearty laugh. 'Quite pointless. He'd be so upset he'd have a relapse on the spot. So we'll just have to put up with the love birds for as long as it lasts. And it's nice to see Lisha looking so happy.'

'And perhaps it won't be so bad this time, when it comes to an end. I think she's a lot steadier now.'

'And a lot older. She's had time to learn some sense.'

'Yes, she's had time to learn that very few people are as lucky as we are, Dick. Which of course,' she added thoughtfully, 'won't prevent her from wanting to be one of the lucky ones.'

'Makes you realize, doesn't it, that a happy marriage is a

pretty immoral thing. Or at least an unsociable one. Gives people the wrong idea.'

'Well, there's no harm in having an ideal, even if it's an unattainable one.'

'No harm at all, so long as you take it with a touch of realism.'

Lisha and Peter were taking their happiness with a touch of realism this time, which made them more relaxed. The first time round Lisha had been so penetrated by her romantic conviction that her love was a once-in-a-lifetime affair that the possibility of losing Peter meant also the prospect of losing love for ever more. She had now loved more than one man, and so had to admit to herself that she might love yet again – and again. Her more relaxed attitude freed Peter from the sense of guilt under which he had laboured in the past, and both felt happier and more secure in their love from the very consciousness that it would not last for ever.

One day in late autumn they were sitting in Lisha's little studio. As usual she was at her drawing board and he was reading.

Suddenly she spoke, without looking up from her work. 'Do you realize that we haven't made love for three days – and three nights?'

Peter put his book down. 'That must be quite a record,' he said.

'It certainly is. Do you think we should discuss its significance?'

'Yes, I think we might. What do you take it to mean?'

'I think it means that the end is approaching, don't you?'

'Yes, probably. In fact, it has occurred to me, vaguely, during the past few days, that perhaps it's time I moved on. I can't go on convalescing for ever.'

'No, not unless you want to become a permanent invalid. And I don't think either of us wants that to happen to you.'

'So, it's time I went.'

'Where to?'

'I think I'll go back home.'

'Back to solitary confinement? Is that wise?'

'Don't forget, I *am* a solitary. You yourself once pointed that out.'

'Yes, but it didn't work all that well, did it?'

'No, but I've learned a lot since then. I was a solitary by default. This time it would be from choice. And I'd be starting from a position of strength, having rebuilt a lot of human relationships. And besides, I think I'd have some company. I wouldn't be entirely on my own.'

'Company? Do you mean Marcus Aurelius?'

Peter laughed. 'Well, yes, I'll certainly have him. But that wasn't what I meant. The post came when you were out shopping this morning. There was a letter from Andrew. He thinks he should be out fairly soon. He was talking of his plans. He still wants to own his own sawmill again, and says he'll work at anything he can get, labouring, anything, and save every penny till he can get started again, even though he knows it will take him many years.'

'So you're going to hand the place over for him to start a sawmill in, is that it?'

'Hmmm . . . not quite. My idea was a sort of partnership. I provide the site and the capital, and he does the work. What do you say to that?'

'I say he's a very lucky man. And I say you've come a long way. When you first told me about Andrew you were quite worried about his penal record and what that could do to you, and now you're prepared to take him into your home and set him up in business.' She got up and crossed over to where he sat. 'I think it's simply splendid,' she said, putting both hands on his shoulders and giving him a kiss.

'And what's more,' he went on, 'I'm prepared to go even

further. He was speaking about the difficulty of getting started again, and said he particularly wanted a business of his own so that he could help other people in his position, particularly the younger ones. He says he's seen it happen several times already since he began his sentence – youngsters, first offenders, going in for a few weeks, on a fairly minor charge, getting out and being back in again in no time, just because they find it so difficult to get started again after a conviction. He wants to set up some sort of liaison between himself and the prison, to offer jobs where possible. But of course it will take years and years if he does it all himself. Now, if I help, it would benefit some of these youngsters as well as Andrew.'

'And it would give you a purpose in life. Yes, I can see, you're on your way.'

'Not quite yet, my generous Lisha. I want to make sure it's all right with you, before I make any moves.'

Lisha was standing beside him, with her arm round his shoulders. 'I'll be all right,' she said. 'I've got my work, and you know I love that. And who knows . . . '

'Yes, who knows? There may be another lame dog just around the corner.'

They decided to have a day in the mountains to mark the end of this period in their lives. They would set off early on the first good morning, drive to the Central Highlands and find some quiet spot to wander about in. Much as they both loved Galloway, they had an intermittent longing for higher mountains every so often. Nothing arduous, of course, for Peter's sake. He still had a bit of a limp, and didn't feel up to anything too energetic. And certainly no rock climbing. Since Frank's death Lisha had been paralysed with fear at the thought.

Three days later the day dawned bright and clear, and they set off, with plenty of provisions, to enable them to wander freely, without having to waste time looking for places to eat.

Besides, as Lisha pointed out, by November there are very few places left open in the Highlands.

They parked the car beside a little hump-backed bridge and, carrying their hamper and a couple of rugs, set off along the edge of the stream. After a few hundred yards they came to the ideal spot. It was so perfect that, without saying a word, they stopped and spread their rugs and sat down. A deep curve in the stream had left a little grassy promontory, facing south, with a raised bank behind it to protect them from the breeze. In this sheltered spot the sun was so warm that they could almost have believed it was summer.

'This is exactly what I was dreaming of,' said Lisha. 'I could swear I saw this very spot in my mind's eye when we set off.'

'It's perfect, utterly perfect. Just listen to the sound of that water.'

They spent the whole day there, looking up at the mountains, talking, making love, eating, listening to the murmur of the water and the cries of the birds. There were no signs of human habitation – even the road was out of sight and out of hearing. When the sun was beginning to sink they got up and collected their belongings in a sort of peaceful daze.

'I feel as if we'd been here for at least five years,' said Lisha, sighing with contentment.

'Yes, I know. Five wonderful years. Or perhaps five thousand.'

They reached the bridge, and before climbing up to the road Lisha stepped down to the water's edge. She stood looking at the running water for some time, then she knelt down and dipped her hand into it.

'It's cold!' she exclaimed. 'Cold but pure and beautiful.' Then she turned to Peter, smiling. 'Come and be baptized,' she said.

Peter came and knelt beside her. She dipped her hand into the stream again and sprinkled the water over his head.

'I baptize you in the name of all creation,' she said, 'and I dedicate you to the Yorkshire moors, to the penal service, and to the two little raspberry pickers who sent you to me by devious paths.'

'Amen,' he said smiling, half laughing, and kissed her hand.

Before standing up Lisha picked up one of the pebbles from the water's edge.

'I want to take some of it with me,' she explained. 'Don't you want one?'

'No,' he said, 'I don't need one. I'm taking it all with me.'

When they got to the bridge they stopped to take one last look at the stream. Lisha held out her arm, with the pebble resting on the palm of her hand. 'You're right,' she said. 'Who needs a pebble?' And she gently tipped her hand over so that the pebble fell into the water with a soft plop. 'Now I can take it all with me.'

37

During his first week in the mental hospital Alan was visited regularly by a psychologist, and eventually began talking to her. In the end he told her all his troubles – problems at work, the book he never could start writing, his sense of his wife's intellectual inferiority, the affair with Rachel, the discovery of his friend's implication in Sheila's writing exploits – all except for the drama of the accident. By now he could allow his own thoughts to dwell on this, but he felt utterly incapable of mentioning it to another living being. He knew he would have to take the secret to the grave with him, unconfessed and unshriven.

But the talks with the psychologist did achieve something, for she spoke to Sheila and learned the real nature of the relationship between the supposedly guilty wife and the best friend, and the very limited extent of her literary achievements. In the end Alan accepted this information as true, and agreed to see Melville again, who took to driving all the way to Manchester at frequent intervals, just to spend a few hours with his friend.

After the first few visits Alan began to tell his troubles to Melville. The business of the accident he still didn't mention; but he told him all about the other problems, including the affair with the pink jellyfish. Sheila he still refused to see, and maintained that their marriage was over, and that there was no point in renewing the relationship on any terms whatever.

Melville took care to see as little as possible of Sheila on his frequent visits, just to make sure that nothing occurred to renew Alan's suspicions. He was sorry about this, as he was very fond of Sheila and pitied her in her difficult position; but he had a suspicion that she was not entirely without help. Herbert Scratchley appeared to be about in the background, or perhaps even in the foreground. Melville was also in communication with Alan's parents, and knew that they were keeping in close touch with Sheila. The ice had at last been broken, and a strong bond of affection seemed to have been formed, especially between the two women, a bond forged, ironically enough, by the very circumstances that seemed to be bringing about the breakdown of the marriage.

As the weeks went past the violence of Alan's distress began to lessen. He realized that none of the things he had told the psychologist about were really beyond bearing, and fell into a sort of twilight apathy, shot through with the quivering consciousness of his guilt over the accident.

Every time he made an effort to take an interest in anything, this guilt stepped in quietly and diverted his attention. This had become the one vital element in his life. Everything else just seemed to be a part of the formless slush that occupied his torpid mind.

He did rouse himself sufficiently to write a letter of resignation to the college. Whatever happened, he felt wholly convinced that nothing on earth could persuade him to teach ever again.

Shortly afterwards he received the following letter:

Dear Alan,

This morning the Principal sent for me and showed me your letter of resignation. After a brief consultation we took the liberty of tearing it up. I have to point out that, as long as you are on sick leave, we have a temporary replacement in the department.

The work of the College therefore does not suffer from your prolonged absence. I presume you know that for the first six months you receive your full salary, and after that half-pay for the following six months. It would therefore seem advisable for you not to resign till the end of that period. If, however, you feel strongly in the matter, there is nothing to stop you from sending in your resignation a second time. In that case we shall be forced to the conclusion that your desire to cock a snook at the College is greater than your wish to support your wife and family.

Yours as ever,

Herbert S.

Alan was furious, and enjoyed his fury, the first good, clean, strong emotion he had felt for a long time. He wrote a second, even more biting letter of resignation. Then, when the fury had subsided, he thought the matter over and realized that a monthly cheque paid into the joint account was a very desirable thing, and that its absence would occasion all sorts of problems that he was in no state to face. He kept the second letter and took it out occasionally to add a few offensive embellishments, knowing by then that he would never send it.

By December the hospital staff had decided that he might as well be discharged, since there was really nothing more they could do for him. They realized that he had no will to live, much less any will to work or participate in any form of social activity; but at least they felt there was no danger of his trying to take his own life. He was too inert for that. Then they all had to face the problem of where he was to go. There was no question of his living alone, and the cottage had been given up long ago.

Sheila was willing to have him at home, but he refused to hear of anything of the sort, and his frequent refusal to speak to her made it evident that there was nothing to be hoped for along these lines. In the end it was decided that he would go and stay with his parents for an indefinite period, till he got himself sorted out.

Georgina and Michael were convinced that this was the best solution to the problem, and were happy to think that they might now be in a position to do something for their unfortunate son, having felt very helpless and inadequate so far. But there were difficulties, and these made them feel rather apprehensive as they sat in the large, comfortable flat, awaiting the arrival of Alan and Melville. The major difficulty lay in Alan's state of mind. They realized his mental state was still far from normal, and wondered whether they would have the skill and the patience to deal with the situation.

The other difficulty was, as it were, the other side of the same coin. For they had to admit that, for a number of reasons, they were not the most suitable of parents to be tackling this sort of problem. Their age for one thing. They just got tired easily, especially with any change of routine – and what a change this would be! And their patience too, they agreed, was more easily exhausted than it had been in their youth – and even then patience had certainly not been Michael's strong point.

As they talked over the impending visit they tried to prepare themselves for whatever trials lay ahead.

'The truth is, my dear,' said Georgina, 'I think we've become a little inflexible in our old age. We must learn to bend a bit more.'

'I'm prepared to bend over backwards, if it's going to help Alan. Only, I suspect I'm not going to be very good at it.'

'Lack of practice, perhaps?' suggested his wife with a smile.

'Probably. I'm afraid I might just lose my balance.'

'Well, we'll just have to try, and keep on trying.'

'The trouble is,' said Michael, 'one doesn't quite know

what to expect. I suppose a certain amount of unreasonable behaviour would be on the cards. And it's something we're not used to coping with. At least, not in the home.'

'That's right, dear. Alan always was so reasonable, even as a child.'

'Yes, he always conformed. That made it so easy for us. It hadn't occurred to me before, but now I wonder whether perhaps he conformed just a little too much. For his own good, I mean.'

'Oh, I don't know,' said Georgina. 'All we did was try to set him a good example.'

'Nothing wrong with that, is there? Well, my dear,' and he patted his wife on the shoulder, 'we'll just have to take things as they come.'

They stood at the window, looking out with a certain amount of apprehension. For they were not particularly good at taking things as they came. And they shared the fear of any form of mental illness which their generation tended to set down as insanity. And so they stood there waiting, two frail, troubled, elderly people, ready to tax their strength to the utmost, screwing up their courage to the sticking place, for the sake of their unhappy son.

In the event, things turned out to be less frightening than they had feared, but more tiring and more depressing. Simply having another person about the house all the time, no matter who, was a great strain. Alan was no bother. He even helped in some of the minor household chores. The problem was his gloom, which spread over the whole family like a dark cloud. It was almost palpable. They tried again and again to find something in which they could arouse his interest. Alan listened politely, answered briefly, and remained untouched. The weather didn't help. It was cold, wet and windy most of the time, and Alan sat in the flat, inert, day after day.

Only during Melville's visits did he show any signs of life.

And Melville, for the sake of the parents as well as for Alan, came as often as he could. He saw with increasing worry the signs of strain on the elderly couple. It wasn't till the beginning of spring that things started to improve a little. With the better weather Alan took to going out for walks in the parks.

'They're too well kept,' he would say on getting back. 'Hardly a weed to be seen.' At first his parents took this to be irony on his part. Gradually they began to realize that Alan's interest in wild flowers was far greater than his desire to see a well kept lawn or an orderly herbaceous border. Seeing that he was unlikely to do anything about it himself, Georgina went to the public library and came back with a selection of books on wild flowers. Michael went to a bookshop and came back with two beautifully illustrated volumes.

When next Melville came he found Alan poring over one of these. 'That's the sort of thing Lisha does,' he exclaimed. 'She's very good. My sister does this sort of illustration,' he explained to Alan's parents. 'She used to do it as a hobby, but she's doing it on a professional basis now, and enjoying it thoroughly. Come to think of it, she's to spend a week with me here at Easter. Perhaps I can bring her over and she and Alan can get together on the subject . . . '

Alan looked up with a spark of interest in his eyes. 'Lisha?' he said. 'Haven't seen her in years. Bring her over.'

Melville had every intention of doing so. He remembered how well Alan and Lisha had got on in the past; and if talking about wild flowers was the way to cheer Alan up, Lisha was just the person to do it. Besides, another idea was beginning to stir in his mind.

That evening he phoned Lisha at her cottage. She consulted her parents and then phoned back. They all agreed that Alan should be persuaded to go back to Auchentoull with Lisha after her week in London. Galloway in April was a paradise of wild flowers, and Lisha was a tonic in herself, quite apart from the liking that Alan had always shown for her. And it would be a respite for the two flagging parents. As for his parents, he felt no scruples at all in saddling them with this sort of an invalid. Like Lisha, they seemed to collect lame dogs and thrive on restoring them to health.

When he went back to the Morleys' the following evening and told them his plan he was delighted to see that Alan obviously approved of the idea, while both parents beamed with gratitude and relief.

'You're sure it won't be an imposition on your parents, especially your mother?' queried Georgina.

'Oh no, not at all. They've no one but my two younger brothers left at home, and a deaf French student – oh, and a budding geologist son of a friend or something. No trouble at all.'

Georgina was horrified. 'But how can your mother be expected to cope with all those people! And to think of adding another!'

Melville and Alan looked at each other and burst out laughing. 'You'd better tell her about the head counting operation, Melville.'

'Head counting?'

'Yes, before meals,' Melville explained. 'When we were all at home in the old days, and we all had friends staying or dropping in, we had to send a scout round the house and garden to count heads before every meal. Just to have an approximate idea of how many to expect.'

Georgina shook her head almost in disbelief. 'Your mother must be a wonderful woman, Melville. It makes me feel quite ashamed.'

Melville laughed. 'Oh well, not everyone wants a houseful of savages. You live a more civilized life here.'

Lisha spent two evenings with them during her stay in London, so that by the time she and Alan left they had got used to each other's company again, and Alan set off in something nearer to high spirits than he had felt for nearly a year. When he said goodbye to his parents he wanted to tell them how well they had done, how much he knew his stay had wearied and worried them, and how much he appreciated it all.

But there was something inside him that still kept all expressions of emotion locked up. It was as if his conviction of his own unworthiness hindered him from doing any of the things that could have earned him praise. To allow that would have been sheer hypocrisy. And so he left, giving his mother a perfunctory peck on the cheek and a 'Thanks, Mother,' mumbled as he turned toward his father to shake his hand.

After he had gone the two old people turned towards each other and gave a sigh, half relief, half regret.

'I know it's only ten o'clock in the morning,' said Georgina, 'but I think I'll go to bed for an hour or two, just to . . . to . . . '

'To celebrate our freedom,' finished off her husband. 'And I think I'll just have a little rest on the couch. Then we can get back into our own routine.'

'Yes,' she agreed, 'it will be nice. And restful. I sometimes wonder how we've got through it so far. Wouldn't it be nice . . . '

'If he didn't come back?'

'Well, if something else more suitable turned up for him.'

After a pause she added:

'I do hope he'll be all right in that wild place.' Her knowledge of Galloway consisted chiefly of memories of reading Crockett's *The Raiders* as a child.

'Of course he'll be all right. The Wilsons seem excellent

people. And don't forget that the father's a doctor. And you know how much we all think of Melville, and his sister seems just as nice.'

'Yes, she does. A nice, motherly sort of a girl, if that's not a contradiction in terms.'

38

As they made for the motorway Lisha said:

'By the way, I had a bright idea last night and phoned a friend of mine in Yorkshire. We're to spend the night there, so we can take our time about the journey. That all right?'

'Anywhere you say. Except Manchester and its environs.'

'Don't worry, we won't go near Manchester. I spent a day or two there last summer and I can't say I cared for it.'

As soon as they had got past the London area they left the motorway and wandered about in a vaguely northerly direction, keeping to the quieter roads. In the afternoon they stopped at a little market town for a cup of tea before tackling the last lap of the day's journey. They went into a self-service café and Alan impressed Lisha and himself by insisting on her sitting down while he went to the counter. He came back with a tray, placed the cups on the table and then took the tray back to the counter before sitting down opposite Lisha.

'There,' he said, 'that was quite an achievement. The first time I've done anything of the kind for many months.'

'Splendid,' said Lisha. 'I see the change is doing you good already.'

'I think it's you. You're a health-giving sort of person. Did you know?'

'I hadn't thought about it,' she admitted. 'But that may have something to do with what the family call my passion for lame dogs. Which, as you know, runs in the family anyway.'

'Well, this dog is feeling distinctly less lame, at any rate. By the way,' he added, 'who is this friend we're going to stay with? Anyone I know?'

Lisha shook her head. 'No. It's a man I met many years ago. We were lovers for a long time. Then we drifted apart, and last summer we came together again. But that's over now.'

'Drifted apart again?'

'No, not quite. It was a decision we took together. Incompatible life styles, I think. You see, he's really a solitary and I'm a gregarious sort of person. So he's gone off to meditate and philosophize in his Yorkshire wilds once again. Only he's not quite alone this time. There's a friend with him.'

'Someone you know?'

'Yes. Only just. I met him once. In jail,' she added, looking up with a mischievous gleam in her eyes, eager to see Alan's reaction.

'Didn't know you'd done time,' was his reply.

She laughed. 'Playing it cool, aren't you? I thought I'd shock you. Anyway, it was Andrew, Peter's friend, not me, that was in jail. Peter had promised to go and see him but he couldn't because he'd been injured in a road accident. So I went instead.'

The words 'road accident' induced a slight feeling of unease in Alan. He turned his thoughts back to Lisha's friends and their problems.

'And why was Andrew in jail and Peter in hospital?' Not sure about that verb, he thought. Should it be plural? He couldn't quite make up his mind, but felt pleased that this sort of consideration was again occupying his mind. I must be getting better, he thought.

'Andrew was in jail because he had stolen some money and Peter was in hospital, with multiple injuries, because he'd been knocked down by a car. A hit and run affair.'

Alan's heart seemed to stop beating. Multiple injuries,

242

hit and run, the name Peter. How far could coincidence stretch? One more question, he told himself, I'll ask one more question, and if it doesn't fit the case I'll know it was just one of those grotesque coincidences, nothing more. He was about to ask her where this had happened, when he remembered she had said she had been in Manchester once – did she say last summer? That just about clinches it, he thought. But still . . . Hoping against hope he asked his last question.

'When was this?'

'Early last summer. May, in fact. I remember now, the hawthorn was in bloom.'

Without saying a word Alan stood up and began walking towards the door.

'Hey, wait a minute. I haven't finished my tea,' Lisha called out.

Alan ignored her and walked on. Suddenly alarmed, Lisha stood up, grabbed her handbag and followed Alan. She reached the door just after Alan had gone out. The door swung back violently and nearly knocked her down.

When she got out he was standing by the side of the pavement, apparently waiting to cross. An enormous lorry was approaching rather fast. When it was just a couple of yards away Alan stepped out into the street. Lisha got there just in time to grab his arm and pull him back, while the lorry swerved violently and drew up with a screech of brakes. Alan was standing on the road, with his face buried in his hands, when a stream of abuse of the most obscene nature made itself heard. It came from the small, wiry man who had just jumped out of the lorry. In spite of her distress Lisha noticed that there seemed to be a ridiculous lack of proportion between the enormous lorry and its tiny driver.

She turned to the man entreatingly. 'Please, he's ill. Can't you see he's ill?'

The flow of obscenities stopped at once. 'Sorry, missis. Can I do anything?'

'You can help me get him back to the car. Over there.'

Between them they half dragged Alan to the car and got him in. Lisha then thanked the driver, got into the driver's seat and drove off in such a hurry that she forgot all about seat belts. A small crowd had already gathered and she was anxious to get Alan away from the scene.

As soon as they were well clear of the town she drew up in a lay-by. Alan was sitting as if turned to stone. He neither spoke nor moved when the car stopped. Lisha turned half round in her seat, resting one arm on the wheel, to face him.

'What is it, Alan? Please tell me what's wrong. Is it something I said? Please, please tell me.'

'If I tell you you'll be sorry. It's something you could never forgive.'

'I can't think of anything I could never forgive. Least of all from you. I know you're not capable of doing anything dreadful. Please tell me.'

'You don't know what I'm capable of doing. Or rather, of not doing.'

'I don't know what you mean.'

'I'll tell you, then. I'm capable of knocking down a man and not stopping. Is that clear enough?'

Lisha was staring at him, appalled, as if paralysed. Alan couldn't look at her, and kept his eyes fixed on the dashboard. Suddenly Lisha snapped out of her state of shock. 'Oh, my poor Alan,' she cried, flinging her arms round him, drawing him to her, cradling him, rocking him gently while she murmured, 'My poor, poor Alan.'

After a while he was able to tell her the whole story – the terrible state he had been in before the accident, his panic, the interminable night he had spent not knowing whether he had killed his victim, the phone call to the hospital the following morning.

'Wait a minute,' said Lisha at this point. 'The nurses told Peter that someone had phoned to ask how he was. They said he gave his name as Lord Jim. Was that you?'

'Yes, of course. Lord Jim in person, that's me.'

'I'm sorry, I don't understand the reference. I know it's a novel by Conrad, because we've got it on one of our book-shelves at home, but I've never read it. Who was Lord Jim?'

'He was a splendid young man who kept dreaming of doing great things, but when the moment of crisis came he did the cowardly thing, and ruined his life. Well, that's me all over. Whenever the big moment comes, I do the wrong thing. And this was the biggest moment of them all and I did the wrong thing and I ruined my life. That's it.'

'No,' she said, 'that's not it at all. Your life isn't ruined unless you want it to be. I know what I'm talking about. I'll tell you about it later. But now we'd better get on. Peter will be expecting us any minute.'

'I'm not going there!' exclaimed Alan. 'That's the one place in the world I can never go to. Can't you see that?'

'That's the one place in the world you *must* go to. Can't *you* see that? It's as if providence had sent me specially to take you to Peter.'

'The good old divinity shaping our ends, you mean? I don't see that meeting this man is going to help matters.'

'Yes it can. It's a chance to blot out your previous failure.'

'Nothing can blot that out.'

'Running away from the meeting won't help, anyway. It's just adding another failure to the list.'

Alan saw he would have to change tactics. 'Besides, can you think what sort of a reception I'll get, once your friend knows who I am?'

'He'll be all right about it. I promise you.'

'Oh, Lisha! Don't be absurd. Who could forgive such an action? It would take a saint.'

Lisha considered the matter. 'Well, I wouldn't claim saint-hood for him. But perhaps he's getting a bit nearer to it than most of us. At least, I think he's trying for something of the sort. But anyway, saint or not, he really doesn't feel he owes you a grudge. In fact, I remember teasing him once, saying we'd have to put up a monument to the Unknown Motorist, because he said the accident had simplified a lot of things for him. And also, it had brought us together again, for he sent for me when he was in hospital. I'm sure, I'm utterly sure that he doesn't hold anything against you now.'

'Well, even so, if we go there and tell him who I am – and I can't go and not tell him – it may revive all sorts of unpleasant memories for him. I don't really think we can risk it.'

'That's very considerate of you. But it does also tie in rather well with your desire to get out of the whole thing, doesn't it? And I'm quite convinced that the most important thing is that this is a chance for you to get things straightened out. And without that you'll never be healed. Can't you see that? Can't you see you're being given the chance once again, the chance to do the right thing, and this time it's without the shock and horror of the accident. You had an excuse for failing then. You'll have no excuse if you run away now.'

Alan sat silent, and Lisha returned to the attack:

'Look, if you're really worried about the effect this may have on Peter, and on the reception you'll get, I'll tell you what we can do. When we get there you stay in the car and I'll speak to Peter. If I'm wrong, if it's going to be difficult, I'll come back to the car and we'll drive away and spend the night somewhere else. How will that do?'

In the end she persuaded him, and some time later the car drove up the drive and stopped in front of the door. Peter and Andrew were sitting on the steps waiting for them. Lisha jumped out of the car and ran to greet Peter with a hasty kiss. Then she shook hands with Andrew.

'Peter,' she said, 'I've got to speak to you urgently, in the house.' Then she turned to Andrew. 'Could you please keep an eye on my friend? If he shows any signs of wanting to get out of the car, call us at once. I'll explain later.'   'What's all the melodrama about?' asked Peter as soon as they were in the house.

Lisha sat down, suddenly weak with the strain of recent events. 'You simply won't believe this. My friend Alan, in the car. Guess, just guess who he is.'

'I'm mystified,' Peter confessed. 'The Lord Chancellor? Elton John?'

'He's the Unknown Motorist.'

'You mean . . . you mean that's the bugger that knocked me down and didn't even stop?'

'Oh, Peter, I didn't think you'd take it like this!'

Seeing her distressed expression Peter suddenly burst into a roar of laughter. 'Well, I'll be blowed!' he exclaimed. 'You really are the most extraordinary person.'

'Me? What's it got to do with me?'

'Well, it's you who's brought him, isn't it?'

'Yes, but I didn't know. I've only just found out.This afternoon. And I had to bring him here, for his sake. It's his one chance of . . . of laying the ghost. He's been through hell, Peter. He was ill when the accident happened, and he's still very ill.'

'So what do you want me to do? Go out there and congratulate him?'

Lisha was staring at him in dismay. 'Honestly, Peter, I didn't think you'd react like this. I certainly didn't expect a sneer. I thought you'd show a little more understanding. Perhaps it was naive of me.' Her voice sounded very near to tears.

Peter softened. He knelt beside her and took her hands in his. 'Lisha, my dear, sweet, naive Lisha. So competent and independent and yet naive at the same time. And you were right, of course. I'm going to take it very well, wonderfully well. I'm sorry I was such a bear. It was a bit of a shock, and it brought back a lot of unpleasant memories. But that's over. Come on, let's go out and be nice to this poor devil. And why, by the way, did you ask Andrew to keep an eye on him? In case he runs away from the encounter?'

'Worse than that. He tried to throw himself under a lorry when he discovered whose house we were coming to.'

They got up and went out. Andrew was still sitting on the steps, whistling. Alan was in the car, still staring fixedly ahead. Peter walked up to the car and opened the door, holding out his hand.

'Hello, Alan,' he said. 'We've met before, sort of, but not socially. Come on in. Oh, and this is Andrew. Let's all go in and have a drink.'

Peter took the first opportunity to ask Lisha not to tell Andrew the whole story. 'I think his reaction might be a bit like my initial one, only more so. He seems to think he's my mastiff, or something.'

So Andrew was told that Alan had been very ill, and was still inclined to display a suicidal tendency if upset, and Andrew, although he was a good ten years younger than Alan, kept a fatherly eye on him for the rest of the evening.

They all felt a slight sense of unreality in the gathering. All except Andrew knew that there was some serious talking to be done, and this put them under a bit of a strain. Alan felt it so strongly that soon after the meal was over he said he thought he'd better go to bed. 'I've not done much travelling lately,' he explained, 'and I tire easily.'

'I'll come up in a little while and say good night,' said Lisha. A few minutes later she got up and said she was going to see Alan. 'I don't like leaving him alone too long,' she explained.

'Well then, what about during the night?' asked Andrew. 'Shouldn't someone stay with him?'

'I'll see to that,' replied Lisha, and left the room.

Andrew turned to Peter in astonishment. 'Does she mean she's going to . . . ?'

'Yes, that's what she means.'

'But I thought . . . I thought you and she . . . I mean weren't you . . . ?'

'Yes, we were. But that's past. Now it's her and him. You see, I'm all right now, and he isn't.'

'I see.' Andrew thought for a moment. Then he looked up with a speculative gleam in his eye. 'I say,' he said, 'what do you have to do to qualify?'

Peter laughed. 'Now, don't you get any ideas. Besides, you've a letter to write tonight, remember? To the Governor of H.M. Prison, telling him we've just got the sawmill set up, so he can look out for any likely lad to be discharged in the near future.'

'Never thought I'd look forward to writing a letter,' said Andrew, as he sat down with paper and pen.

39

Alan was lying in bed, looking at the pattern the lamp-shade made on the ceiling, trying to concentrate on that to keep himself from plunging once again into his earlier panic, when Lisha came in. She was wearing a long pale grey dressing gown that fell from her shoulders in gentle folds.

'Very classical,' said Alan. 'You look like a Greek goddess.'

'Let's hope it's Minerva,' she replied.

'Why Minerva? I'd have thought Juno was more like it.'

'It's Minerva I need, to give me the wisdom for what I've got to say.'

'You're going to tell me everything's all right now, aren't you? The fairy has waved her magic wand, Peter has been nice to me, and I can now forget about the whole miserable business.'

Lisha sat down at the foot of the bed.

'I'm simply going to tell you that your life needn't be ruined unless you want it to be.'

Alan was giving the pattern on the ceiling his full attention.

After a while he said:

'Nothing has changed. There's really nothing to talk about.'

'A lot has changed.'

'Nothing that matters.'

'Oh, Alan, how can you say that? Two very important

things have changed. First of all, you know Peter is all right. He's none the worse for the accident.'

'Has he always had a limp?'

'No, but it's very much better than it was. Soon it will be completely gone. And the other thing that's changed is that you know he doesn't bear you a grudge. Surely that's important too?'

'Yes, it's important, both things are important, especially for him.'

'But not for you?'

'Only superficially. Neither of these facts does anything to alter the real, unchangeable problem.'

'Which is?'

'That I'm the man who injured another and didn't even stop to try and help. How did I know he wasn't going to bleed to death before help arrived?'

'Well, he didn't, did he?'

'Lisha, for goodness's sake stop being so bloody pragmatic. So all that counts is the result, is it? It's a splendid way of shaking off responsibility.'

'No, that's not what I'm saying at all. You were responsible for what you did, or rather, what you didn't do. That doesn't mean you have to stick with it for the rest of your life. You have a choice, you always have a choice. You can either go on wallowing in your guilt, or you can decide you're going to put the whole thing behind you and move on. It would be a pity if you chose to stick at one of the lowest points in your life.'

'If I chose . . . As if one had a choice. I can't *not* be the man who ran away from his crime.'

'No, but you don't need to spend the rest of your life looking at it.' She took hold of his hand and held it in hers. 'I know what I'm talking about when I say you can put this behind you. You remember that I was once nearly engaged to the young man who died in a climbing accident?'

Alan nodded. 'Yes, I was sorry to hear about that.'

'Well, I was, to a certain extent, responsible for his death.'

'But I heard that you didn't even go on that climb!'

'Precisely. If I had gone, the accident wouldn't have happened. They only did that particular climb because I ratted at the last minute. As I was a beginner they always did easier climbs when I was with them. But that day I took fright and got out of it – and in a rather feeble, shameful manner into the bargain. And as a result they did this other climb and he died.'

'But that's not the same at all. You couldn't possibly have known that he would die as a result.'

'I'm not saying it's an exact parallel. The point is that I was left with the memory of a failure on my part that had resulted in Frank's death. And death is a lot more final than injury. So you see, I had quite a weight of guilt to bear.'

Alan nodded.

'And after that,' she continued, 'I had the choice: either to go on blaming myself for the rest of my life, or to forgive myself and try to piece my life together again.'

'And a great success you've made of it. But then, your life has been one long series of successes. Mine a long series of failures.'

'I've had my failures too, just like anyone else. The first time Peter and I broke up, for instance. And then Frank's death. And my work in the museum wasn't exactly a success. I never got the promotion I hoped for.'

'Was that why you gave it up?'

'That was why. I could have gone on, feeling undervalued and frustrated for the rest of my working life. Instead I tried something else, and it's all worked out wonderfully well. I enjoy my present work far more, and I feel I'm really getting somewhere. But, as you see I've had my failures too. You haven't got a monopoly, you know.'

'Perhaps not. But I think I've got more, and more serious failures to my credit than most people. My marriage, my job, my writing, which has never even got off the ground, and . . . and other things. And then this thing, the worst of them all.'

'Tomorrow,' she said, 'tomorrow you can make a fresh start. Tomorrow you can put all these failures behind you.'

'It's too much, Lisha. Nearly forty years of failures.'

'But you've had successes too. You got a first at Cambridge. And I gather you had quite a number of other successes at Cambridge.'

Alan smiled. 'All those girls, you mean? That was a long time ago.'

'And do you mean to say you've had no more successes of the kind since then?'

'I've been leading a very respectable life since then. Except, that is,' he added, 'for the Pink Jellyfish. And that ended in failure too.'

Lisha stood up. 'Alan,' she said, 'I don't want to hear the word 'failure' again. Not tonight, at any rate. And there's only one way I can think of that will stop you.'

She unfastened her dressing gown, then slipped it off and laid it on the chair beside the bed. Then she leaned over and lifted the bedclothes.

'Move over,' she said.

40

Peter spent a restless night. There were two things worrying him. The awareness that, a couple of rooms away, Lisha was spending the night with Alan disturbed him more than he would have thought possible; and the recollection of how he had reacted on hearing that the man responsible for the accident was under his roof also caused him a good deal of mental discomfort. He remembered the anger, resentment and scorn he had felt during his first days in hospital, and the sudden resurgence of these emotions had definitely taken him aback. For Lisha's sake he had tried to master his feelings that evening, but he wasn't at all sure that the friendliness he had shown to Alan was genuine. He had thought he had overcome these negative feelings long ago. Now it seemed that all that had happened was that they had lain dormant, and still had to be faced.

As for his feelings about Lisha and Alan, probably asleep in each other's arms by now, he kept telling himself that he had no right to have any objections or to feel any jealousy. After all, he and Lisha had agreed that their affair was over. She was therefore free to sleep with anyone she liked. It was none of his business. But it did seem a peculiar twist of fate that she should have chosen the very man who had behaved so disgracefully to him.

And in his own house, too.

In anyone but Lisha he would have thought it was a case of

deliberate provocation. With Lisha, of course, that was out of the question. She was too straightforward for that, too honest, too delightfully yet maddeningly naive. What does she take me for, he thought angrily, a bloody saint?

These thoughts kept churning over in his mind, till he was afraid he wouldn't be able to face his guests at breakfast without showing something of what he really felt. And yet he knew he had no right to do anything of the kind. He had agreed, willingly and spontaneously, that he and Lisha should go their separate ways; and he had assured her that he no longer had any hard feelings towards Alan.

Shortly before dawn he got up and dressed, and slipped quietly out of the house. He had a great longing to be out alone on the moors, watching the dawn coming up over the hills. He walked along the deserted road till the light was strong enough for him to strike out across the moor. As he walked his anger and jealousy and resentment began to fade and he was able to examine the situation more clearly. What, after all, did he want?

Did he really want to go back to the old relationship with Lisha?

Much as he loved her, he had come to see her as a stumbling block in his life. His true path he felt sure, lay in a sterner landscape than Lisha inhabited. Life with Lisha was delightful, and stimulating, and eminently human. But it was easy, too easy. It lacked the spiritual challenge that he had, belatedly, come to recognize as an indispensable element in his life.

As he walked, still trying to find out what he really wanted, he cast his mind back to the different periods in his life, trying to see whether he could find any consistent pattern, any indication of the direction his life was taking as a whole. First a reasonably happy childhood, then his studies and the start of his career, which he had enjoyed during the first years.

A marriage which had at no time fulfilled him, but which had seemed tolerable, till its sudden ending when Susan ran off with the Italian scholar.

Then Lisha, and his increasing disillusion with his work, and the retreat to the family home after his father's death. And it was some time after settling in Yorkshire that he had realized he had truly lost his way. He had become a hermit without a vocation. It was then, when the two little girls had run away from 'the hermit' that he had reached his nadir. After that, especially during the first months of his wanderings, life had been hard, but it had acquired a new quality that made the hardness bearable. He now had a sense of purpose. He was on his way back to humanity. And he had been helped by Andrew, and by Lisha and her family. And if it hadn't been for the accident, he told himself, his path and Lisha's might never have crossed again.

When his thoughts reached this point he gave a sigh of satisfaction and, turning his back on the sunrise, began walking back to the house. With this clearer perspective of the link between his life and Lisha's he was able to accept her new relationship with Alan. And the memory of the part Alan had played, however unwittingly, in bringing him and Lisha together was enough to allow him to forget his anger. The evil Alan had done him had brought with it a far greater good. The accident had given him back the help and comfort of Lisha's company, but he needed this no longer. He had got back on to the path he had first glimpsed in his discovery of *The Meditations*. The severed branch was learning to grow back and become one with its neighbour again.

Soon the sawmill would be in operation ready for the first of the young offenders. He and Andrew had a job to do.

Making love with Lisha had been such a dream-like experience that the following morning Alan could hardly say he had enjoyed it physically. What he was sure of was the immense comfort that the gift of her body had brought him. This was something that went far beyond the physical. He turned over on to his side to get a good view of her profile as she lay sleeping. That seemed to be the best proof that it had actually happened.

Lisha was sleeping very peacefully, and Alan was glad to see her resting so fully, aware that the previous day must have been a trying one for her too. He lay beside her quietly, happy to let her sleep as long as she needed. It was a lovely, peaceful start to a day that he realized had some trials in store for him. Yesterday he had faced the meeting with Peter, and he was thankful that this was over. But he knew some sort of apology or explanation on his part was called for, and wondered how he could go through with that.

Suddenly Lisha opened her eyes and turned towards him with an expression of alarm on her face.

'Oh, you're here,' she exclaimed in a tone of relief.

'Of course I'm here. Where else could I possibly be?'

'I was just afraid you might have . . . '

'Gone off in search of a lorry, you mean?'

'Well, something like that.'

'No chance. Not with you in bed beside me.'

'Lisha', he said after a while, 'why did you do it? Just pity?'

'I told you why. I wanted to stop you going on and on about your failures.'

'I'm sorry. I know I went on and on. But then, you see, I've plenty of material to keep me going in that strain. And you must remember, I was still in shock. First of all, leaving the protecting environment of my parents' home, then the discovery of whose house I was going to and my reaction . . . '

'Which was a shock to both of us,' put in Lisha.

'Yes, I know it was, and I'm sorry. And then being bullied by you into actually meeting Peter. You must admit it was enough to leave anyone feeling pretty feeble.'

'Well, I must admit, for a man in shock, you did rather well last night. That was a pretty good opportunity for failure that you missed out on.'

'You're laughing at me, you wicked woman.'

'No, I'm only teasing.'

Alan gave a great sigh of satisfaction. 'You've no idea how wonderful it is to be considered well enough to be teased. The trouble about being ill, mentally ill, is that everyone takes you so bloody seriously. They're so afraid of hurting your feelings and causing a relapse . . . '

' . . . that you nearly get one through sheer boredom?'

'Exactly. It was like that with my parents. I know they must have suffered dreadfully, poor dears, but I'm sure we'd all have been the better for a good laugh. Thank goodness for Melville. He managed to treat me like a normal human being, even though I know I wasn't.'

'Yes, thank goodness for Melville. I sometimes think his main purpose in life is cheering up other people.'

'He was like that even at university. It seems to be a Wilson characteristic.'

'I don't think we can take too much credit for that. There are times when it can really be very pleasant.' Lisha looked at him with a mischievous smile.

'Like when?' he prompted.

'Like last night.'

'Bless you, Lisha, you really are the most generous person. You manage to give the impression that you are the beneficiary even when it's you who are conferring a favour.'

'How do you know I haven't been lusting after you all my life?'

'That's just not true. What about Peter, and Frank?'

'Yes, I did love them. And I still love Peter very dearly, though not in the same way any longer. But, if we go back to our student days, when you first came to stay with us . . . If you hadn't met Sheila, who knows?'

'Lisha, Lisha,' he groaned 'if you only knew . . . I thought of you as quite inaccessible in those days. But I meant to try, all the same, once I'd got my studies out of the way. And I waited, and then I met Sheila . . . '

' . . . and married her before you'd got your studies out of the way . . . '

' . . . with predictable results. Oh, Lisha, if only I'd been a bit bolder then, if only I'd dared to ask you . . . '

'We would have been married right away and lived happily ever after?'

'Well, why not?'

'Life's not like that, Alan, we'd have had other problems, we'd have *made* other problems.'

'We'd have been too happy to have made problems for ourselves.'

'We'd have made them all the same.'

'Well, I expect *I* would have. I'm good at that. But instead of talking about hypothetical problems, we've got a real one to talk about. I suppose there'll have to be some sort of confrontation between Peter and me. I mean, I can't just go off and not say a thing about the accident. What am I say to him?'

'What do you want to say him?'

'Nothing. I want to run away.'

'Then perhaps we should leave it for some other time.'

'You mean I've got to go on seeing him? Isn't once enough?'

'Well, *I* want to go on seeing him. And I rather hope to go on seeing you, so . . . '

'Well then, we might as well put the thing off, if I'm to go on seeing him all the same, don't you think?'

259

'Let's just play it by ear, shall we?'

'I haven't got a conspicuously good ear. In fact, I have what amounts to quite a talent for making a mess of even the simplest situation.'

'Well, this one isn't all that simple. Perhaps you'll get it right.'

'For once? You never know.'

Andrew slept little that night.

The more he thought about it, the angrier he felt about Lisha's apparent infidelity to Peter. And his anger, naturally, spilled over to include Alan. It was true, Peter appeared to be taking it remarkably well. But then he would, wouldn't he? Any other man would have been fuming. But Peter showed more self-control than most, and Andrew had a great respect for his ability to see someone else's point of view. Hadn't he seen his, Andrew's, and refrained from judging him when most other people would have condemned him?

In Andrew's eyes Peter was above all other men. You'd need to be, to see your girlfriend hop into bed with another man under your very own roof, and show no signs of resentment. And yet, in spite of the cool way Peter had taken things, Andrew was close enough to him to sense a certain tension in Peter as they discussed the letter Andrew was to write. As he lay in bed thinking it all over he came to the conclusion that both Lisha and Alan had behaved shockingly badly, and that Peter must be feeling very hurt. He wished he could think of some way of showing his solidarity with Peter, but could come up with nothing better than a firm intention of being as rude as possible to both guilty parties.

He was in the kitchen preparing breakfast when Peter came back from his walk, and before they could exchange more than a few words Lisha and Alan appeared and greeted the two men. All they got from Andrew in return was a grunt while he bent over the sink. Alan was too concerned with the thought of his possible forthcoming conversation with Peter to pay much attention. Lisha was surprised, but decided Andrew must be one of those people who take a while to get over the angry bear stage in the morning. Peter noticed Andrew's rudeness and guessed the reason but felt he could do nothing about it in the presence of the others. The integration of the whole, he thought, is not without its difficulties.

Breakfast was rather an edgy affair, with everyone except Andrew trying to sound natural and none of them quite succeeding. Lisha tried to draw Andrew out on the subject of the sawmill, but was unable to dent his taciturnity. Peter would have prefered Lisha to be with them when he and Alan discussed the accident, as he knew they must do. But with Andrew in his present aggressive and resentful mood he was afraid to suggest any arrangement that would exclude him from the whole company. He compromised by inviting Alan to go for a walk with him as soon as breakfast was finished. Lisha, anxious on behalf of both of them, was a bit disappointed that she hadn't been included in the invitation.

She was puzzled by Andrew's sudden change of manner, especially to Alan, whom he seemed to have marked out for the greatest share of his rudeness. And yet he had been so protective towards him last night after they had explained about his breakdown and suicide attempt. She didn't know what to make of it, and wondered whether Peter had changed his mind and told Andrew about the accident. Yes, she decided, that was it. This must be the mastiff response Peter had predicted. And the rudeness to her might be because it was she who had brought Alan. Once this explanation of the matter had dawned upon her she felt less irritated by Andrew's attitude, and set about winning him over.

She made several attempts at conversation, all of which were snubbed. She was on the point of walking out of the kitchen, leaving him to get on with the washing-up by himself, when he suddenly rounded on her.

'I suppose you're perfectly happy about what's going on out there with those two, aren't you?'

'Well, yes. It was bound to happen, sooner or later. If things were ever to be cleared up properly that is. So yes, I'm glad they've gone off together.'

'Women!' he exclaimed in tones of the deepest scorn. 'A feather in your cap, that's all. Never mind the outcome.'

'A feather in my cap? Oh well, it's certainly what I've been hoping for, if that's what you mean.'

Andrew gave a grunt of disgust. 'And I thought you were such a nice girl. And here you are putting them up to this sort of thing, and enjoying it. Bitch!'

'I haven't put them up to anything. It's got nothing to do with me.'

'Don't come the little innocent on me. I know perfectly well where you spent the night. You even told us you were going to.'

Lisha opened her mouth to protest, then shut it again. She now realized her mistake, but could do little to clarify matters without referring to the accident, the very thing Peter had begged her not to do. The idea that Andrew thought the two men had gone off to fight over her struck her as very funny, and for a moment she thought she was going to burst out laughing. She could think of no two men less likely to indulge in this type of behaviour than Peter and Alan.

'Look,' she said, 'I think there's been some sort of mis-understanding. Do you think that Peter and Alan have gone off to have a fight?'

'That's obvious, isn't it?'

'Over me?'

'Who else?'

'No, really, it's not that at all. Peter and I agreed months ago that we should go our separate ways, so he can't possibly mind about my sleeping with Alan.'

Andrew's eyebrows rose sceptically. 'Well then, what are they fighting about?'

'They're not fighting. Do you think I'd have let them go off if I'd thought they were going to have a fight? So that's why you called me a bitch!'

Andrew looked slightly sheepish. 'Well, what have they gone off like that for?'

'They've got something to discuss. And I can't really tell you what it is. I've already said it has nothing to do with me. I'm sorry I can't say any more. But they're not going to have a fight, I can promise you that.'

'In that case,' Andrew conceded, 'it looks like I owe you an apology. I see I've got it all wrong.'

'So I'm not a bitch?'

'No. Just a bit . . . insensitive, perhaps.'

'Insensitive! Me?' Lisha was shocked.

'I don't think you realize how a man, any man, even Peter, is bound to feel about your changing partners just like that.'

It was now Lisha's turn to look a bit crestfallen. 'I didn't think of it as changing partners,' she said. 'It was just that I was so worried about Alan and . . . and that seemed the best thing to do.'

'I've no doubt it's a good way to keep a man's mind off suicide,' Andrew admitted. 'But it can lead to complications.'

A truth Lisha felt unable to deny.

41

For the first few minutes of their walk the two men chatted casually about this and that, neither of them paying much attention to what they were saying, each of them concerned with the conversation that was to come, if only they could get it started. Gradually they lapsed into silence. Alan was perfectly clear as to why they were there. He had to make some sort of apology, give some sort of explanation. He knew he owed it to Peter, and he realized that his own self-esteem depended on how he acquitted himself.

For Peter the matter was not quite so clear-cut. He knew that for some time after the accident he would have liked to meet the unknown driver and vent all his anger and outrage on him. But Lisha's reappearance in his life had changed that, and he genuinely thought that all his feelings of resentment had vanished, and been replaced by an amused realization that he owed his new-found happiness to the accident.

At this point he had virtually ceased to think of the matter, and no longer had any desire to meet the culprit. Lisha's announcement of Alan's identity plunged him right back into all his earlier emotions, but he felt he had overcome them during his long walk that morning. Now that he wasn't sure whether he wanted this discussion because he realized how important it was for Alan, or whether there was still inside him some unfinished business to be settled, his doubt made him feel slightly apprehensive. Added to his awareness of Alan's state of extreme anxiety, it made him hesitate about broaching the subject. Alan, he felt sure, would never be able to speak the first words. It's up to me, he thought, and racked his brains for a diplomatic way of getting the conversation going.

So they walked on, in anxious silence, till suddenly Alan stopped and said, 'Do you think we could sit down somewhere? I'm getting a bit breathless.'

'Yes, of course.' Peter looked at his companion and saw that he had turned very pale. 'Look, there's a fallen tree trunk just over there. Can you make it?'

Alan nodded. In a moment they were sitting side by side on the fallen trunk.

'I'm sorry, I forgot you were ill. Lisha told me. In fact,' Peter went on, seizing his chance, 'she said you were ill at the time of the accident. That would account for . . . for quite a lot.'

Alan was sitting on the trunk, with his elbows resting on his knees and his chin in his hands. He looked the very picture of despair and defeat, and showed no signs of taking up the opening he had been given. Peter waited, increasingly aware of the silence and gloom emanating from his companion. It was something almost physical, like a dense pall of smoke or fog. After a moment Peter stood up and walked a few paces away, as if to get clear of the miasma. He turned and looked at Alan, who sat motionless, staring ahead of him. Suddenly he felt a wave of anger rising in him. He moved towards Alan almost threateningly.

'Well, don't just sit there looking like the sacrificial victim. For God's sake man, show a little spirit!'

Alan stood up and faced the other. His face was contorted with fury, his fists clenched. If Lisha and Andrew had seen them at that moment they would have thought all Andrew's fears were justified, and that they were about to attack each other any minute.

'What do you know about it? What do you bloody know about it? All you've had to do is be the victim, the innocent victim. No guilt for you, no nightmare leading up to the situation, nothing, just self-pity, and all the world's sympathy.'

'You seem to be pretty good at the self-pity bit too, if it comes to that. And as for sympathy, it seems to me you got quite a lot of that last night.'

'You leave Lisha out of this. You know nothing about her motives.'

'I know quite a lot about her reactions. If it hadn't been for your melodramatic suicide attempt she would never have thought of spending the night with you.'

And if Andrew and Lisha could have heard what was going on up on the hill they would have come to the conclusion that the quarrel was about Lisha after all.

'Leave her out of this, I said.'

'We can't leave her out. She's the one link between us. Well, apart from the accident, that is.'

'And you won't let me forget about that, will you?'

Peter sighed with exasperation. 'Look, I could forget about it quite easily. I nearly had till you turned up. For me it's past. I can let it go. It's you that can't.'

'I've no right to. It's something I've got to live with.'

'Till you do something about it.'

'Like what?'

'Like facing it, and then putting it behind you.'

'You sound like Lisha.'

'You see,' said Peter smiling, 'we can't really leave her out of it. Look, let's sit down again. I want to tell you a story.'

They sat down and Alan resumed his defeated attitude.

'I'm not good as a raconteur, I'm afraid,' said Peter. 'I can only tell you the bare bones of the story, with no embellishments. It's about two monks, two Buddhist monks, walking along the road. They come to a river, and there's a girl standing at the ford, afraid to cross in case she gets her clothes wet. The younger monk picks her up and carries her across, to the horror of the older one, who continues the journey muttering and mumbling about this unholy action. At last the younger one turns to him and says, "Are you still carrying that girl? I put her down at the ford." Not a brilliant piece of story-telling, I'm afraid, but I think the message is quite clear. You've got to put the girl down.'

'I can't. To continue your metaphor, she won't let go.'

Peter sighed. 'Look,' he said after a while, 'earlier on you said you had no right to put the thing behind you. That is, you feel you have a moral obligation to go on making your own life miserable. And yet you've just said that you can't put the girl down because she won't let go. Which is it?'

'Both. I can't put this experience behind me, and even if I could I mustn't, because it would be wrong. It would be like pretending to be someone I'm not.'

'You don't believe people evolve?'

'No, I suppose not. Not that much.'

'So you've always been the sort of rotter that knocks a man down and doesn't even stop to see whether he's alive or dead?'

Alan looked up, startled.

Peter continued. 'Because, if you have, I don't see why you're worrying about the moral issues. And if you haven't, then you have to admit that human beings are capable of change. Or do you think we're only capable of change for the worse? And if so, on what grounds do you hold this uncomfortable belief?'

'I can't answer all this. I'm not a philosopher. My interests are hardly metaphysical.'

'What are they, then?'

'Well, lately I've become very interested in the world of nature, especially wild flowers. But all my life the main thing has been literature. I like books. I've always wanted to write. I'm at home with books. My wife complains that I'm more concerned with the characters I read about than with real people.'

'Lord Jim, and such?'

'Oh, you know that? Did Lisha tell you?'

'No, the nurses at the hospital. That was your pseudonym when you phoned to find out how seriously I'd been injured, wasn't it?

Alan nodded.

Peter went on. 'You know, even then – when I knew nothing at all about you – it made me wonder.'

'Wonder what?'

'Whether this Lord Jim idea was perhaps a sort of habitual attitude of the Unknown Motorist. Whether he was perhaps inclined to shelter behind this label.'

During the silence that followed Peter decided that this was perhaps the moment for shock tactics.

'Why did you run away?' he asked. 'Why didn't you stop when you hit me?'

Alan's answer came right away, before he'd had time to think. 'Panic,' he said.

'Do you always panic when things go wrong?'

This time there was some hesitation. 'No, probably not always. But I do have a gift for doing and saying the wrong thing, for letting myself down, if you like. I call it the Lord Jim complex. And perhaps you're right, perhaps I do shelter behind this label. A sort of "I'm Lord Jim" thing, so this is how I've got to behave. I suppose that does lead to a tendency to give up and panic. Nothing else has ever gone so violently and dramatically wrong, but I've certainly had a number of minor panics.' Suddenly he looked up and laughed. 'Like when I hid in a cupboard in my own house when I heard my wife coming in.'

'And why did you do that?'

'Well, it was just before the accident. That was one of the reasons why I was so unstrung, by the way, why I nearly missed my turning. Anyway, why was I hiding in the cupboard? I'll tell you, only I don't quite know where to start. Where does a circumstance begin? Incidentally, that's one of the problems I found in trying to write – how far back do you go before you can get started? And before we can make sense of the cupboard episode I suppose we have to go right back to my undergraduate days. I had the misfortune to get a First at Cambridge. If it hadn't been for that I suppose I'd have had a less inflated idea of my abilities. I wanted to write and I wanted a university job to live on. But I didn't make it. All I could rise to was a technical college. And I married the wrong woman . . . '

'Who doesn't?' put in Peter quietly.

Alan went on, trying to paint a reasonably accurate account of his life and the circumstances that led up to the accident – Scratchley's appointment, the cottage, Rachel, the discovery of Sheila's writing . . .

When he came to the bit about the cupboard he said:

'You can laugh if you like. It was a real sitcom piece of clowning, one of my best efforts. There I was hiding in the cupboard, waiting for my wife and the girls to go out so that I could sneak away and I fell asleep, and I was having a dream about that bloody Rachel woman, and she turned into a huge pink jellyfish that was smothering me, and I woke up with a yell that must have put the fear of death into them, and there they were, all four of them neatly disposed on the stairs, wanting to know what I was doing in the cupboard.'

'What did you say?'

'God knows. I was hardly rational by that time. All I know is that I pushed past them and got into the car and drove away. I was looking for a cliff to drive off, but I couldn't think of where to find one. And I had the most appalling headache. So I decided to go home – back to the cottage, that is – and have a rest and then look out a map. I really did want to kill myself. And instead I nearly killed you.'

'Can you remember what you felt, after you got the car under control and drove off?'

'Shock, horror, panic . . . The thing that shook me most was that I hadn't stopped automatically. Funny how you've got to go through something yourself before you really know what it's like. I'd always thought that hit-and-run drivers were utterly unspeakable. The scum of the earth. And suddenly I'd turned into one of them myself. It's the speed with which it happens that really gets you. You've no time to make any decisions. It just happens. Before you know where you are, that's it. You're one of them, a hit-and-run driver, one of the scum the earth. At the moment of the accident all you're guilty of is bad, no, dangerous, driving. And then, seconds later – it only takes seconds – it's turned into something quite different, and it's going to take ten times as much courage to turn and go back. And if I hadn't even had enough courage in the first place to stop right away and see . . . God knows what I might have seen, a mangled corpse, God knows . . . So how could I go back and face it all, the mangled corpse and the consequences of not having stopped in the first place . . . '

'That first night, before you phoned the hospital and found out that I was mangled, but not a corpse, how did you get through that?'

'Thinking I'd got murder on my hands?'

'Hardly murder. Manslaughter, I think would have been the verdict.'

'Yes, I suppose so. I think that the only thing that got me through that night was the need to make plans. I had to phone Sheila in the morning to make sure she didn't bring the girls over as usual on a Saturday, and then I had to read through the local paper till I found what I was looking for. After that at least I knew I hadn't killed you outright. But you might have died after getting into hospital. So I had to phone.

'After that I thought all I had to do was lie down and die. It shows how deranged I must have been. I really thought all I had to do was go to bed and wait for death. And two days later Sheila and bloody Scratchley came and dragged me out. And I've refused to have anything to do with Sheila ever since. I could never forgive her for not letting me die.'

'But you wouldn't have died anyway, would you? Someone else would surely have found you before you starved to death, if that was your intention.'

'I don't know that I had any such concrete intention, not at that point. Once I was in hospital, yes. That's what I was trying to do, only they won't let you. Back in the cottage I think it was just an ardent desire for death. I was convinced that death was on its way. And then Sheila came and spoilt it all.'

'How long did it take you to forgive her?'

Alan thought for a moment, then said:

'Till last night, I suppose. Yes, I think that till last night I really wanted to die, more than anything else. I had nothing to live for, and too much to live with. I still had that bloody hedge in front of me all the time.'

'She's got a great instinct, Lisha has. She's given you something to live for. And rather less to live with, now you've spoken about it.'

Alan nodded. 'You know,' he said, 'I'm beginning to think that perhaps I can let that girl go after all – the one at the ford.'

'She's not holding on quite so tight?'

'I don't think she's holding on at all now.'

'In that case it's up to you, isn't it? Come on, we'd better get back. The others will think we've got lost.'

As they approached the house they saw the other two coming to meet them. They had been away so long that even Lisha was beginning to wonder whether she'd been over-optimistic in assuring Andrew that there was no question of a quarrel between the two men.

'Where on earth have you been?' Andrew asked rather querulously as they approached.

'Oh, just walking,' Peter said airily. 'We got quite far, didn't we, Alan?'

'Yes, quite a long way,' Alan agreed.

Peter put a hand on Andrew's shoulder. 'Let's go and see that stuff that arrived yesterday. We'd better check that they've sent the right size this time. You'll excuse us, won't you, you two? Sawmill business.'

As soon as they were out of hearing of the others he said:

'Now I can tell you what it's all about. But you've got to make me a promise first.'

'That I won't tell another soul?'

'No, that you won't try to kill that poor chap, or even bite him.'

Andrew grinned. 'Promise. I won't even growl at him.'

Alan and Lisha went back to the house in silence. In the sitting-room Alan dropped into an armchair and gave a great sigh.

'Well, that's over, anyway.'

'All right?' asked Lisha, standing in front of him.

'Yes, I think so. He's all right, anyway.'

'And you?'

'I think I'll be all right too. Once I get used to it.'

'To what?'

'To letting bygones be bygones.'

'You mean you're actually going to forgive yourself?'

'I hope so. But I'll need help, Lisha. I've got a lot of changes to make. I'll need help.'

'I'm here,' she said, and knelt down beside him.

Alan put his hands on her shoulders and was leaning forward to kiss her when he suddenly straightened up with a look of horror on his face.

'My God!' he said. 'Oh, my God! I just don't believe it!'

'What is it, Alan? What on earth's the matter?'

'All that talking out there, all those ages talking, going over it all, and do you know what I forgot?'

Lisha shook her head.

'I forgot to say anything, anything at all about being sorry. Can you believe it? Not even the shadow of an apology.'

'Is that all? You had me worried.' Lisha laughed with relief. 'I thought there was something seriously wrong.'

'There is. With me. Who else could forget? What on earth can Peter be thinking of me?'

'I shouldn't worry. I don't suppose he's even noticed. No doubt he's much too busy trying to unruffle Andrew.'

42

It was a great relief to Sheila when Alan was discharged from the mental hospital and went to stay with his parents in London. It meant the end of her weekly ordeal of spending some time sitting in the presence of a husband who disregarded her entirely. And she no longer had to go home every week and try to think of something cheerful to say to the girls. Without this weekly semi-contact with him the girls would have a better chance to settle down. She thought she saw signs of strain in two of them – Beth more remote than ever, and Jane rather more aggressive, with a tendency to put her mother down at every turn. Perhaps that was just due to approaching teens. As for Tessa, she romped her way through life with her usual zest.

Apart from the suppression of the weekly hospital visits, Alan's absence in London made little difference to Sheila's life. She had already got used to not having him about after he went to the cottage, and found she could cope remarkably well without him, after she got over the initial panicky feeling about being on her own with the children.

And then there was Herbert, who came once a week at least, and did a lot of the things that Alan could have been expected to do, and sometimes had done. Herbert was more active, more methodical, and much more use whether it came to broken-down machinery or an argument with a tradesman.

Her mother-in-law phoned her once a week, after Alan had

gone to bed, and confided her hopes and fears and frustrations to Sheila, who soon realized what a strain Alan's presence was putting on the old couple.

The weeks went by quietly, peacefully on the surface. But Sheila was aware of a great sense of waiting in her life, waiting to see if Alan's state improved, to see if he would ever be well enough to come back and live with them again, to see what was going to happen about Herbert. For she felt certain that he was not spending so much time with them out of mere charity. She thought she knew his character well enough to exclude that possibility. But they all seemed to be caught in this web of waiting. Herbert must feel, as she did, that no plans could be made till the situation with Alan resolved itself. And this it showed no signs of doing. So they lived on provisionally, week after week.

She often wondered whether she should marry Herbert if it were to become clear that her present marriage was at an end. Assuming, of course, that this was what Herbert wanted. She liked him, she imagined she might even grow to love him, though not in the helpless, totally committed way in which she had loved Alan. But surely a marriage founded on respect and admiration stood as good a chance of success as one founded on Hollywood-based ideas of romantic love?

She had thought a good deal about what Herbert had said at the beginning of the crisis – about the way Alan had undervalued her and how she had taken herself at his valuation. She was now convinced that this was indeed the case. Perhaps she wasn't so useless after all. Without Alan's denigratory view of her she might have managed her life much more competently. But she wasn't quite sure where this new view of her own capabilities was going to lead her. If Alan were to come back, would she be able to hold her own a bit better?

Or would it just lead to even greater discord? And if the

marriage broke up and she were to marry Herbert instead, would things be any better? For she felt that Herbert, in spite of his obvious admiration of her, was clearly the sort of man who feels it is his right and his duty to guide and protect his woman. With Alan it wasn't a sexist thing at all – he just happened to think he had married an utter twit. But with Herbert it was a matter of conviction, part of his world-view. Even the most intelligent of women must be subservient to her husband. It looked as if, either way, she was going to have to keep to her subordinate role. Unless of course she struck out on her own . . .

The idea of being responsible, permanently and voluntarily responsible, for herself and the children suddenly came to her with such force that it took her breath away.

Shaken, her thought settled back to the possibility of marrying Herbert. That at least would mean security for her and the girls. And the girls liked him, there could be no doubt about that.

There was no denying that marriage to Herbert would certainly put an end to the financial worries, which were now beginning to loom quite large. Alan was now on half-pay, and in a few months this income would stop completely. Her work for Melville's firm was a help, but not enough to bridge the gap. Soon the situation would be really serious.

She spoke of this one day to the girls, when the demands for new clothes and increased pocket money made it clear that they must be told something of the way things stood. All Sheila had hoped for was to stem the flood of incessant demands. Their response was touching, and typical.

After a solemn pause, Jane spoke first. 'I'll give up my violin lessons,' she said, not without some satisfaction. 'That will be a saving. And we could sell my violin. Pity it's not exactly a Stradivarius. If only you'd bought me that dearer one I wanted, think how much more money we could get now.'

Beth announced that she didn't want any more pocket money, not till Daddy was better, anyway, and Tessa produced a few coins from her pocket and handed them over to her mother. 'That's all I've got left of this week's,' she said. 'You can have that. But I'm not making any promises about next week.'

'Well, my dear, I've got rather better news for you today.' Georgina's voice sounded brighter than it had for a long time. 'Alan's going to stay with Melville's parents in Galloway. His sister Lisha is here and she's going to drive him back, so he'll be in good hands.'

'I'm so glad. That will be a bit of a break for you. And perhaps it will do Alan some good. I know he was always very fond of the place.'

'And the people,' added Georgina. 'You know what a darling Melville is. Well, his sister is just as nice. I do hope they'll be able to do something for poor Alan. I'm sure he just ought to enjoy himself for a while. What he needs is a really good laugh. And we seem to have run rather short of that commodity here.'

'From what I know of Melville, he'll probably get plenty of laughter in that house. I'm so glad, for all of you.'

For the first time since the beginning of Alan's illness Sheila felt a spark of hope. Was it possible that things were moving at last?

When she told the news to Herbert his comment was:

'About time, too. I can't stand much more of this waiting.'

'*You* can't? What do you think it's like for me?'

'No worse, and I hope no better, than it is for me. It's been a long wait, Sheila. And yes, I know, it may be much longer still. But I think we're entitled to . . . to clarify things between ourselves. Sooner or later a decision will have to be made as to what's to happen between you two. When that happens I want you to know that I very much hope the decision will be to put an end to the marriage. That would be the sensible thing to do. And then you'd be in a position to marry me. Which, I may add, would be an equally sensible thing to do.'

Sheila smiled. 'It's not the most romantic of proposals, you must admit,' she pointed out gently.

'Agreed. But you must remember that it has to be a provisional one. Once you are free to accept I'll make you a proper offer, with flowers and bended knee and all the usual rhetoric. Will you accept?'

'Once I'm free,' she said, 'I'll tell you.'

Sheila was a little taken aback by the tone of her answer. As soon as she had spoken she realized that her words sounded a little arch, perhaps even coquettish. What, she wondered, had made her adopt this almost flirtatious tone?

It was so utterly out of character that she felt she must try to account for it. She had never told a frivolous lie in her life, never used ambiguity as a weapon (she got enough of that from Alan), she had always spoken in a serious and straightforward manner. Perhaps, she reflected, she had been too serious, not to say just plain dull. That red-haired vampire, for instance, she thought, I bet there wasn't anything very straightforward about her conversation. And that was perhaps the attraction – well, one of them, anyway. She had to admit that even a quick glance had revealed quite a number of other attractions on display.

Perhaps I'm learning, she thought. Perhaps part of Alan's problem was that I bored him stiff. There may be something inside me warning me not to do the same thing again. And then her previous half-formed thought came back to her:

Could it be, could it possibly be, that what she really wanted was to be married to neither Alan nor Herbert?

Could it be that her rather saucy reply was a way of preparing the ground for a completely different type of set-up, in which she would take control of her own life?

She found herself facing the awesome possibility that a new Sheila was about to be born.

Herbert had received her answer with a little nod of the head and a meditative 'Uh-huh!' as if he were amused at this example of a little sauciness from the usually demure Sheila. He had never quite worked out why he wanted to marry her. All his life the most important thing for him had been his career, and marriage to Sheila would not be a step up as far as that was concerned.

But then, it wouldn't be a step down, he reflected. A man has to please himself in some things, as long as he doesn't ruin his chances of promotion. Satisfied that his career would not be placed in jeopardy by such a marriage, he felt at liberty to follow his tastes in the matter of a life partner. As to why he was so attracted to Sheila he couldn't quite make out. True, he had always prefered fair women, and Sheila's delicate, rose-petal beauty had lost little of its charm, even now in her mid-thirties. And then there was her expression, her whole attitude – wistful, even forlorn-looking at times. The less selfish side of his active, aggressive character responded to the appeal of the helpless, when the helplessness was clothed in so comely a garment. Sheila needed protection, and he was only too willing to be the protector. He interpreted her rather pert reply to his provisional proposal as a sign that she was beginning to respond to his love with a little long-overdue playfulness.

I can give her the security she needs, he thought, I can make her blossom like a flower.

43

'Can I have a word with you?'

Alan was on his way up to his room to pack. They were to leave after lunch, as Lisha's parents expected them that evening. He turned and saw Andrew following him up the stairs.

'Yes, of course.' He tried to sound more confident than he felt. 'Come in and talk to me while I get my things together.'

'It's about this accident business. I'm just wondering how many people you're going to tell.'

'Oh, I don't know. I haven't really thought about it yet. Up till I told Lisha yesterday I had the firm intention of never telling anyone. So I've not got used to the idea yet.'

'Well, you'd better think. Hard. Don't you realize that you've committed a criminal offence? I wouldn't like to think how *you* would get on in one of Her Majesty's prisons. It was bad enough for me, and I'm pretty tough.'

'Well, I hadn't exactly reckoned on telling the police, you know.'

'No doubt,' said Andrew drily. 'But you told Lisha . . . '

'And Lisha told Peter.'

'Quite right. And Peter told me.'

'Quite right. We agreed that on our way back to the house. He could see you were going to be pretty bolshy one way or another, so you'd better be told.'

Andrew grinned. 'Quite right,' he said again. 'But the point is, where is it going to stop? If you have one or two more dear friends who have to be told, and those friends have friends . . . '

Alan realized he had once again been taken under Andrew's energetic wing. 'I see this is something I'll have to think about. Friends, even the best of them, can be a danger, you mean.'

'Exactly. I've only got one friend, and he already knows, so you're all right there. Peter won't tell anyone else, I'll take my oath on that. And I don't suppose Lisha will tell anyone without your permission. So you yourself are the only danger.'

'Well, I've been warned. Thanks. Up till yesterday I'd told no one, absolutely no one, as I said. Not even my best friend. And now that I've got over my hang-up about it I suppose there is a danger I might go too far in the other direction. I promise you I'll really think about it.'

'Don't you think we should have a conference on the subject?'

Alan seemed a bit amused by this idea.

'What's so funny?' demanded Andrew. 'Why not?'

'Oh, very well. I'll leave you to make up the agenda and tell the other members of the committee. And now I'd better get started on the packing.'

Andrew took the hint and turned to leave the room. As he went towards the door he picked up Lisha's dressing-gown, which was still lying on the chair by the bed.

'Nice taste in nightwear you've got,' he remarked as he threw the shining garment on to the bed.

After the lunch table had been cleared they all sat down again and Peter said:

'We're here, I gather, to save Alan from himself. The point at issue is, how many more confessions are we going to allow him to make? Have you thought about who else you want to tell?'

'I've really got to start speaking to Sheila again, to sort out the whole situation. And I don't see how I can do that without telling her.'

'And who else is *she* going to tell?' asked Andrew.

'Bloody Scratchley, I suppose.'

'But would he tell anyone?' asked Lisha. 'From what Melville tells me, I don't think he dislikes you as much as you dislike him.'

'You don't need to dislike a man to shop him,' put in Andrew. 'You just do it without thinking.'

'That seems to me to be the real danger,' Peter agreed. 'It's very difficult to keep a secret to yourself, even with the best of intentions.'

'And I don't think Scratchley's got too many of those.'

Lisha looked at Alan and sighed.

'I'm sorry,' he said, 'I just can't be objective about that man. But you never know,' he added, looking at Lisha more cheerfully, 'perhaps I'll get over it now that I'm no longer in his power.'

'That makes two, with possible additions,' came from Andrew, who was not to be put off. 'Who else, then?'

'And I simply have to tell Melville.'

'Who'll he discuss it with?'

'Me,' said Lisha. 'And I already know, so that's not an addition.'

'And I feel I ought to tell my parents. They've had to put up with a lot from me.'

'So you want to reward them by telling them all about your criminal past?' Peter sounded distinctly amused.

'You might as well have a circular printed while you're at it,' groaned Andrew.

They all laughed.

'No, seriously,' Andrew went on, 'that's five already, not counting any additions. Can anyone guarantee that not one of them would tell anyone else?'

This was greeted with silence. Then Peter spoke:

'I think you'd better limit it to Melville, where it would certainly go no further, and Sheila, who has a right to know. As for her telling Scratchley . . . '

'Suppose you begged her not to tell anyone else, not even Scratchley? Would that work?' suggested Lisha.

Alan thought for a while. 'I think it might. She has a strong moral sense and, yes, she's loyal. I think she could keep the secret.'

'As for your parents,' added Lisha, 'I don't think it would make them any happier to know the truth, even though they would appreciate your confiding in them. If only they can see you improving, getting back to a normal life . . . I'm sure that's all they want.'

Alan was nodding thoughtfully. 'A normal life,' he repeated. 'Yes, I suppose that's all a parent really asks for his children. And if I get things straightened out with Sheila, I'll be able to see the girls again. It's been a long time.'

'Well, there's a carrot for you,' said Peter. Once again his mind flew back to the two little raspberry pickers, and he thought of how much he owed them. Less than two years ago, he mused, I was alone in this house, with no human contacts. And now . . . There was Lisha, once again his former lover, but this time with a firmer core of friendship to keep them in touch. And Andrew, a friend and partner in an enterprise full of hope and promise.

And the Unknown Motorist himself, also playing his part in the integration of the whole.

Epilogue

After the waitress had brought him his coffee and the cream
cake he could never convince himself he didn't really need,
Melville sat back and pulled the book out of his pocket.

There it was, published at last.

It had taken them five years, with all those ups and downs
that Alan's moods were still subject to, but the book had at
last appeared, the husband-and-wife team had at last got into
print. Before opening it Melville gazed with satisfaction at
the jacket.

Very, very nice, he said to himself, as he admired the
delicate drawing of a spray of hawthorn blossom.

He had intended to look inside the book while eating his
cream cake, but then decided that each – book and cake – was
worthy of his undivided attention. So he set to on the cake,
meanwhile continuing to contemplate with pleasure the jacket
drawing. He knew this was a drawing Lisha had done for Peter
long ago, he knew the significance of the hawthorn hedge, and
he was particularly glad that Peter himself had suggested they
should use this drawing on the front of the book.

And Alan had agreed – which meant he really had laid the
ghost of the hawthorn hedge, and all that it signified.

'Mind if I sit here?'

'Not at all.' Melville glanced up at the tall, elegantly
dressed woman standing beside his table, then let his gaze
be drawn once more to Lisha's illustration.

'Mind if I smoke?'

Tiresome woman, he thought. Is she after a pick-up? As he looked up at her again he noticed that most of the other tables were unoccupied, which seemed to confirm his suspicion. Oh well, he thought, I'll give her a run for her money.

'Not at all,' he repeated amiably. 'I'm only sorry I can't offer you a light. You see, I'm one of the unpopular minority who don't smoke.'

'And I'm one of the unpopular majority who does?'

'I shouldn't think *you*'d be unpopular, whatever you did,' he retorted gallantly, beginning to enjoy the conversation. She certainly was a very striking-looking woman, and he liked the slightly mocking tone of her voice. He was looking forward to continuing a lighthearted, creamcake-style conversation, when his companion's eye fell on the book lying on the table.

'Oh, that's pretty,' she said.

Melville pushed the book along the table towards her.

'Yes,' she went on, 'a lovely piece of work.' Then she noticed the name of the author. 'Good heavens! Alan Morley! It can't be the Alan Morley I used to know! Or yes, I suppose it is. *Wild Flowers of Scotland.* He was very keen on wild flowers. Got me quite interested too, for a while. But what a comedown! Poor Alan!'

Melville felt a surge of vicarious irritation. 'Why a comedown?' he asked.

'Oh, he was always going to write a masterpiece. A combination of Kafka and Thomas Mann, or something of the sort.'

'I should have thought the two would be quite difficult to combine!' Melville spoke with a touch of acerbity. He was beginning to suspect he knew the identity of the communicative lady.

'I mean their stature, not their style or content. He certainly saw himself as a great author, fit to rank with those two – some time in the future. Meanwhile he peppered his discourse with quotes from other people's works. A study in inauthentic living. As for this, it may be a charming book, but it's hardly going to rank with the great works of the twentieth century, is it?'

'I haven't read it yet,' Melville said solemnly, as if that left the question open. 'It has only . . . just arrived this morning.' He had been about to say it had just been sent to him by the author, who happened to be his brother-in-law. Then he decided it would be wiser not to reveal the relationship. If this really was Rachel, he felt both Alan and Lisha should be protected from her. She'd done quite enough damage in the past. He thought of the long, hard struggle Alan had had in getting back to normality, and remembered the part Rachel had played in his breakdown.

Meanwhile the woman was turning over the pages, murmuring words of approval about the illustrations. 'He's certainly got hold of a good artist, I must admit. Who is it? Oh, Alicia Morley. His wife, I suppose. Only, her name wasn't Alicia, was it? I'm sure it wasn't that.'

'Some people remarry,' Melville pointed out.

'Yes,' she laughed. 'There's no end to human folly, is there?'

For once Melville found himself ready to defend the institution he had scorned all his life. He couldn't claim that Lisha and Alan's marriage had been free from difficulties, what with Alan's inability to face taking a teaching job again, and their childlessness. And yet, he felt, it was the right thing for both of them. Lisha had no children of her own, but she had three part-time stepdaughters of whom she was very fond, and her maternal instincts were given full-time employment looking after Alan. And their collaboration on this book, with another in the pipeline, was a great bond. Altogether it seemed that the marriage worked very well.

So Melville's views on marriage were undergoing a bit of a change. Enough at any rate to make him resent this woman's scornful attitude. He took a good look at her, now confident that this was indeed the Pink Jellyfish. She was wearing well, and had apparently landed on her feet again, judging by the style and quality of her clothes. Or else, of course, it could all be another tremendous bluff. Perhaps instead of owing thousands of pounds she now owed tens of thousands.

'Where did you meet this Alan Morley?' he asked.

'Believe it or not, in the heart of the country. We were next-door neighbours.'

'Why shouldn't I believe it?'

'Do I look like the bucolic type?'

'Far from it! So what was a woman like you doing in the heart of the country?'

'You might well ask! But you needn't bother, for I'm not going to tell you. It was a rather surprising chapter in my discreditable pasts. And this man helped to entertain me for a while in my rustic exile. He wasn't exactly exciting company, but I put up with him, *faute de mieux*.'

If I stay much longer, Melville thought, I'll hit her. Alarmed by the strength of his uncharacteristic desire to hurt this mocking, dangerous woman, he didn't dare say anything that might reveal his identity to her. But he could at least allow himself the pleasure of disconcerting her. He stood up suddenly and put the book in his pocket.

The woman glanced up and looked about to express indignant surprise.

Just before turning away, Melville bent over her and asked in a confidential whisper:

'Ever heard of the Pink Jellyfish?'

'Pink Jellyfish? Sounds perfectly horrible.'

'How right you are,' he said, and walked away, humming: *'La donna è mobile.'*